QUEERVILLE

RISE OF THE RED DRAGONS

BOOK 3

ABOUT THE AUTHOR

Callisto, a visionary storyteller with a passion for authentic representation, initially conceived 'Queerville' as a captivating drama series. The vibrant world they envisioned, filled with diverse characters and complex narratives, was a testament to their commitment to showcasing the realities and complexities of LGBTQ+ lives.

However, despite the strength of their concept, Callisto faced a disheartening reality; without the proper representation, they were unable to pitch it to any major studios.

Undeterred, Callisto embarked on a strategic shift, deciding to adapt 'Queerville' into a novel series, each chapter mirroring an episode of the original drama. This novel format proved to be a turning point, allowing Callisto to directly connect with readers and build a dedicated fan base who yearned for stories that reflected their own experiences.

The novel series' success fueled Callisto's vision, and they are now diligently working on a cinematic trailer, a visually stunning masterpiece that will capture the essence of 'Queerville' and entice audiences worldwide.

CHAPTER 1

Present Day, 1960
O Town, USA

O Town, once a thriving community, now stands as a desolate ghost town. Abandoned homes, their windows boarded up and paint peeling, line the deserted streets. Unkempt grass, once neatly manicured, now grew wild in the unkempt front yards.

Shuttered businesses, faded and dilapidated, stand as silent witnesses to the town's decline. The few remaining citizens, their faces etched with resignation, have no choice but to endure the remnants of their shattered lives.

The old O Town, with its bustling streets and vibrant community, is but a distant memory, a haunting reminder of what once was. The future holds nothing but uncertainty, a bleak and unknown path stretching out before them. The 'Welcome to O Town' sign had been defaced with a stark red X, a symbol of the town's tragic demise.

* * *

QUEERVILLE

Over in Queerville, Charlotte's Diner, once a beacon of warmth and community, was now a charred husk. The windows, once sparkling with the promise of a good meal, were blasted out, gaping holes in the building's facade. The landscaping wilted and forgotten, overgrown weeds choking the once-pristine beds.

As a mysterious car pulled up and parked outside the wreckage of the diner, an unsettling silence enveloped the scene. The engine's rumble faded, giving way to the soft crunch of gravel beneath black boots that stepped out with purpose. Zack emerged from the car, the weight of anticipation heavy in the air, only to be met by the stark reality of what remained.

Their gaze fell upon the remnants of Charlotte's diner, a place once vibrant with life, now reduced to twisted metal and shattered glass. As Zack took in the extent of the destruction, their heart sank like a stone. Memories surged forth unbidden, cascading through their mind—echoes of laughter that had danced through the air, intimate conversations shared over cold vanilla milk shakes, and the warm embraces of friendship that had flourished within those very walls.

With a heavy heart, Zack stepped closer, reaching out a hand as if to touch what once was, grasping at the threads of nostalgia that kept them tethered to this place. The diner had been more than just a structure; it had been a canvas painted with the stories of countless lives, a witness to the joys and heartaches that shaped their community. The realization that it lay in ruins struck deeply, igniting a flicker of determination within Zack. Though the walls may have crumbled, the spirit of what Charlotte's diner had represented could not be extinguished. It was time to honor the past and perhaps, in the ashes of this loss, to dream of a new beginning.

Three years ago…
Queerville, 1957

Zack laid sprawled in bed, surrounded by the remnants of a debauched night: two nude women, empty beer bottles, pizza boxes, and vinyl records scattered across the floor. As Sandy stormed into the loft, the darkness and drawn curtains enveloped her, casting an eerie ambiance. The room was in disarray, a testament to the night that had transpired.

Sandy flung open the drapes and the windows, letting in fresh air and sunlight to dispel the lingering haze. She approached the bed and yanked off the covers, tapping the sleeping women on their legs to awaken them.

"All right, ladies, it's time to go. The party is over," she announced, her voice firm.

The girls awoke lethargic.

Sandy gathered their clothes from the floor.

"Here you go. I'm not sure whose clothes belong to whom, but I have a feeling it doesn't matter."

"Wait. Who are you?" One of the women inquired.

Sandy's patience waned. "I'm the girl politely asking you to leave, but I can be the girl dragging you out of here if you want," Sandy said with a smirk.

The girls sucked their teeth and rolled their eyes before they quickly dressed and dashed out the door.

Zack chuckled while observing their hasty departure, terrified by Sandy.

She then turned to face Zack, saying, "Oh, I haven't even started on you." Sandy's sharply sarcastic voice cut through Zack's haze of grief. "Are you done feeling sorry for yourself?" she asked, but her words were met with a cold, silent stare. Zack's heart ached; a raw wound left open by Kelly's departure.

Sandy, sensing Zack's pain, tried to offer a mix of empathy and tough love.

"I know you're hurting, and I really feel for you, but you have got to pull yourself together. You can screw every poodle skirt that walks by, but none of them is Kelly. She's gone, and you need to move on."

Zack, trapped in their sorrow, merely groaned, "Get out, Sandy." But Sandy, refused to budge.

"No, I will not get out. You need to get up." With a gentle but firm hand, she dragged a sluggish Zack out of bed, their feet stumbling towards the bathroom.

"Let's go," Sandy commanded, pushing Zack into the tub and turning on the cold water.

"Sandy!" Zack shouted, with water cascading down their face. "Clean yourself up," she replied, closing the door behind her.

Sandy took a step back, surveying the chaotic mess of Zack's loft. With a flick of her wrist, she pulled her hair into a ponytail, ready to tackle the daunting task of cleaning.

Meanwhile, back in the bathroom, Zack sank into the tub, submerging themself beneath the water's soothing surface. As the warmth enveloped them, they closed their eyes and allowed their thoughts to drift to Kelly. Her voice reverberated in their mind, *I'll always find a way to you, Zack,* a haunting promise that stirred something deep within them.

The intensity of those words startled them, and they shot up from the depths, gasping for air, the water cascading down their face like a waterfall of mixed emotions. Shaking off the weight of their introspection, they took a quick bath, desperate to wash away the lingering confusion that tainted their thoughts.

Zack finally emerged from the bathroom, fully dressed and feeling somewhat refreshed, only to be met with an unexpected sight—the loft was immaculate. Sandy had transformed the chaotic mess into a sanctuary of creativity. The neatness was almost surreal, a stark contrast to the whirlwind of clutter that had previously occupied the space. Zack's heart swelled with gratitude as they took in the sight, realizing the depth of her kindness. A sigh of relief escaped their lips as they uttered, "Wow, thanks Sandy."

"It was no problem really. You would do the same for me." "You were right—I needed a bath."

"Well, a nice warm bath always works for me, so I just figured."

"Thank you, Sandy, for not giving up on me."

"I'll never give up on you, Zack," she replied, hugging Zack tightly. "Now, come on, let's go to this town hall meeting."

―――――――――――――

A large crowd had gathered outside the Town Hall. The sheriff was about to make a huge announcement.

"Good morning to the good people of O Town and Queerville. I'm here to introduce your new mayor, who will share with you his plans for the future of both towns. Now, without further ado, please welcome Mr. Allen Lewis as your new Mayor."

There was partial applause, with the crowd divided between O Town and Queerville on opposite sides.

Dawn and Rose seemed compelled to stand on the O Town side.

Amidst the bustling crowd, Sandy and Zack spotted Charlotte and Freddie. "Hey, babies," Charlotte greeted them warmly. Zack took their place beside Freddie, who seemed visibly displeased with the mayor.

"Thank you, sheriff and thank you to the good people of this community. First, I want to thank you all for electing me your new mayor."

"Who elected this guy?" Freddie mumbled to Zack.

"I've never seen this man before. How do you elect someone?" Zack asked.

"You have to vote. Did you vote?"

"I guess not because I don't know who this man is." "Zack, you need to vote." Freddie chuckled.

"I vote for a new mayor," Zack remarked.

Mayor Lewis continued, "I, like the rest of the world, heard about what transpired here. Hearing about what happened to those poor innocent youngsters made me sick to my stomach. In order to ensure we do not repeat our history. I've already issued the order to return O Town back to Queerville."

The residents of Queerville erupted with joy.
What does that mean? Cries came from the crowd.

"Given that this was previously a single settlement, we shall restore it as such. Meaning there is no longer an O Town. The O Town students will now attend one high school, and that is Queerville High..."

Chaos broke out between both O Town and Queerville.

"...there will be a separation of church and state in this town. Any preaching or testimony forced upon a youngster outside the doors of the church and the sanctity of your own homes is illegal and will be prosecuted."

The people of Queerville rejoiced while O Town residents grasped their chests and appeared dumbfounded. A chorus of boos and jeers reverberated through the crowd, raining down humiliation upon Dawn and Rose, who had valiantly defended these same rights. With their heads bowed low and their faces hidden behind their hands, they retreated to the Queerville side.

"All O Town students will be transferred over to Queerville with their same GPA and academic schedule to finish out their senior year. All shop signs that refuse service to anyone due to their ethnicity, gender, weight, height, skin color, or sexual orientation will result in the loss of your license…"

Charlotte was amused by the O Town residents' reaction to the new mayor.

"Okay, Mr. Mayor is flipping these squares wigs." Charlotte chuckled. "Wow never thought I'd see the day. Someone would come and clean up this town." Freddie stated. "Yeah, he seems to want to make a real change," Sandy chimed in, her eyes shining with hope.

"I don't trust him," Zack mumbled, crossing their arms defensively. The others turned to face them, intrigued by their reluctance to join in the optimistic chatter. Zack's brows furrowed in skepticism, their instincts telling them that not everything glittered was gold.

As if on cue, Mayor Lewis said, "Please if you have any concerns my office doors are always open," a sly smile gracing his lips, the kind that raised more questions than answers.

Yet, as soon as he entered the comfort of his own space, the facade fell away. He slammed the door shut and locked it, eager to indulge in a private moment of self-admiration. Staring into the mirror, he whispered words of encouragement, "They fucking love you, man." A sense of bravado surged through him as he reached into his jacket and pulled out a joint, the ritual soothing his nerves. With a flick of his lighter, he inhaled deeply, the smoke swirling around him like the promises he was weaving—a swirling dance of ambition and deception.

———————————

Back at Charlotte's diner, the atmosphere was electric. Patrons packed the establishment, their faces beaming with satisfaction over the newly elected mayor and his vision for the future. Charlotte diligently collected orders behind the counter while Sandy deftly served meals.

At the jukebox, Zack was posted up, enjoying a beer.

Their stoic demeanor was shattered by the entrance of Maria, whose excitement was impossible to ignore. With a mischievous glint in her eye, Maria made a beeline for Zack, her body language radiating allure. Her, licking her lips and twirling her hair, were an irresistible flirtation.

Sandy, witnessing the interaction from the sidelines, couldn't help but cast a curious glance.

"Hey, Zack, haven't seen you in a while."

"Yeah, what's it to you?"

"I guess I missed you is all."

"Where's your little friend Val?" Zack asked.

"Oh please, Zack, you know I was only using her to get to you." "Ain't nothing like the real thing, huh?"

"Boy, don't I know it." Maria's flirtation reached new heights as she pressed her body against Zack's, her eyes filled with desire, "Let me get some of that beer."

With a seductive gesture, she reached for Zack's beer and used it as a sexual plaything, licking the brim in a provocative manner that left Zack mesmerized.

"Are you busy right now?" she asked while licking her lips. "No, not really."

As Maria whispered enticingly in their ear, Zack could sense their resistance crumbling. With a quick caress of their crotch, Maria sealed the deal, and Zack eagerly finished their beer before dashing out of the diner with Maria.

* * *

In the confines of his room, Freddie animatedly narrated an embellished tale of what transpired at town hall to Mark.

"The mayor was like; I will throw all of you bible thumpers in jail. They were all angry clutching their pearls."

"This town needs someone to come shake things up." Mark stated.

"So, you know what this means right? Tomorrow we all will be in one school all together. Squares and Queers."

They shared a moment of contemplation, recognizing the profound implications of this impending merger.

Yet, as they sat in the bubble of their dreams, Mark felt a familiar tension coil in his stomach. "Freddie, I don't know about me going back to school."

"What? We talked about this."

"I know but I make good money down at the shop with Zack," Mark explained.

"Don't you want to run your own store instead of working for someone else? You need a diploma for that."

"Zack did it without a diploma."

"Zack is also the child of a gangster. It's in their blood. Just give it a week for me please." He pleaded with his eyes.

Freddie kissed Mark on the lips, trailing his neck. He planted sweet kisses from his neck to his grind. Mark's eyes widened, and Freddie's head sank onto his lap.

* * *

Meanwhile, in the midst of the diner's lively atmosphere, Sandy's radiant presence captivated the room. She **was reading the newspaper on the rise in crime while manning the counter.** Male patrons couldn't resist stealing glances at her, admiring her striking beauty.

Amidst the throng, one man summoned his courage and approached her, his demeanor betraying a hint of shyness. "Hello, Sandy, how are you today?" The man's voice was warm, tinged with an earnest enthusiasm that made the corners of her lips curl into a genuine smile.

"I'm just fine how are you?" she replied, her eyes sparkling with a light that could brighten even the dullest of days. His heart skipped a beat as he noticed her joyful spirit and infectious warmth, instantly putting him at ease; it always did. Sandy had a way of making everyone feel special, from the regulars at the diner to the passersby who dared to stop and chat for a moment.

"Well, any day I can come to the diner and see your gorgeous face is always a good one," he confessed, his cheeks warming slightly under her gaze.

"Awe, thank you. You are far too charming," Sandy said, playfully swatting away the compliment as if it were a blushing butterfly.

"You have a birthday coming up soon, right?" Eagerly, she nodded, "Yes, I do; it's my 23rd. How nice of you to remember?" "What do you have planned?" The sparkle in her eyes danced even more brightly as she revealed, "Oh, just the finest party Queerville has ever seen."

Intrigued, he leaned in, "Oh, gee, is this a private party?" As if savoring the moment, she replied, "Oh, no, sweetie. Everyone is welcomed, but you must show up in nothing but your best threads."

His enthusiasm ignited. "Oh, I see. Well, will you save me a dance?" The question hung in the air, filled with hopeful anticipation.

But Sandy shook her head with a playful smirk, "Oh, sugar, I never dance with anyone. I enjoy being alone in my element, just me and the music." Her independence only made her more appealing, and he said with a twinkle in his eye, "That's what makes you so captivating. You're untamable, Sandy. I'll still come just so I can watch you move." He took a moment, donning his hat with a theatrical flourish before retreating gracefully.

At that instant, Val approached, raising her eyebrows in curiosity. "Where do you find these cowboys?" she asked, glancing between them with a knowing smile.

"I honestly don't know," Sandy replied, her voice light and teasing. "Have you seen Maria?"

"Yeah, she was in here earlier speaking with Zack."

"Zack?" Val inquired angrily. "Yeah, why?"

"She's never going to leave Zack alone. No matter what I do," Val stormed off, consumed by jealousy and frustration at Maria's persistent pursuit of Zack.

* * *

Zack's eyes glazed over as they and Maria sipped beer in the isolated backseat of Maria's car, a hazy euphoria engulfing their mind. "You ever wonder how many times you have actually been alive."

"What do you mean? What are you talking about?" Maria was lost. "Reincarnation...you're just born over and over again. Until you finally get it right. I wonder what life I'm on right now."

"I miss all your crazy talks." Maria giggled.

"If you missed it so much, why did you cheat on me?" Maria's laughter died down, replaced by a flicker of guilt. "I was young and dumb," she admitted.

"**You still are young and dumb.**" Zack retorted with a wry smile. Suddenly, their banter gave way to an undeniable longing. Maria's gaze locked with Zack's, her eyes burning with desire. "And I haven't grown any wiser," she whispered, her voice a mere breath.

With lightning-fast reflexes, she pulled Zack towards her and captured their lips in a fiery kiss. Zack's heart raced as they lifted Maria onto their lap, her body trembling with anticipation. Her fingers deftly unbuttoned her top, revealing her ample breasts. Zack's hands eagerly unhooked her bra, and their mouth descended upon her nipples, suckling them gently. Maria gasped, her breath coming in shallow pants as Zack's grip tightened on her breasts. "I've missed you so much," she murmured into Zack's ear, her voice a seductive whisper. With trembling hands, Maria unbuttoned Zack's pants, her eyes sparkling with lust.

She gasped as Zack penetrated her. "**Oh, Zack…oh my!**" she panted excitedly, leaving hickeys on Zack's neck as she thrust up and down in Zack's lap. Zack remained emotionless; their mind focused solely on the physical sensations of the act. But Maria was lost in the moment, her body moving in time with Zack's as they thrust together. She leaned in close, murmuring soft words of love and longing into Zack's ear.

When it was over, Maria collapsed against Zack, her body slick with sweat and overwhelmed by the remnants of pleasure. Zack sipped on their beer, choosing not to break the moment with words. They both knew that this was just a physical release, nothing more. But for Maria, it was enough. She had missed the feel of Zack's body against hers, and she was grateful for the opportunity to experience it again, even if it was just for one night.

._____

Charlotte pushed through the doors of the diner; her eyes immediately drawn to the spectacle unfolding before her. Every man in the place, from the grizzled old-timer nursing a coffee to the young fella in a leather jacket, had their eyes glued to Sandy. She was perched on a stool at the counter, her back straight, her chin tilted, and a playful smirk tugging at her lips. "Okay, what is going on? Were you in here stripping again?" Charlotte demanded, her voice laced with a blend of amusement and exasperation.

"What? No," Sandy countered, offended.

"Why are all these men sitting here gawking at you?"

"Per usual." Sandy shrugged, her nonchalance bordering on arrogance. Charlotte couldn't help but let out a snort, "Well, ain't you a cocky bitch." "I don't want any of these men," Sandy declared, her tone matter-of-fact. "Oh, we know, darling," Charlotte retorted, her eyes twinkling with knowing. "What's that supposed to mean?" Sandy pressed; her curiosity piqued.

"Oh, nothing," Charlotte brushed it off, her gaze shifting to the clock, "**Where is Zack? I asked that child to be here on time.**" "With Maria still, I presume."

"What? She got her claws back into Zack. Oh, Lord!" Charlotte threw her hands up in defeat, her frustration growing with each passing second. She marched to the back, muttering under her breath.

A moment later, Zack walked in, their casual swagger momentarily halted as they too caught sight of the men's blatant admiration of Sandy. "**Why are all these men sitting here looking at you like some freak show in the circus.**" Sandy, unfazed, brushed off their concern, "Forget them. Where have you been?" she countered, her voice firm. Zack, seemingly oblivious to the tension, nonchalantly requested, "Can you give me a glass of water. My throat is little dry." Sandy, with resigned obedience, poured a glass of water.

Her curiosity, however, remained undeterred.

"Where did you go with Maria? Val was here looking for her," she pressed. Zack replied, "We went to lover's lane. Like some love drunk teenagers." They drained the water in one gulp, their actions mirroring their casual approach to the situation.

Sandy, trying to be subtle, but her curiosity getting the better of her, remarked, "Oh, you must've really had a good work out."

Zack, seemingly unaware of the hidden meaning behind her words, simply replied, "I just needed to blow off some steam." Sandy, her patience waning, finally pressed, "Wait. So, you did sleep with her?" Zack, with a casual shrug that betrayed a lack of understanding of the gravity of their actions, simply confirmed, "I wouldn't call what we did sleeping." Sandy's face fell, her agitation evident, "You had sex with Maria just now?" Zack, seemingly unfazed, nonchalantly confirmed, "Yeah."

Sandy, unable to contain her dissatisfaction, sighed heavily as she loosened her apron, a futile attempt to release the tension that had been building throughout her long shift. "My shift is over. I'm going home," she declared, the words tumbling from her lips with a mix of relief and frustration. "Do you want a ride?" Zack offered, genuinely caring for her well-being, but just then, Charlotte emerged from the back, "Zack, you're here," she chirped, a warm smile lighting up her face. Sandy, feeling the air thicken with unspoken emotions and knowing it was best to let Zack and Charlotte speak, turned on her heel and left the two of them to their conversation.

"Tell me this plan of yours again." Zack asked.

"My Queer Youth House has its grand opening next month, and I want you to hold a class and speak with the kids."

"Charlotte, I'm a high school dropout and a gang member. I'm probably not the best role model for the youth." "Yes, but you are also a successful business owner and street racer. You're a beatnik they will relate to you. Give them a tour of your auto shop."

"Gee whiz, Charlotte ask for a kidney why don't you." Zack felt overwhelmed.

The night air was crisp, filled with the scent of a cool fall night and distant laughter from nearby houses. Sandy sat at her kitchen table, a bowl of half-eaten noodles in front of her, mindlessly pushing the pasta around. She was lost in thought—when the doorbell rang, pulling her back to reality.

Sandy hesitated, glancing at the clock. It was well past eight, and she wasn't expecting anyone. With a sense of curiosity, she walked to the door, the atmosphere tinged with anticipation she couldn't quite place. When she opened it, she froze.

Standing there, bathed in the warm glow of the moon light, was a face etched deeply into her memory, a visage she never thought she'd see again—her father, Mr. Myers. The years seemed to melt away as he beamed at her, his smile wide and genuine. The resemblance she bore to her mother was startlingly uncanny, flooding him with a maelstrom of nostalgia and bittersweet.

Mr. Myers stood in awe, seemingly lost in thoughts about how his child had grown, her beauty illuminating the entrance to her home. It was as if he was seeing a piece of her mother brought back to life in the form of Sandy, an overwhelming mix of pride and remorse flickered across his face.

"You look just like your mother," he finally managed to say, his voice thick with emotion, rendering Sandy momentarily speechless as she struggled to reconcile this unexpected reunion with the life she had built.

"Dad?" she uttered hesitantly, the word feeling foreign yet comforting, her heart racing as he nodded.

"Hey Samuel," he replied, a hint of pride lacing his tone, even as she felt the need to correct him.

"I go by Sandy now," she said softly, a smile creeping onto her lips as a sense of curiosity mingled with the remnants of their shared history. "Hello, Sandy, nice to meet you," he responded, his eyes sparkling with a warmth she hadn't anticipated, and in that moment, the door wasn't just an entryway into her home but a threshold between years lost and possibilities regained.

Mr. Myers and Sandy settled into the warmth of her living room. The soft glow of the table lamps cast gentle shadows on the walls, creating an inviting atmosphere that enveloped them like a comforting embrace, a stark contrast to the years of silence that had stretched between them.

"I'm so sorry," Mr. Myers said, his gaze falling to the floor. "For everything. I've thought about you every day. It's… not easy to face you after all this time."

"You missed a lot of things, Dad. I went through a lot, too." "I know. I was a coward," he admitted, his voice wrought with regret. "When you told me you were… I didn't know how to process it. I— I didn't know how to raise you, so I ran away from it all, ran away from you."

His confession hung in the air, raw and unfiltered, echoing in Sandy's heart. "It wasn't your choice to make for me," she said softly, "I needed you."
"I'm sorry Sam…"
"I wanted a father I could turn to," she continued, her eyes shining with unshed tears, "I needed to know you loved me."

His eyes met hers, and she could see the glimmer of hope flickering in his gaze. "I do love you, Sandy. I've always loved you. I just didn't know how to show it." He stumbled over her name at first—"Sandy" felt foreign on his tongue, a shift he needed to adjust to—but he tried. With each sincere attempt, each nod of understanding, the walls between them began to crack.

"I want to try," he said, his voice steadying, "I want to be a part of your life. I want to understand everything— who you are now. I want to get to know… my daughter."

Sandy felt the weight of those words, warming her from within. It wouldn't be easy. There would be bumps along the road—miscommunications, awkward moments, perhaps even setbacks. Yet, the love in his voice, the earnestness in his eyes, ignited a small flicker of a future she dared to consider.

For hours, they talked, their voices a blend of laughter and tears, each word tearing down the walls of hurt and misunderstanding that had built up over time. He started by apologizing for his absence, for the milestones he had missed in her life, and slowly unraveled the difficult tapestry of events that had led him to send her to live with Zack and their mother.

He explained his rationale, that he believed Mama Zack, with her nurturing spirit and stability, could provide Sandy with a better life than he could ever offer as a broken man stumbling through his own struggles. Sandy listened intently, her heart balancing the weight of pain and empathy, and as he spoke, she felt a flicker of understanding kindling within her.

As they shared their stories, they cried over lost time but also laughed at the small memories that still lingered, discovering that healing was not just possible but necessary. Amidst the flow of emotions, a shift occurred in the air between them, transforming their years of estrangement into a newfound connection.

They both recognized the profound truth in their conversation—while the past could not be changed, the future was still unwritten, a blank canvas that now offered the promise of a fresh start. With a tentative but optimistic agreement, they embraced their roles anew, as father and daughter, vowing to nurture their relationship with patience and love, no longer held hostage by the weight of their past but propelled forward by hope and the shared desire to rewrite their narrative together.

* * *

As darkness enveloped the quaint town of Queerville, Zack noticed a silhouette of Mayor Lewis's car parked outside their shop. With cautious steps, they approached the vehicle as the mayor emerged, a slight smile playing upon his lips. "**Zack Calhoun, I presume?**"

"**Yeah,**" Zack responded, a hint of curiosity coloring their tone. "**Pleased to meet your acquaintance,**" the mayor replied, extending a cordial handshake. Zack couldn't help but wonder why the mayor would pay a visit to their unassuming residence. "What brings the Mayor of Queerville to my pad?"

"I'm glad you asked; I think we could both help each other." "How's that?" Zack inquired, doubtful.

"Well, I did my due diligence, and I discovered the **people in this town** hold you in high regard. Your opinions are valued and respected. I am in need of your assistance in gaining their trust."

"Why would I do that?" Zack asked, a hint of amusement in their voice. Mayor Lewis's expression grew serious.

"I possess something that may be of great interest to you," he replied. Zack's skepticism began to wane.

"I doubt that," Zack scoffed, turning to walk away.

However, Mayor Lewis's next words brought them to an abrupt halt, sending shivers down their spine.

"I beg to differ, Zack Calhoun. If you can persuade the people of Queerville to place their trust in me. I will return the love of your life to you... memories intact."

Zack's eyes widened in astonishment.

They spun around, their gaze fixed upon the mayor. "That's right," Mayor Lewis continued with a sly grin. "I can give you back your precious Kelly."

Zack listened intently, their heart pounding in their chest.

"How?" they whispered, barely able to contain their emotions. "That, Zack Calhoun, is a secret I shall reveal in due time," the mayor replied enigmatically. "But trust me when I say that the path to Kelly's heart lies through the trust of Queerville." With these tantalizing words, Mayor Lewis turned and strode towards his car, leaving Zack alone in the darkness, their mind reeling from the possibilities.

CHAPTER 2

Mississippi, 1957

In the bustling halls of academia, a set of dainty feet raced across the polished floor, their rapid movement creating a soft patter that echoed through the air. A pastel poodle skirt billowed out behind its wearer, dancing in the gentle breeze that swept through the corridor. A pristine white sweater, as delicate as a snowflake, clung to her petite frame, adding an air of elegance to her hasty steps.

It was Kelly, dashing into class with a flurry of motion.

Professor Clarke, seated behind his cluttered desk, raised an eyebrow as Kelly's tardy form appeared in the doorway.

"Ah, Ms. Hamilton," he drawled sardonically, his voice dripping with condescension, "How wonderful for you to join us this morning."

Kelly, one of only three women in the entire class, felt a pang of unease as she realized the professor's thinly veiled disdain. "Sorry, professor, I..."

"No need for excuses, Ms. Hamilton," Professor Clarke interrupted brusquely. "Take your seat." His manner was dismissive, as if her absence had disrupted the cosmic order. Clarke was the epitome of a male chauvinist, firmly convinced that women belonged in the kitchen, their primary roles being childbearing and meal preparation.

As Kelly made her way to her desk, she caught the fleeting gaze of a handsome blonde boy seated in the front row. His piercing blue eyes sparkled with a hint of amusement, as if he found the professor's antics equally absurd. A small smile played upon his lips, offering a silent beacon of camaraderie in the face of academic adversity.

Queerville, 1957

The arrival of the O Town teens at Queerville High was a whirlwind of confused stares and muttered comments. The Queerville students, with their vibrant clothes, bold hairstyles, and seemingly effortless confidence, were a stark contrast to the O Towners' more conservative attire and nervous demeanor. The O Town teens felt the eyes of the Queerville students on them, their own self-consciousness magnified by the colorful chaos that surrounded them.

The culture shock was palpable, a silent language spoken through the clash of differing styles and attitudes. Some Queerville students offered friendly smiles and welcoming nods, but others, their faces etched with amusement or disdain, made the O Towners feel like they were stepping into a foreign film.

The anxious O Towners, already overwhelmed by the strange new environment, found themselves further disoriented when Queerville students knocked their books from their grasp and shoved them into lockers, ~~leaving them feeling vulnerable and exposed~~.

Amidst the chaos, Rose and Dawn, with their unwavering composure, seemed unaffected by the hostility.

They strolled down the corridor, with heads held high. "I can't believe this new mayor is making all of us repeat our senior year." Rose complained, her voice carrying a hint of annoyance, but not fear, as they reached the door to their first class.

"He's not making us repeat it. He's more like extending it." Dawn explained.

"Well, what for? I was counting the days till graduation."

"Rose, the entire town has been through a calamity, and many teens have missed school as a result."

"We were this close... Wait do we get a second prom?" Rose asked excitedly.

"No, Rose, we don't get a second prom."

"Ugh, I hate it here." Rose scoffed.

"At least we finally get to hang with some hip kids and not those squares. Huh, Rose?"

Rose barely registered what Dawn was saying as her eyes locked onto Daron, the star running back for the Queerville football team. With his almond-shaped hazel eyes that held an intense gentleness, full lips that made her wonder how they would feel against her own, and glowing cinnamon skin, he was nothing short of breathtaking. Rose couldn't believe it, but she had fallen for him instantly.

She felt a nudge from Dawn and turned to face her.

"Rose are you okay?" she asked, sounding genuinely concerned. Rose forced a smile, trying to shake off her infatuation. She knew it was ridiculous - she didn't even know Daron. And yet, she couldn't help but feel drawn to him, like a moth to a flame.

She couldn't take her eyes off him.

"Rose?" As Dawn's voice trailed off, a gentle tap on her shoulder broke her reverie. She turned around to see.

"Max!" she said, her eyes wide with surprise.

In an instant, she leaped into his arms, her laughter mingling with his. "Hey, Dawn. It's so good to see you."

"What are you doing here? I thought you were settled in Mississippi with Kelly and your parents?"

"I came back I wanted to stay and finish school and try to undo some of the damage I help cause."

"Well, good. I'm glad you're here," Dawn said excitedly.

Sandy nervously approached Zack, her heart racing like a wild drum, the words she had rehearsed in her mind seeming to dance just out of reach as she prepared to broach the delicate topic that had been weighing heavily on her thoughts for days.

In the soft glow of Zack' Auto shop, she gathered her courage, her fingers fidgeting with the buckle of her belt as she approached Zack.

"Zack, I need a hug favor," she murmured, her voice low and shaky, but it was enough to catch their attention, their eyes glistened with warmth, clearly indicating their willingness to help, as they asked, "Sure, what is it?" Sandy took a steadying breath, "I need you to give my father some work, if it's possible. I know you've been at your neck in orders, and you and Mark have been buried under piles of tasks, but he's eager to stand on his own two feet again. He sees my support as a burden, and I think a job would really help him regain his sense of dignity."

The moment hung thick in the air, and Zack's brow furrowed as they processed this new information.

"Wait, Sandy, your father is in town, and this is how you tell me?" they said incredulously, disbelief mingling with a dawning realization.

"I'm sorry; we got so lost in catching up that I totally forgot to mention it," she replied, guilt washing over her. But then, as Zack's eyes softened and they registered the big smile on her face, they couldn't help but hug her in a warm embrace, their heart swelling with support.

"I'm happy for you, Sandy," genuine warmth flooding their voice, even as a hint of apprehension curled at the edges of their thoughts. Zack knew how much Sandy cherished her father and how profoundly it had hurt her when he chose to leave years earlier, the scars of that abandonment still fresh in her heart.

It felt unjust to forget those painful moments, and yet, as they looked into Sandy's pleading eyes, they knew that her well-being mattered more than old grudges. Sandy had always been a shining light in their life, and her unwavering loyalty and kindness had earned their respect and affection over the years. Zack hesitated, balancing their feelings of loyalty to their friend with their dislike for her father.

After a heavy pause, they sighed, realizing that there was nothing they wouldn't do for her, knowing that in helping him, they were ultimately standing by Sandy.

"Yes, of course Sandy." She bear hugged Zack.

Zack recognized that sometimes, the path to healing involved taking steps that feel uncomfortable but necessary.

* * *

Rose's boredom, a constant companion in the sterile halls of her new high school, began to dissipate as she noticed Daron seated alone, hunched over his notebook, his brow slightly furrowed in concentration. The usual monotony of her day melted away as her heart skipped a beat. She discreetly adjusted her blouse, a nervous habit she'd developed around boys like him, boys whose smiles seemed to possess the power to melt glaciers and warm even the coldest of environments. They had a way of drawing her in, captivating her attention and setting her heart racing.

Every step she took toward his table felt like traversing a tightrope, balancing her growing courage with anxiety; she was acutely aware of the gaze of her peers, their whispers blending into a background hum that she diligently tried to tune out. With each careful movement, she navigated the classroom's aisle, her eyes fixed unwaveringly on the empty seat beside him, fueled by an almost subconscious desire to be closer to his magnetic aura.

The closer she got, the more she could feel the cautious optimism brewing within her; perhaps this was her chance to breach the wall of isolation that had surrounded her since the first day at this unfamiliar place.

"Excuse me, is anyone sitting here?" she inquired, her voice a soft whisper, an attempt to mask the fluttering in her chest.

Daron, caught off guard, looked up, his gaze lingering on her face, making her feel as if she were the only person in the room. "Um, no, I don't believe so," he replied, his voice a warm baritone that sent shivers down her spine.

Rose, unable to resist the pull of his charm, slid into the seat, feeling an instant connection with him.

"Let me guess…" Daron began, a playful glint in his eyes, "You're from O Town?"

"What gave me away? My pale skin." Rose teased back, a nervous laugh escaping her lips.

"There are plenty of white girls in Queerville," Daron countered, his gaze unwavering, "None as pretty as you though."

Rose, overwhelmed by his compliment, turned a bright shade of scarlet, her cheeks flaming with a blush that rivaled the crimson of a blooming rose. She grinned, unable to meet his eyes, her heart pounding a frantic rhythm against her ribs. The classroom walls suddenly seemed to melt away, leaving only her and Daron, two souls drawn together by an invisible thread of attraction.

* * *

Douglas was at the tender age of nineteen. With the chiseled physique of an All-American quarterback, he was a force to be reckoned with. A party boy turned drug dealer. Hailing from the nearby O Town, Douglas had adopted the greaser style, complete with slicked-back hair and a tough-guy attitude.

He had a liking for the abandoned homes of O Town, using them as the venue for his infamous parties. It was behind the school bleachers that Douglas and a group of spaced-out juniors, smoking marijuana, spotted a group of squares from O Town walking by. Dressed in their old letterman sweaters, the squares were a stark contrast to Douglas and his group of misfits.

"These O Town squares are wired to fucking tight."

"Are those sweaters sewn on?" One spaced out junior asked as they all chuckled. "What's up with their hair?"

"I think it's crazy glued." Douglas chuckled.

"And those colors? It's like watching a black and white flick but in person."

Despite their differences, Douglas and his group couldn't help but be intrigued by the squares. They represented a world that Douglas had left behind, one of conformity and tradition. Yet, as he took another hit of his joint, Douglas couldn't help but feel a sense of satisfaction in his newfound freedom and identity as a Queerville greaser.

The squares may have looked down on Douglas and his group, but Douglas knew that they were the ones who were truly living life on their own terms.

"We should invite them to the bash tonight." Doulgas suggested.

"No way! No squares." "Squares equal dollars and we need dollars. Spread the word," Douglas demanded.

Douglas's flunkies played a pivotal role in disseminating the information, whispering into the ears of passing teens who then became unwitting messengers. Douglas parties were renowned for their grandeur and exclusivity, and the prospect of missing one was enough to send shivers down the spines of any self-respecting teen.

With lightning speed, the news reached every corner of the school, igniting a collective buzz of anticipation. From the boisterous gym, where basketballs thumped against the hardwood, to the sterile science lab, where test tubes bubbled with scientific curiosity, to the grease-stained auto shop, where engines roared, and even the home ec classes, where the aroma of freshly baked cookies wafted, the news spread, igniting a palpable sense of excitement among the teenage students.

As the evening approached, the school was transformed into a hotbed of preparations, with students rushing to secure their outfits, hairstyles, and dance moves, all eager to make a grand impression at Douglas' illustrious bash.

The scent of fresh paint and wood hung heavy in the air as Val and Maria hustled about Charlotte's Queer House, readying it for its grand opening. Val, her usually vibrant energy dimmed by a cloud of jealousy, couldn't shake the rumors of Maria and Zack leaving the diner together; a tiny spark igniting a fire of insecurity within her.

"Where did you go with Zack?" Val blurted out; her voice laced with a bitterness that surprised even her. She knew Maria still held a flame for Zack, a fact she often conveniently forgot in her own wishful thinking.

But Maria, with a practiced air of nonchalance, countered, "What are you talking about?"

"Don't lie, people saw you drive off." "We went for a drive?" "Where to Maria?"

"Love's lane. You happy now?" Maria's words dripped with sarcasm, a subtle jab at Val's possessive tendencies.

Val, unable to contain her suspicions, spat out, "You had sex with Zack didn't you."
"That's why people go to Lover's Lane. Don't flip your wig." "How could you Maria?" Val's words were barely a whisper, a testament to the turmoil brewing within her.

Maria, finally losing her patience, snapped back, "You and I aren't even together." "How could you say that?" "We screwed a few times Val that's it. I never said we were together." With a final, scathing glance, Maria stalked off, leaving Val alone amidst the chaos of the preparations.

On the other side of the building, Charlotte was giving Zack a tour of Queer House, her safe haven for LGBTQ+ teens. The living area, with its mismatched furniture and vibrant artwork, was buzzing with youthful energy. Passing through the well-stocked kitchen, they moved towards the communal bathroom, a haven of fresh paint and calming colors.

Each space, though modest, was imbued with a sense of warmth and belonging.

"I want these babies to have a clean safe space they can come to." Charlotte declared, her voice tinged with both pride and a hint of weariness. She was providing shelter and support for the kids who had been cast out of their homes, forced to flee the clutches of the cruel P.G.A conversion camp.

Zack, taking in the scene, couldn't help but be moved.

"Charlotte this is really amazing what you're doing. These kids are lucky to have someone like you looking after them."

"You know how it is. We're always trying to give our kids the childhood we never had. The love our parents didn't give us." "What do you need from me? How can I help?" "As good as this place looks, don't nothing work." Charlotte chuckled, a hint of desperation in her voice. "Please find something and hammer it or screw it. I can't afford no handyman." "Okay, Charlotte I'll see what I can do." "Thank you, baby."

With newfound purpose, Zack retrieved their tools from the car and delved into the task at hand. They fixed stoves, repaired outlets, installed beds, mended TV's, placed knobs on doors, and patched up holes in the walls. Each task they completed brought them closer to Charlotte's vision of creating a safe and nurturing environment for the young people who were about to call Queer House, home.

Sandy sat cross-legged on the living room floor, nostalgic warmth enveloping her as she recounted stories from her childhood to her father, a gentle smile painting his face as he listened intently. She spoke of summers spent laughing under the sun, the way Zack had always been right by her side, a constant companion through every adventure and misadventure that life threw their way.

There was a sweetness in her laughter as she recalled the silly arguments over who would have the last slice of pizza or how they had teamed up for their school projects, their teamwork unwavering despite the occasional bickering.

As the tales unfolded, Mr. Myers couldn't help but feel a swell of appreciation for Zack, recognizing the unwavering support and friendship they had shown to Sandy throughout the years.

"You know," he said thoughtfully, pausing for a moment, "I always thought you two would end up together."

Sandy erupted into laughter, shaking her head as if the very notion was absurd. "Together? No way! Zack is like my brother, always there to tease me about my terrible cooking and who hogs the last slice of pizza."

Yet, Mr. Myers persisted, "But come on, Sandy. You have to admit there's a special bond between you two. I mean, remember how you both fought tooth and nail to finish that science project, but somehow always ended up laughing by the end of it?" Sandy playfully rolled her eyes.

"True, but it was more of a 'let's not kill each other' kind of teamwork! I can't picture us as anything other than friends."

"You say that now, but the way you light up when you talk about Zack... it's pretty clear there's something deeper there." Sandy, scoffing lightly, "Oh please! I just appreciate having a partner in crime who knows how to escape detention with style."

"Think about it: you share so many memories and support each other through everything. That kind of connection doesn't just disappear."

"I know, I know. But I love that we can be silly together without it getting complicated. I mean, would you really take that last slice of pizza from the person you loved?" she argued, attempting to retreat to her fortress of logic. Open her heart? It seemed an unwelcome idea when simplicity felt so comfortable. Sandy was in denial she refused to believe there was something between she and Zack.

Mr. Myers reminded her of the deep connection they shared, the way they could finish each other's sentences and the ease with which they navigated life together.

"I appreciate that, really. I just... I don't want to risk losing what we have. It's too precious."

"Fair enough. Just remember, the best friendships often evolve into the strongest relationships. Don't close yourself off to that possibility."

Indeed, their bond was something special—an unbreakable friendship forged through countless shared experiences, laughter, and tears. Mr. Myers pointed out that through every challenge Sandy faced, Zack was always her anchor, the one person who had never let her down or caused her pain, always there to lift her up and make her smile even on the toughest of days.

Still, as Sandy mulled over her father's perspective, her laughter faded into a thoughtful smile. Mr. Myers had a way of illuminating truths she often overlooked, the rhythm of their friendship that flowed effortlessly—could there be something more? Inner turmoil churned within her as she weighed the possibilities, unsure whether to embrace the complexity or retreat to the safety of friendship.

———————

As the O Town students made their way to the house party, they were greeted by a scene that shocked their conservative sensibilities. The raucous atmosphere was fueled by an abundance of drugs, scandalous sexual activity, and the pulsating rhythm of rock & roll music. However, instead of being frightened away, these square teenagers found themselves drawn into the vortex of debauchery.

Douglas was in the backyard, transforming some square into a greaser. He yanked off the boy's sweater, greased up his hair, slicked it back and cuffed his pants. "Now, you a hip cat..." He executed a dramatic spin with the square, showcasing the transformation.

"Hey ladies, would you ride in this square ragtop?" His words flowed with an infectious bravado, and to his delight, the nearby girls couldn't help but smile, their expressions revealing a mix of intrigue and excitement. The square couldn't quite believe the sudden attention; the sparkle in the girls' eyes was electrifying, and the thrill of acceptance filled the air. "Sure!" one of the girls chirped, her enthusiasm infectious.

"Now, you come back and see me if you really want to seal the deal..." Douglas slid a joint in the squares pocket. "...that one is on me." The square grinned and walked off with the two girls under his arm.

Inside the lively abode, the infectious rhythm of Little Richard's 'Good Golly Miss Molly' filled the air, propelling the Queerville teens into an energetic frenzy. They jived and swayed their bodies pulsating to the beat of the jitterbug. The square kids, not to be outdone, attempted to emulate their counterparts, their clumsy movements adding a touch of comic relief.

Rose and Dawn, upon entering the scene, were instantly captivated by the infectious vibe. "Oh, wow, look at them go," Rose exclaimed, her eyes wide with excitement. "Now, this is a party," Dawn chimed in, as they joined in, their own bodies surrendering to the rhythm.

Meanwhile, Freddie rummaged through the refrigerator in the kitchen, searching for more drinks.

"Okay, where are the rest of the beers?"

"Here have mine," Mark offered.

However, Douglas interjected with a tantalizing alternative. "I got something better than beer." Freddie and Mark looked at him with curiosity.

Daron strode into the party, his arrival heralded by a chorus of greetings and backslaps. He was a magnet for attention, a whirlwind of laughter and boisterous camaraderie, soaking up the adoration like a sponge.

Amidst the swirling chaos, Rose, quietly observing from the sidelines, caught his eye. A fleeting glance, a shared smile, flickered between them. Her hand instinctively went to her hair, smoothing down a stray strand as she straightened her dress, a subconscious attempt to tidy herself up for the moment.

Meanwhile, Dawn, on a mission to replenish her dwindling supply of beer, navigated her way through the crowded living room. She stumbled into the kitchen, her eyes scanning the counter, only to be met by Max. "Max, you made it. I'm happy to see you."

"Yeah, I thought I should try to make some new friends." "And get better acquainted with some old ones?" "Yeah, that too." Max smiled.

Dawn turned cherry red from blushing.

Freddie leaned back against the weathered fence post, the night moon warming his face. Beside him, Mark expertly rolled another joint, his eyes narrowed in concentration. The air thick with the scent of marijuana and the buzzing of cicadas.

"Douglas, aren't you doing your senior year for the third time?" Freddie asked. Douglas chuckled, his eyes twinkling with mischief. "Yeah, I keep flunking homeroom," he admitted, puffing out a plume of smoke.

"All you have to do is show up." Freddie snorted. "I know," Douglas muttered, taking a long drag from his joint.

"It's just...sometimes it's easier to not show up at all, you know? Then I don't have to face the disappointment, the expectations, the..." he trailed off, his gaze drifting towards the distant horizon.

For a moment, the three sat in comfortable silence, each lost in their own thoughts, the smoke swirling around them like a silent promise of carefree days and the escape they sought from the pressures of their final year.

* * *

The unexpected arrival of Mr. Myers disrupted the quiet solitude of Zack's evening. The older man, visibly wearied by the years and perhaps the weight of his own conscience, had come to express his gratitude for the job opportunity.

However, Zack had been wrestling with an internal rage and sadness regarding the man who had once abandoned Sandy, leaving behind a legacy of pain that had molded her into the resilient, yet fragile woman she was today. Summoning the courage to confront Mr. Myers, Zack laid bare their emotions, articulating how profoundly Sandy's life had been affected by his absence—her struggles, her hesitations in trusting others, and the lingering shadow of abandonment that haunted her heart.

"I know how you must feel about me. And you have every right. I walked a long road of despair with my own guilt. I want to thank you for being there for Sandy. I know how much I hurt her, and I know it was less of a blow because she had you in her life." His words, laden with a sincere acknowledgment of pain and regret. It was a bittersweet moment, the kind that called for vulnerability and honesty, an effort to bridge the chasm created by past wounds. "We had each other. Sandy is family," Zack responded. "It's because of you and Mama Zack that she even knows what a happy family is," he added, a hint of gratitude in his voice, a recognition of the warmth and safety that they had strived to provide for Sandy. Yet Zack felt an unsettling urgency to clarify the dynamics at play.

"I wouldn't say we're the example of a happy family, but she definitely is kin."

It was important for Zack to make it clear that while they appreciated Mr. Myers' acknowledgment of their role in Sandy's life, that sentiment could not cloud the undeniable truth of their past.

"If you're not prepared to be a part of her life, then I suggest you leave now," Zack urged, their tone resolute yet weary. There was no room for half-hearted attempts at reconciliation; the stakes were far too high for Sandy. As Mr. Myers stood there, grappling with the confrontation, Zack hoped that the gravity of the moment would bring some clarity to a man who had seemed lost for far too long.

Zack wished for Mr. Myers to understand that it wasn't just about him—it was about the little girl who had learned to cope without her father's presence, who had built her world on the ashes of disappointment. They dared to believe that facing this truth might allow Mr. Myers to finally confront his own shortcomings.

It was a delicate balance of past pain and future possibility, a moment where redemption could either blossom or wither away, depending on the choices made in the seconds that followed. "I'm not going anywhere. I'll be here for Sandy." Mr. Myers assured Zack.

Daron, holding a drink, presented it to Rose with a playful, yet loaded, remark: "I got this for you, or should I give it to another white girl I might see."

Rose, catching the subtle jab at her earlier comment, took the drink with a smile and apologized, "Thank you and sorry about my comment earlier."

"It's okay, I get it. Tensions are high, squares are mixing with queers, blacks and whites mixing, everyone is on defense."

"Just so you know, I'm not like the other squares. My best friend and I kick it in Queerville all the time."

"Oh, do you?" Daron chuckled at the unexpected revelation. Rose, continuing to break down the walls of assumptions, shared, "Yes. Do you know Zack? We're real good friends with them."

"Of course, I know Zack. Everyone in Queerville knows who Zack is."

Rose was relieved she and Daron actually had one thing in common at least.

"Wait," Daron exclaimed, "Are you the Rose that helped uncover the conversion camp?" "Yes, I am," Rose confirmed, her voice brimming with pride, "I didn't do it alone. It was my best friend, Dawn. Well, it was mostly her, but I drove."

Daron, visibly excited, declared, "Wow, you guys are like rock stars in Queerville." Rose, perplexed by the praise, asked, "Really?" Daron elaborated, "Yeah, you saved a bunch of kids and helped take that some of the town's most influential."

Rose, realizing the impact of their actions, said, "I guess we did. It's good to know you guys think so. Because it's the complete opposite here in O Town. They practically want to burn us at the stake."

Daron, sensing her apprehension, extended his hand with a genuine smile. "Well, it's an honor to meet you, Rose." Rose, touched by his sincerity, gladly shook it.

The familiar melody of The Five Satins *"To the aisle"* filled the room, drawing them to the center. "Would you care to dance?" Daron asked, his eyes twinkling. "With you? Yes," Rose replied, a radiant smile blossoming on her lips. Daron took her hand, leading her into the warm embrace of the music.

Her gaze locked onto his, and she felt a spark—a palpable connection that sent shivers down her spine. It was a feeling she had never truly known, a yearning that transcended the superficial layers of fleeting encounters. In that moment, the desire for temporary thrills faded away, giving way to something more profound. She longed to dive deeper into Daron's world, to peel back the layers of his experiences and thoughts, to understand the man behind the charming smile.

She wanted to take it slow, to unravel the layers of Daron, to fall in love. The thought of sex, usually an immediate and unavoidable impulse, was completely absent. She was lost in the moment, lost in Daron's eyes, lost in the rhythm of their dance, and for the first time, she felt a flicker of hope that she would find love.

Freddie and Mark had indulged in some mind-altering drugs, and their make-out session in the backyard was a testament to their heightened senses and desires. The atmosphere was thick with anticipation and the hazy clouds of smoke that hung in the air. Meanwhile, Douglas, who had also partaken in the fun, sat nearby, his eyes glazed over as he watched the two men with rapt attention.

Freddie gazed at Douglas, who chewed his lower lip, eager to join. He could see the hunger in Douglas's eyes, the desire to join in on the sensual activities.

Freddie licked his lips, feeling a surge of excitement as he unfastened his pants, exposing himself.

Douglas, unable to control himself any longer, began rubbing on his crotch, his erection straining against his pants. Freddie snatched Douglas's head and forced it onto his lap. Douglas eagerly took Freddie into his mouth, his head bobbing up and down as he pleasured him.

Meanwhile, Mark stood up, freeing his own hard erection. Freddie, still with Douglas's head in his lap, eagerly took Mark into his mouth. The three men moved in a rhythm, their bodies swaying and thrusting in time with each other. It was a scene of pure, unadulterated pleasure, as the three men lost themselves in the moment, their senses heightened and their desires unleashed.

The backyard, which had been quiet and still just moments before, was now filled with the sounds of moans and heavy breathing. The air was thick with the scent of arousal, as the three men explored each other's bodies with a fierce passion. It was a night of wild abandon and freedom, as they surrendered themselves to their desires and the power of the substances that flowed through their veins.

Back in the house, Daron, emboldened by the warmth of their shared laughter, felt the need to address the elephant in the room. It was time to lay his cards on the table, to finally ask the question that had been gnawing at him all day. "Rose," he began, his voice slightly shaky, "Do you think you could see yourself... going out with a fella like me?" Rose tilted her head, a flicker of confusion crossing her features.

"Do you mean a colored boy?" she asked, her tone gentle but curious.

Daron swallowed hard, his nervousness bubbling to the surface. "Yeah," he managed, "You ever dated a colored boy before?" Rose's smile faltered. "No," she admitted, "I can't say that I have." Daron pressed on, his heart pounding in his chest. "Why not? You don't fancy them?" Rose's eyes softened as she replied, "They don't seem to fancy me."

A silent understanding passed between them. Daron took a deep breath, gathering his courage.

"Well, Rose," he said, his voice firming, "consider yourself fancied." Rose's lips curved into a slow, knowing smile.

"Are you asking me out on a date?" she replied, a twinkle in her eyes. Daron, caught off guard by her directness, stammered, "Yeah, I am. I'm sucking at it," he confessed; his face flushed with embarrassment. Rose chuckled, her warmth radiating towards him.

"No," she said, "You're doing just fine."

"Is that a yes then?" Daron asked, his voice laced with hope. "Yes, Daron," Rose answered, a genuine smile lighting up her face, "I would love to go out with you." The air crackled with a newfound energy as they shared an excited grin, a silent promise of a future where their differences wouldn't matter, their feelings would speak louder than any prejudice.

As darkness enveloped the street, casting an eerie glow upon the backyard, Freddie and Mark had long since departed from the raucous party. Amidst the shadows, Douglas, his nefarious dealings continuing unabated.
With practiced precision, he dispensed illicit substances to a group of impressionable teenagers.

Among them was a familiar face, the square boy from earlier, his eyes wide with anticipation. With an eagerness born of desperation, the boy returned, his voice trembling slightly as he addressed Douglas. "Earlier, you said you had something that would get us really high."

"Well, well, well, look who it is," Douglas drawled, a hint of amusement in his voice, "You came to the right place," Douglas replied, a sinister grin spreading across his lips.

Reaching into his concealed stash, he retrieved a small plastic baggie with **a phoenix, in a defiant pose, rising from the ashes, emblem.** "What is it?" the boy inquired, a mixture of curiosity and excitement coloring his voice.

Douglas leaned in close, his breath warm and heavy with the scent of danger. "This, my friend, is called heroin," he whispered conspiratorially. "And it will take you places only imaginable in your wildest dreams."

The square boy's eyes sparkled with excitement as he reached out to take the baggie, unaware of the treacherous path he was about to embark upon.

CHAPTER 3

Mississippi, 1957

Amidst the morning rush to class, Kelly stumbled and dropped her precious books. As dismay washed over her, a helping hand emerged from the crowd. It was Martin, the handsome classmate known for his conservative charm. With his piercing blue eyes, sandy blonde hair, and a warm smile, Martin gracefully bent down to retrieve her scattered belongings.

As he handed them back to Kelly, she uttered a hesitant, "Thank you," her mind preoccupied with the task at hand.

Martin, ever the southern gentleman, introduced himself, his resonant voice carrying a hint of curiosity.

"You're Kelly, right? Kelly Hamilton?" **"Yes,"** a polite smile gracing her lips.

However, despite Martin's undeniable charisma, a certain spark was missing in their interaction. Kelly's eyes remained focused on her books as she politely shook his hand, her mind already racing ahead to the lecture that awaited her. "Nice to meet you," she murmured, her voice polite yet devoid of any genuine warmth.

"I'm Martin, Martin Campbell."

"What are you studying, Martin Campbell?" Kelly inquired. "Political science, you see I'm going to be president of this fine country one day." "Great," she quipped, her voice laced with sarcasm, "Another man to lead us."

A chuckle escaped Martin's lips, "You trust a woman to lead us?" "Why not?" she retorted, her eyes flashing with defiance, "We're capable of the same as any man." The air crackled with unspoken tension. "A woman's place is in the home," Martin stated, his words a stark reminder of the outdated societal norms that Kelly loathed.

"I think it's time I get to class, or should I be home cooking dinner for when my husband gets home?" she shot back, her voice dripping with mockery. With a final, disdainful glance, she turned on her heel, leaving Martin to stand alone, a bemused expression on his face. "That's a fiery one," he whispered to himself, a flicker of intrigue replacing his initial amusement. "This won't be easy."

Queerville, 1957

Mr. Myers had truly become a great help around the shop, his steady presence transforming the place into a more welcoming environment as he immersed himself in the day-to-day tasks that made the small business function smoothly.

At first, Zack had been hesitant about Mr. Myers working there, skeptical of the sudden changes and grappling with their own childhood memories, but they were slowly beginning to come around, recognizing the comfort and stability his presence brought.

The three of them would gather for dinner most nights, sharing meals that turned into lively conversations peppered with laughter, and after they finished eating, they would huddle together in the living room, engrossed in watching scary movies that sent shivers down their spines.

For Sandy, these moments were reminiscent of her childhood; she felt like that ten-year-old kid all over again, relishing the warmth of snuggling under her father's protective arm, reliving the safety and joy she had long missed. Occasionally, she would catch herself uttering the word "dad," and while the term felt foreign on her tongue, it was also imbued with a twinge of newfound normalcy that was slowly setting in, like a comforting blanket wrapping around her heart.

On one particularly exciting evening, she decided to bring her dad to the diner, a place that had always been bustling with her many male admirers. To her delight and amusement, he scared off all the men who were gaping at her, his mere presence radiating a kind of protectiveness that made her heart swell. It was as if he had donned a knight's armor, standing tall and sturdy, ensuring her safety while simultaneously allowing her to rediscover the bond she so dearly craved.

In those moments, the gaps of years apart began to fill with laughter, warmth, and an undeniable sense of family—a strange symmetry blossoming in their lives that felt as if it had always been meant to be.

* * *

The sheriff, his face etched with the weariness of too many similar calls, entered the sterile, cold confines of the morgue. The body on the stainless-steel table was young, barely more than a boy. It was 'The Square,' kid from the party. His face pale and slack. Another teenage overdose, another life cut tragically short.

"What is with these young kids and drugs," the sheriff muttered, his voice heavy with frustration.

"Just killing themselves for a five-minute high."

He went through the boy's meager belongings, finding a small, crumpled plastic baggie tucked inside a worn wallet. It contained a white powder, the remnants of the heroin that had claimed his life. But his eyes drifted to the emblem embossed on the baggie – a phoenix, its wings spread in a defiant pose, rising from the ashes. He couldn't understand it, this desperate need to numb everything, to escape the world, even if it meant losing it forever. As he left the morgue, the phoenix emblem burned in his mind.

O Town, 1957

Val arrived at the abandoned warehouse, where Douglas, Lisa, Robin, Maria, and the rest eagerly awaited her arrival, anticipation in the air as tension hung like a thick fog around them. As she pulled up in her vehicle, the gravel crunching under the tires, Val stepped out with a determined stride, addressing her gathered crew with a sense of urgency that immediately commanded their attention.

"Listen up, everyone," she declared, her voice cutting through the murmurs and anxious whispers that had filled the space. "We certainly didn't anticipate running out of product so quickly. Is anyone still in possession of any inventory?"

The question hung in the air, heavy with implications, as her eyes scanned the faces of her team—each one reflecting a mix of worry and frustration. They all shook their heads no, a collective gesture that echoed Val's growing concern; she could see the weight of their disappointment mirrored in their expressions.

Val popped open her trunk, revealing an abundance of large bags filled to the brim with marijuana. The crew's eyes sparkled with excitement as they took in the sight of their newfound fortune.

"I guess for now just finish selling this Mary Jane. But only to the Queerville side. That way it's just a normal day in Queerville, high teens in tight jeans."

"Any word on the next shipment?" Douglas inquired.

"No, but don't worry. If our shipment doesn't come in. My guy knows where to find more."

"Are we ever going to meet this mysterious guy that we're making rich?"

"In due time Douglas. You just keep throwing those bashes and bringing in these customers. You'll be meeting him sooner than you think."

* * *

Mr. Myers found himself at a crossroads, grappling with complex emotions and conflicting beliefs. He decided to visit Mama Zack.

As he entered her warm, inviting home, he was filled with a mixture of hope and trepidation. His heart felt heavy as he reflected on the struggles he faced regarding Sandy, who was bravely embracing a transgender lifestyle.

Mr. Myers loved Sandy deeply, but the teachings of his faith weighed heavily upon him, creating a storm of uncertainty and inner conflict. He longed for guidance, hoping Mama Zack could offer him some clarity on how she had managed to reconcile her faith with Zack's trans identity.

During their conversation, Mama Zack listened attentively to Mr. Myers, allowing him to express his fears and doubts. She gently encouraged him to

51

consider a different perspective regarding the scriptures. With a compassionate demeanor, she explained that many interpretations of the Bible have been misunderstood over time. Mama Zack emphasized that the texts often condemned behaviors like pedophilia, not the loving relationships that exist between consenting adults, regardless of gender.

She spoke passionately about the essence of God being love, urging Mr. Myers to focus on the importance of acceptance and understanding rather than condemnation.

"God is not about hatred or rejection," she said. "They are about unconditional love. Embracing your child for who they truly are is one of the greatest expressions of that love."

Her words resonated deeply within Mr. Myers as he began to process the idea that loving and supporting Sandy for her authentic self could align with his understanding of faith. Mama Zack's wisdom and kindness provided a glimmer of hope, helping him to envision a future where he could reconcile his love for his child with his religious beliefs.

As he left Mama Zack's home, Mr. Myers felt a newfound sense of determination. He realized that while the journey ahead might be challenging, he wasn't alone. With the right support, love, and acceptance, he could find a way to embrace both his faith and his beloved child's identity.

———————

Zack had been monitoring the petty cash drawer for weeks, and the unsettling realization that money was vanishing, little by little, gnawed at them. Even though the evidence suggested that Mr. Myers might be involved, Zack hesitated to make any accusations without solid proof. Determined to uncover the truth, they devised a plan with Mark to set up a sting operation; they would leave some petty cash around and wait to see if it went missing again.

After a few days of anxious waiting, they discovered that the money had indeed disappeared, giving Zack the heartbreaking evidence they needed. However, despite having proof, Zack found themself paralyzed by the thought of confronting Mr. Myers. The last thing they wanted was to shatter Sandy's perception of her father or to deliver such devastating news to her. As the weight of the secret pressed down on their conscience, it became increasingly difficult to bear.

One afternoon enjoying burgers, in a moment of thoughtless casualness, Mark let it slip, that Mr. Myers was stealing from Zack. Sandy's expression shifted from joy to disbelief as she processed what she heard. Unable to fathom the idea that her father would steal from Zack, she confronted Mr. Myers directly.

Initially, he denied the allegations, but the hurt in Sandy's eyes and her unwavering belief in Zack's integrity compelled her to investigate further. To her shock, she discovered the missing petty cash tucked away in shoulder bags belonging to her father, and in that moment, the reality of the situation hit her like a freight train. Faced with undeniable evidence, Mr. Myers had no choice but to come clean.

Yet in a surprising twist, Sandy found it within herself to forgive him, recognizing the complexities of human flaws and the desperate measures some might take in challenging circumstances. The revelation of betrayal weighed heavily on their relationship, but it also opened a path toward healing and understanding, as Sandy navigated the difficult terrain of forgiveness and trust.

* * *

Sandy was positively buzzing with excitement as she eagerly planned her birthday celebration, a masquerade ball that she had envisioned since childhood, where elegance and mystery would reign supreme. Every detail had been meticulously sorted out with her closest friends, Patty, Charlotte and Zack, who shared in her enthusiasm as they dove headfirst into the preparations. From the decorations that transformed the venue into a whimsical wonderland of shimmering lights and delicate lace masks, to the enchanting live band that would fill the air with music, Sandy had thought of everything to make this birthday unforgettable.

Perhaps the most heartwarming aspect of the evening was the anticipation she felt about sharing the occasion with her father, who had promised to attend and celebrate alongside her.

Sandy's 23rd birthday party was an absolute smash hit, a vibrant celebration that lit up the heart of Queerville as friends and well-wishers flocked in from every corner to honor their beloved queen, Sandy.

The atmosphere buzzed with excitement as folks from Bronxville and Northside turned out in droves, eager to partake in the revelry and shower Sandy with affection on her special day. Her regulars from the diner, those familiar faces who had watched her grow into the dazzling woman she is today, arrived bearing extravagant gifts that reflected the deep bonds of friendship and appreciation they shared with her.

As the live band played a tune that pulsed through the air, the infectious rhythm and vibrant melodies wove their way into the very fabric of the night, irresistibly drawing everyone onto the dance floor in a celebration of life.

With each note resonating like a heartbeat, the large crowd transformed into a swirling mass of color and movement, where laughter bubbled over and spilled into the surrounding atmosphere, creating an irresistible magnetism that pulled even the most reluctant dancers into the fray. The room, aglow with soft lighting that kissed the walls and sparkled off the dance floor, became a sanctuary of shared experiences, where faces lit up with smiles and voices harmonized, blending into a delightful cacophony.

Couples twirled, friends spun each other around, and strangers exchanged glances, all partaking in the rhythm that connected them in a fleeting, yet profound, moment of unity. Amidst the rhythmic echoes of happy voices, was Duffus, the quirky yet endearing boy from the northside, his whimsical spirit and messy hair.

As he approached Sandy, with an infectious grin, his heart raced with a mix of excitement and nervousness, like a schoolboy with a crush. "Hey Sandy, happy birthday! Me and the boys on the northside wanted you to have this," he said, offering a beautifully wrapped gift, the paper glimmering under the twinkling lights decorating the space. "Oh, gee, thank you, Duffus, and tell the boys I said thank you," she replied, with a genuine smile. His presence was a testament to the love and camaraderie that unified the community as they all gathered to celebrate Sandy.

The night unfolded brilliantly; Lisa and Robin spent the evening gazing into each other's eyes, lost in a world of their own while making out in a cozy corner, their laughter mingling with the music, radiating the warmth of young love.

Meanwhile, Maria was on a determined quest, doggedly following Zack, who was masterfully attempting to evade her charming advances at every turn, while Val playfully chased Maria, turning their pursuit into an amusing spectacle that drew chuckles from nearby on lookers.

Further fueling the raucous atmosphere, Freddie and Mark, the party's mischief-makers, indulged in a bit of experimentation with drugs, their wild dance moves sweeping them up into a euphoric rhythm.

As Charlotte and Patty engaged in a spirited vogue battle, showcasing their fierce fashion sense and exaggerated poses, it felt as if time stood still, with each pose and twirl echoing the very essence of fun and celebration. In this kaleidoscope of camaraderie and joy.

As the night unfolded, drinks flowed and the dance floor became a swirl of vibrant colors and infectious energy, capturing the essence of friendship and shared memories. Each moment was a reminder of the beautiful connections that Sandy had nurtured over the years, solidifying her status not just as a queen in title, but as a true queen of hearts, adored by everyone who crossed her path.

With each passing hour, she glanced at the clock, her excitement slowly turning into unease. Zack, ever the observant friend, noticed her growing despondency as she tried to mask her worry with a smile.

When her father finally arrived, the initial joy she felt quickly transformed into something else entirely; he seemed overwhelmed by the colorful expressions of queerness that surrounded him. Instead of the warmth she had hoped for, she sensed his discomfort, a tightening grip on his face that betrayed his unease.

In a life-altering moment that Sandy could scarcely comprehend, her father revealed the truth she had feared: he could no longer bear to stay in Queerville, unraveling his words with a painful clarity that shattered her heart. He told her he was leaving and wouldn't be coming back, and just like that, her dreams of a harmonious birthday celebration were eclipsed by heartbreak, leaving Sandy standing amidst the joyous crowd, feeling utterly isolated while surrounded by loved ones, drowning in the sting of rejection from the very person she had wished could embrace her fully.

The weight of disappointment and betrayal rested heavily on her heart, crushing her spirit and leaving her feeling more isolated than ever. She knew she couldn't bear to face anymore—bright, cheery faces that seemed so oblivious to the chaos that had erupted in her personal life. Spotting Zack across the room, she felt a flicker of hope.

With a sense of urgency, she approached them, quietly pleading for an escape from the festivities which had turned into a hollow celebration.

"Zack can you please get me out of here?" she said, her voice barely more than a whisper, her eyes brimming with tears that threatened to spill over at any moment.

Zack, sensing the distress in her eyes, nodded without hesitation, ready to help their best friend salvage what little remained of her special day.

Without a word, they slipped away from the party.

———————————

As they reached the familiar comfort of Zack's loft, the door closed behind them softly, shutting out the chaos and clamor of the outside world, and soon she felt the pressing weight of her troubles begin to lift, if only slightly. In that private sanctuary, with its soft lighting and cozy corners, the harsh realities of the day began to dissolve, replaced by the comforting presence of someone who truly understood her heart, allowing her to breathe just a little easier as she finally felt safe to release the tears that had been building beneath the surface.

In an attempt to lift Sandy's spirits, Zack carefully retrieved the birthday cake they had painstakingly baked just hours earlier.

As they unveiled the cake, its enticing layers of rich chocolate frosting glistening under the soft glow of the room, the sight of the cake, adorned with delicate sprinkles that danced like confetti across its surface, sparked an immediate twinkle in Sandy's eyes, restoring a bit of the joy that had been missing moments before.

As they set the cake on the table, the aroma of fresh chocolate wafted through the air, enveloping Sandy in a cocoon of comfort; it reminded her of all those late-night baking sessions they had shared, filled with laughter and flour-covered smiles. And chocolate being her favorite. Sandy was thrilled not just because of the cake itself, but because it symbolized Zack's commitment to making her feel cherished on her special day.

As she gazed at the beautiful creation, a wave of happiness washed over her; she felt deeply loved and appreciated, knowing that Zack had taken the time to ensure her birthday was as magical as she could imagine.

With a radiant smile, she couldn't wait to cut into the cake and share it with them.

As they sat on the couch, fork in hand, savoring the sweet cake and washing it down with cold beers, they found themselves drifting into nostalgia. They reminisced about childhood adventures, silly pranks, and dreams that once felt vibrant and achievable. With each shared story, Sandy felt a small fragment of her burden lift.

Grateful tears shimmered in her eyes as she turned to Zack, her voice a fragile whisper as she thanked them for always being her unwavering support—the one person who knew how to distract her from the storms of life that threatened to engulf her. It was in this comfort that she finally revealed a hurt she had buried deep for far too long; how devastated she felt when Zack left after their 18th birthday, a wound she hesitated to bring up before.

The truth poured out of her heart like an open floodgate, and she realized how much she had missed having her best friend, her anchor, by her side through the tumult of life. Zack's expression softened, "Why didn't you just ask me to stay?" they inquired gently, their eyes searching for understanding.

Taking a deep breath, Sandy reflected on the moment, shaking her head slowly as she replied, "Because I knew you needed to go."

In that moment, a profound understanding settled between them—an acknowledgment of sacrifice and the bittersweet nature of growing up, that it often meant letting go of what was cherished to allow for the possibility of future happiness, even if it came at a great cost.

The night transformed from one of despair into a celebration of connection and resilience, their spirits rising as they danced freely around the loft, laughter echoing off the walls, finding solace in one another's presence, as they created new memories.

―――――――――――――――

The next morning, Sandy woke up on Zack's couch, feeling the remnants of a good night's sleep mixed with the lingering haze of the previous night's activities. The warm morning light filtered through the half-drawn curtains, casting a soft glow across the room, while the sound of water splashing against tile floated in from the bathroom — *Zack must be taking a shower,* she thought. Stretching her arms and legs to shake off the stiffness from the couch, she glanced around at the remnants of their late-night escapade: dirty dishes in the sink and crumpled beer cans. The sight of the clutter invoked a sense of responsibility in her, and Sandy began to tidy up the mess they had made.

Zack finally emerged from the bathroom in a towel. Sandy, her back turned to Zack, pivoted slowly, her gaze sweeping over Zack's towel-clad form. Their sculpted chest gleamed, abs taut, and biceps chiseled with the precision of a master artisan. Zack's tall, muscular frame exuded power even in their comfortable setting.

Sandy couldn't avert her eyes from their broad shoulders and rippling muscles. Zack was truly unique; their androgynous appearance captivated her, making it feel like she was seeing Zack for the first time.

Her attention drifted to the tantalizing glimpse of Zack's bulge beneath the towel, and she was struck by an overwhelming surge of attraction.

In her distraction, the plates she held slipped from her grasp, shattering on the floor.

"Oh, shit. I'm sorry, Zack," Sandy stammered, her voice thick with embarrassment. Zack's gaze softened with amusement as they approached Sandy, their footsteps soundless on the tiled floor.

"Just leave it; I'll get it later. Thanks for cleaning up."

"Yeah, it's becoming my thing every time I come over here," Sandy responded, shaking off her hormones.

Zack reached out, gently brushing a stray hair from Sandy's face. Their fingertips lingered on her skin, sending a shiver down her spine. Sandy met Zack's gaze, her heart pounding in her chest.

In that moment, time seemed to stand still as she lost herself in the depths of Zack's eyes.

"Are you calling me dirty?" Zack teased, breaking the spell and eliciting a genuine laugh from Sandy that rang like music in the air.

"I didn't plan on staying over. I need to change before my shift." "No worries I can drop you off home to change before taking you to work."

"Really Zack? Thank you so much," She replied and they headed out.

* * *

Charlotte was delighted when she spotted Zack and Sandy walking through the entrance of the diner, her usual sunny disposition amplified by their presence. "Well, if it isn't the king and queen of Queerville! Sandy, darling, why did you leave your own birthday party? I mean, really, child..." she exclaimed, her voice warm but laced with playful admonishment.

However, Sandy barely registered Charlotte's words; her attention was unwaveringly fixed on Zack, her heart racing with fragmented memories of what had just unfolded between them in the loft. Despite the clamor of the diner and Charlotte's continued chatter, Sandy found herself lost in thought, grappling with the realization that her feelings for Zack were evolving into something far deeper than mere friendship. This revelation ignited a tumult of mixed emotions within her—excitement intertwined with fear, longing tinged with insecurity.

Just then, Charlotte snapped her out of it with an abrupt shift in tone, her demeanor shifting to one of authority.

"I'm glad you two are here. I need you guys to move some boxes in the back," she commanded, cutting through the haze in which Sandy had been engulfed. Zack, ever the good-natured friend, let out an audible sigh, taking a deep breath as they headed toward the storage room.

The air in the room was thick with the smell of old pizza and dusty inventory, but as Sandy followed behind them. Her mind, still reeling from the knowledge of Zack's brief affair with Maria, couldn't help but surface her frustration as she muttered, "You know, Zack, I'm still mad at you."

She was surprised at how the bitterness laced her words, her heart fluttering with a mix of unresolved anger and unacknowledged attraction.

"Why?" Zack replied, confusion etched across their face.

"Because, I can't believe you had sex with Maria." Sandy's words carried a hint of jealousy or perhaps disdain.

"So, what."

"I just don't want to see you get hurt. And you know Maria is with Val now. You're just looking for trouble."

"I don't want that girl. It was just one moment of fun. It won't happen again."

Sandy gave Zack a doubtful look.

"I'm serious," Zack said with a straight face. Sandy's doubtful gaze softened as she perceived the sincerity in Zack's eyes. "Okay, now you can help me. Are you okay with being in here?" Sandy asked, her voice laced with concern for Zack's claustrophobia.

"Yeah, it's not that small and there's windows. Plus, I have you here," Zack said winking at Sandy, before placing a box on the shelf. "What is all of this stuff?"

"Extra inventory for the singles bash and the Queer off contest." Sandy replied.

"Are you going?"

"Yeah. Are you?"

"Hell no." Zack chuckled.

"Don't laugh. Why aren't you going?"

"Sandy, do I look like the singles bash type?"

"I forgot Zack is too cool to look silly for love," Sandy sneered, her words dripping with playful sarcasm.

"Exactly," ~~Zack agreed, a sense of satisfaction in their voice~~.

A sudden crash startled them.

A crate full of packing peanuts had toppled over, scattering its contents across the floor.

They exchanged surprised glances, then, in a moment of shared impulsiveness, dove into the mound of fluffy white peanuts, like two children rediscovering the joy of simple pleasures. Zack grabbed a handful of peanuts and hurled them at Sandy's face.

Sandy, not to be outdone, returned the gesture, and soon the room was filled with the playful chaos of a peanut fight. They wrestled playfully, covering each other in the soft, white fluff, making peanut angels in their impromptu snowdrift.

As Sandy ended up buried under the mountain of peanuts, Zack reached down to pull her up.

She sprang up quickly, coming nose to nose with Zack.

Their eyes met, it began innocently, a shared look of amusement, then the moment hung heavy...becoming an intimate exchange, a silent communication between two people who had just discovered a new dimension to their friendship.

Sandy peered into Zack's alluring green eyes; her gaze drawn to the fire burning within them. But these flames were different; they weren't roaring, they were calm, steady, and profound. She felt butterflies flutter in her stomach, a sensation she had never experienced before. It was as if she were standing on the precipice of something beautiful and unknown, looking into the soul of her hero, her protector, her safe place.

Zack, in turn, stared into Sandy's eyes, a mixture of surprise and wonder washing over them. They had always seen her as a close friend, a confidant, but this moment unraveled the tapestry of their usual playful banter, revealing threads of vulnerability and deeper emotion.

Zack was lost in the warmth of her gaze and felt the tentative stirrings of something more profound than friendship. It was exhilarating and terrifying all at once.

However, just as the realization dawned upon them, the bubble of their intimate connection burst. Zack snapped back to reality, their heart racing as they instinctively released her hand.

The air between them thickened with an uncomfortable silence... "Um, I got to go," Zack mumbled, barely meeting her eyes as they both leapt up in a rush, the exhilaration of their moment replaced by a hurriedness to escape the very feelings they had unearthed. They fled, leaving behind the electric tension, both aware that their friendship would never be quite the same again.

Zack returned to the front of the diner, where they spotted Freddie and Mark, a familiar scene that provided them a sense of comfort amidst the chaos of their thoughts.

As Zack slid into the booth across from Freddie and Mark, they felt a mix of relief and lingering discomfort;

the encounter with Sandy still hung in the air like a thick fog, her teasing smile and playful glances replaying in their mind. It had been an innocent exchange, but something about it felt charged, almost electric, and it left them feeling flustered as they tried to transition back to the familiar camaraderie of their friends.

"What's up, love birds?" they murmured half-jokingly, hoping to overshadow their own turbulent thoughts with the lighthearted banter of their friends.

Freddie, ever the social butterfly, wasted no time getting to the point, "Hey, are you going to the singles bash?"

"God, no, why does everyone keep asking me that?" Mark, never one to miss an opportunity to poke fun, chimed in, "Because you're single." He punctuated the statement with a sneer, his eyes twinkling with amusement.

Zack, however, was not amused. "Single, not desperate," Zack retorted, their tone sharp and defensive.

Before they could elaborate further, Sandy approached the booth, her hand landing on Zack's shoulder with a warmth that felt suffocating in that charged moment. The weight of her touch, the way her fingers lingered a moment too long, sent shivers down Zack's spine. The air thickened with the tension of their unspoken feelings hanging heavy between them.

"Hey guys, what can I get for you?" she asked softly.

Zack, unable to meet her gaze, tried to ignore the sensation of her hand, but then Sandy, to their utter horror, slid into the booth, her body pressing against theirs.

"School was a drag, so I'll take a vanilla milk shake, cheeseburger and double fries." Freddie sighed. "Okay. Anything for you Mark?"

"Just a burger, small fry and a coke. Thanks Sandy."

Sandy's gaze fell on Zack.

"Zack, are you having anything?" Zack, unable to speak, shook their head.

Sandy nodded and headed towards the counter to prepare their drinks.

"Did you see that?" Zack asked Freddie and Mark, who appeared perplexed. "See what?" Freddie inquired.

"Sandy practically sitting on my lap."

"Sandy always sits on your lap," Mark remarked indifferently. "Come to think of it, you're the only person I've ever seen Sandy even touch," Freddie added with a hint of sarcasm.

Mark looked at Freddie, a flicker of realization crossing his face as he caught the depths of Freddie's comment.

"You're right," he exclaimed, exasperation seeping into his voice, "I've never seen her shake anyone's hand. Have you ever touched Sandy?" he asked Freddie. "No, not anymore," Freddie replied trailing off, "I touched her once and it made me... feel things." Mark burst into laughter. "Sandy will definitely do that to you. She can turn a gay man straight."

Zack glanced over at Sandy at the counter.

Shook it off.

"Are you okay?" Freddie asked.

"Yeah. Are you speaking at this queer house event for Charlotte?"

"No. But she asked Mark to speak a little about what he's been through."

"I think that would be a great idea." Zack replied, their gaze drifting back to Sandy...

Suddenly, Sandy looked up, her eyes locked with Zack's across the diner. As she lifted a perfectly ripe strawberry to her lips, she could feel the weight of their gaze.

She held it up, licking it before biting into the juicy fruit, its sweet nectar spilled forth, trickling down her chin in a way that felt both innocent and scandalous. She savored the rush of sweetness, then deliberately suckled her fingers with an exaggerated slowness, each slow movement calculated to draw Zack's attention further, amplifying the intimate atmosphere that surrounded them.

With a playful flick of her tongue, she sucked teasingly at her fingertip, letting out the slightest sigh of indulgence, as if the simple act were a delicious secret meant just for them.

"Are ya'll seeing this?" Zack exclaimed, their mouth agape. Freddie and Mark turned to look, but Sandy was simply adding whip cream to Freddie's milkshake.

"Zack what's going on with you?" Freddie asked, his voice laced with concern.

Clearly, Zack was imagining things.

"I think I'm tripping," Zack muttered under their breath, before abruptly standing up and storming out, leaving Freddie and Mark bewildered, just as Sandy came over with their drinks.

"Why is Zack freaking out?" Freddie asked Sandy. Sandy exhaled deeply, the weight of the situation settling on her shoulders as she slumped into the booth. "We had a moment earlier," she explained, her voice laced with a hint of frustration, "And Zack... well, Zack doesn't know how to deal with their emotions, so they're freaking out."

"Wait... what? What's the tale?" Freddie was shocked.

"That's it. That's the tale. It was a moment nothing more."

Mark, ever the mischievous one, leaned in with a sly grin.

"So, you've never thought about being together?" he inquired, his voice dripping with playful innuendo.

Sandy, however, remained resolute.

"No! Never, not once."

"You guys are actually very compatible." Freddie added. "Okay, I have to get back to work now." Sandy's eyes rolled skyward as she returned to the counter with a dismissive chuckle.

Freddie, however, couldn't contain his excitement. For years he'd watched the undeniable chemistry between Sandy and Zack, the unspoken connection simmering beneath the surface of their friendship.

This, he thought, could finally be it.

The two most desired people in town, finally falling for each other. His two closest friends, finally realizing the love they have for each other. He couldn't contain his happiness, radiating it with a broad grin.

"Those two will be in bed together by the end of the week," he whispered to Mark, his voice brimming with hope.

Back at the counter, Charlotte and Sandy tended to their duties. Charlotte engrossed in reviewing receipts, while Sandy's mind wandered to Zack's recent peculiar behavior.

"Charlotte," Sandy finally spoke up, "Has Zack seemed...odd to you lately?" "Odd in what way?"

"I'm not sure," Sandy replied with uncertainty, "Just different."

Charlotte's eyes sparkled with a knowing glint as she leaned closer, a mischievous smile playing on her lips.

"Oh, I see."

Sandy, caught off guard, tilted her head in confusion, "See what?" she asked, scrutinizing Charlotte's expression.

"It's that time."

"What time?"

"The time when best friends realize they're in love." Charlotte stated with unwavering confidence, her grin widening. "No, Zack and I are just friends. What is it with everyone?" Sandy insisted, her voice a mixture of amusement and denial.

"Please, Chile," Charlotte exclaimed, "I've known both of you for an eternity. You've always harbored a soft spot for Zack."

"No, I have not," Sandy felt a rush of heat to her cheeks.

"Look at you, blushing," Charlotte teased. Sandy's initial reaction was a sputtered protest, **"I'm not blushing, this is just absurd. Zack is my best friend."** But even her protest felt weak against the backdrop of her growing smile.

"And you were just being Zack's best friend when you scared Maria away right?" Charlotte asked, her tone laced with playful sarcasm.

"Yes, Maria was no good for Zack."

"And what about Kelly? You threatened that poor girl the first time you met her. You don't like any woman Zack dates because they're not you. No one is good enough for your Zack except you."

The weight of Charlotte's words hung in the air causing her to pause and reflect. She was lost in deep thought. The echoes of her father's words about a possible future with Zack ringing in her ears.

A flood of memories washed over her, sparking a familiar warmth along with a new confusion. Could it really be true? Was her love for Zack more than mere friendship? Maybe there was a grain of truth in Charlotte's playful accusations. The nagging thorn of confusion pricked at her heart; a clash of emotions made her question everything.

As she grappled with this revelation, her voice trembled with curiosity as she asked Charlotte, "How can you be so sure about me and Zack?"

"I watched you both grow up, become best friends and fall in love with each other. I always thought in the end you would be together."

"Really?"

"Absolutely," Charlotte affirmed, "You're a libra and Zack is a Leo. You two are perfectly matched."

Yet, despite Charlotte's resolute assertion, Sandy remained enveloped in denial, "Sandy, can you honestly say that you don't have romantic feelings for Zack?" Charlotte probed gently, her voice softer now, as if to coax forth Sandy's hidden truth. Sandy hesitated for a moment, a tense silence stretching between them as she searched her soul for answers.

Suddenly, clarity washed over her like a tidal wave, an epiphany that took her by surprise. She looked Charlotte in the eye, and with a gasp that was almost a whisper, she exclaimed, "Oh, fuck!" The revelation crashed into her, raw and unfiltered—this was more than just a fleeting infatuation; this was love, the kind that set off alarms in her mind and awoke feelings she thought she'd buried. Charlotte erupted into laughter; her joy infectious yet maddening.

"Love, done snuck up on you and bit you in the ass. I know it hurts." That laughter rang in Sandy's ears, a stark contrast to the internal tempest swirling inside her.

Sandy's breath hitched, her chest constricting as a wave of panic washed over her. Hyperventilation seized her, leaving her gasping for air.

"What am I supposed to do now?" she stammered; each word punctuated by the frantic drumming of her heart. She felt trapped between the thrill of the realization and the fear of what it meant.

"Well, breathe child. This is not supposed to be a bad thing," Charlotte mocked, teasingly, but Sandy was far from convinced. Her mind raced, darting through memories of late-night talks and shared laughter with Zack, each moment now infused with meaning she hadn't dared acknowledge until that very second. It was a terrifying and exhilarating realization all at once. Yet as she contemplated her feelings, no matter how daunting, she could not deny their depth; she undoubtedly had feelings for Zack.

"You don't understand," she blurted, her voice taking on a frantic edge, "I have an Aquarius rising sign. We do not fall in love. We run from it, we sabotage it, booby trap it, set it off with explosives and leave. Then cry about it later to our next partner," her voice, a jumbled torrent of anxieties, echoed her internal struggle.

Charlotte, with a firm hand, pulled Sandy closer, grounding her with a gentle hug. "Breathe, calm down. It is not the end of the world to learn that you're in love with your best friend."

"No, not in love. We still do not know that. You asked do I have romantic feelings for Zack. Which clearly, I do but no one said anything about being in love."

"So, what are you going to do now that you know?" Sandy's shoulders slumped, a wave of disappointment washing over her. "Nothing. Zack is clearly still hung up on Kelly, it doesn't matter," she muttered under her breath, the words tasting bitter as they escaped her lips.

"I'm gonna go get ready for the singles bash."

The sting of acceptance settled in her chest, mingling with her heart's lingering hope. And with that, she walked away, leaving Charlotte to watch, concern etched on her face, as her friend wrestled with the unexpected, overwhelming truth of her heart.

* * *

Daron's gaze was fixed on the corner of Main Street outside the cinema, his heart pounding in his chest. He had been waiting for this moment, for Rose, for what felt like an eternity. The sun hung low in the sky, casting long shadows that danced across the pavement, while the familiar hum of the evening crowd blurred into a soft murmur that barely touched his ears. Each tick of the clock seemed to echo louder than the last, amplifying the anticipation that churned within him like a storm.

Finally, a flash of white caught his eye, slicing through the sea of everyday life, and his breath hitched as he strained to catch a glimpse of her. There she was, radiant as ever, her white sundress fluttering gently in the warm summer breeze, each step she took a graceful note in a symphony composed just for that moment.

Rose was a vision in a stunning white dress that accentuated her fiery red curls. He marveled at how she appeared even more beautiful than he'd remembered, a breathtaking blend of classic grace and contemporary allure, reminiscent of a modern-day Marilyn Monroe.

"Wow, Rose," he finally managed to say, his voice hoarse with awe, "You're really a doll." Rose smiled, her eyes sparkling with joy. Daron, regaining his composure, pulled a beautiful bouquet from behind his back.

"I got these for you," he said, his heart soaring as her face lit up with pure delight. "Awe, thank you," Rose gushed, her voice laced with disbelief. "No one's ever brought me roses before." Daron grinned, feeling a surge of pride.

"Good. So, I'm the first."

As the two settled into the cozy confines of the cinema seats, their gazes met furtively, each stolen glance holding a promise of unspoken desire. Daron's fingers danced tentatively on his knee, their movements mirroring the subtle rhythm of his heart. They were both too nervous to make the first move. Daron, mustering his courage, settled his hand on his knee. Rose, mirroring his action, did the same.

Daron slowly slid his hand closer, and Rose, as if guided by an invisible force, followed suit. Their fingers brushed, a jolt of electricity running through their bodies. Daron gently caressed the back of Rose's hand, his touch sending shivers down her spine. A smile bloomed on her face; a smile born from the purest, most innocent joy she'd ever known. Daron, emboldened by her response, pulled a classic move, stretching his arm around Rose's back.

She leaned in, welcoming his embrace, their bodies close, a silent promise hanging in the air.

* * *

Over at the shop, Zack was completely absorbed in their craft, meticulously applying the final touches to a custom order that had consumed their attention for the better part of the day. Tools and materials scattered across the workbench testified to the labor they had poured into the project, a perfect visual metaphor for the monotony that had begun to characterize their life—a relentless cycle of working late into the night, followed only by a series of fleeting one-night stands that offered nothing more than temporary distraction.

As the door swung open and Freddie walked in, to pick up Mark for the singles bash, he couldn't help but feel a jolt of surprise at the sight of Zack still glued to their work.

"Zack, why aren't you ready?" Freddie called out, the urgency in his voice palpable, but Zack only looked up, momentarily puzzled.

"Ready for what?" they replied, brow furrowed like a sculpted work of art itself. "The singles bash," Freddie insisted, his expression a mixture of excitement and disbelief.

"I told you I'm not going to that," Zack shot back, their voice steady yet edged with a hint of annoyance, "Wait, is that where you guys are going?"

"Yeah, you should come," Freddie urged, trying to coax some spontaneity into his friend's rigid routine.

"Why are you going? You're not single," Zack pointed out, their skepticism creeping in as they closed their tools with a deliberate finality.

"We're going to mingle with the singles," Freddie replied.

Zack chuckled at their friend's humor, the kind that never failed to lift their spirits no matter how heavy the day felt.

"So, what are you going to do, sleep?" Freddie mocked with an exaggerated expression, his eyebrows raised, and a grin plastered across his face, clearly relishing the chance to tease Zack. But Zack just shook their head, "I can't sleep, got a lot on my mind," they sighed, the words escaping their lips with an air of resignation, as if the very idea of resting was both foreign and impossible at that moment. The truth was, sleep seemed elusive; their mind was a whirlwind of thoughts and emotions, each one colliding with the next, making it hard for them to settle down.

"Oh, you got Sandy on the brain," Freddie teased.

Zack gave Freddie a quizzical look. "What?"

"Zack you were practically freaking out at the diner earlier. What was all that?"

Unable to suppress their thoughts any longer, Zack blurted out, "Back in the storage unit, something happened between me and Sandy."

"What?"

"I don't know... something." Zack stammered. "You looked into her eyes, didn't you? I looked in Sandy's eyes once. She almost turned me, that body, that face." Freddie's voice trailed off as he became lost in his own musings. "Will you stop joshing!" Zack snapped, their patience wearing thin.

"Listen, Zack, if you think there's something between you and Sandy go for it."

Zack shook their head, "No, way."

"You guys are best friends. You know each other better than anyone. You're compatible, you're both smoking hot. What's the problem?"

Zack turned their head away, their gaze falling upon the flickering lights of the machinery.

"Oh, I get it. You still think Kelly is going to walk through that door and remember everything. It's been nine months already Zack, that's not happening. You can't keep hanging onto that ghost. Kelly's gone, and you've got to move on. Can't you see that? You deserve happiness, and Sandy may just be the one who can give that to you." Freddie's voice was imbued with a sense of urgency, an imploring tone that desperately sought to penetrate Zack's stubborn soul.

The words hung heavy in the air; a painful reminder of the reality Zack desperately wanted to escape.

"I don't know how to move on," Zack whispered.

"You can start by asking Sandy out," he suggested, their tone both understanding and encouraging.

"If Kelly being gone taught you anything, it should be that you never know how long you have with someone. So, make each day count."

Just then, Mark emerged from his room, looking handsome and ready for the night, his shirt perfectly pressed, and his hair styled just so, radiating an effortless charm that set the tone for the evening.

"You're looking nifty," Zack remarked, an approving nod punctuating their compliment.

"Thanks, Zack," Mark replied, a hint of gratitude evident in his smile as he adjusted his collar. Freddie, ever the excited one, blurted out the news, "Zack is going to ask Sandy out."

Mark's face lit up at the revelation, his expression transforming into one of pure excitement as he threw his arms around Zack in a tight hug.

"I'm happy for you guys," he exclaimed.

However, Zack's reaction was strikingly different from the lively and animated enthusiasm that radiated from Mark, whose eyes sparkled with possibilities as he envisioned a romantic rendezvous between his two friends. "I'm not asking Sandy out."

The weight of their denial hung thick.

"Well why not?"

"I don't see Sandy that way. She's just a friend," Zack replied, their voice devoid of the thrill that Mark seemed to find in the idea.

"You should ask her out that's an easy yes."

"That's what I said," Freddie agreed.

Zack sucked their teeth, a gesture of resignation, and returned to work on the car. "You guys have fun tonight," they muttered, a faint echo. Zack, oblivious to the fact that sometimes, the heart operates on a frequency entirely different from that of the mind.

* * *

Charlotte's single bash was a vibrant spectacle, thronged with men and women adorned in their most alluring attire. The club pulsed with an eclectic mix of straight couples embracing in rhythmic dance, gay men exuding confidence, and lesbians radiating allure. The atmosphere was thick with anticipation as love permeated the air.

Amidst the lively crowd, bursting with exuberance and animated conversations, Lisa, Val, and Maria made their grand entrance into the bustling singles bash that was pulsating with music and laughter.

The vibrant colors of the decorations swirled around them, setting an electrifying backdrop as Lisa's eyes sparkled with an irresistible desire, her gaze eagerly scanning the room in search of her beloved Robin, who had promised to join them but was nowhere in sight.

"Where is my baby?" Lisa sighed dramatically, her voice rising above the cheerful cacophony, a hint of anxiety flickering in her otherwise bright demeanor.

Val raised an eyebrow and leaned closer to Lisa; curiosity tinged with mischief evident on her face. "Hey, why are you at a singles bash anyway?" she inquired, her tone teasing yet genuine.

Lisa, attempting to brush off her disappointment, replied with a playful smirk, "For moral support." The subtle implication hung in the air, prompting Val to counter with a mischievous glint in her eyes, "Moral support for who?" Val draped her arm affectionately around Maria, who stood beside them, her brow furrowing as she pivoted the conversation towards her own concerns.

"Where is Zack?" Maria asked, her voice tinged with expectation.

Lisa cast an amused look at Val and quipped, "I guess for Maria."

Charlotte ascended the stage, her presence commanding attention. "Look at all you beautiful colorful Queer people out there. Tonight is the night to find love. So, don't be shy. The theme of the night is, if you see an orange rose, they swing both ways. Yellow for my trans babies, blue for my gay boys, violet for all you sexy fems..."

The crowd peered around at all cups in hands. "And green means go, that's right, go get you one. Like what you see, then just simply take them by the hand and go dance. If you see someone with a red rose in their hair, baby just enjoy the show. Those hotties are out of your league."

Sandy's entrance was a force of nature, a whirlwind of crimson and ivory that swept through the room, demanding everyone's attention. Her white and red dress, a masterpiece of form-fitting silk, clung to her curves like a second skin, the high split revealing a flash of long toned legs with each step.

It was a dress that whispered of confidence and allure, the kind that made hearts skip a beat and jaws drop. Her curly hair, styled in a sophisticated updo, framed a face that seemed to glow with an inner light. A single red rose, pinned behind her ear, added a touch of feminine grace, contrasting beautifully with the red of her dress. Her eyes, the color of warm honey, scanned the room, taking in every reaction – the hushed whispers, the awestruck stares, the men who instinctively straightened their ties. Sandy knew she was the center of attention, and she reveled in it. Every step she took, every glance she cast, was a calculated move, a silent proclamation that she was the queen of the room, and everyone else was just waiting for her to speak.

On the other side of the dance floor, Val and Maria engaged in a heated and jealousy-filled conversation.

Val, their face flushed with a mix of anger and desperation, cornered Maria, their voice a low, urgent growl.

"You said you would be my girl if I lead the Red Dragons," she spat, her eyes burning into hers.

"No, I said I would be with you if you ran the crews. You lead the dragons, that's it. Zack is still in charge."

"I beat Zack in the race. I'm the top guy now." Maria, her voice laced with a biting sarcasm, replied, "No, Val, Zack let you win the race. Everyone knows that. Why do you think no one wants to race you? You're not the one to beat." With a final, dismissive shove, Maria turned and walked away, leaving Val standing alone, the music blurring around her as the weight of her delusions crashed down upon her. The promise of a future with Maria, a future she believed she had secured, evaporated into the smoke and sweat of the dance floor, leaving her with nothing but the bitter taste of betrayal and an overwhelming sense of her own inadequacy.

Lisa's eyes scanned the vibrant ballroom, searching for Robin amidst the swirling gowns and dapper suits. The air buzzed with laughter and conversation, yet she felt a nervous anticipation, her heart thumping a frantic rhythm against her ribs. Then, in the corner bathed in the warm glow of a chandelier, she saw her.

Robin, radiant in a sunflower yellow dress that seemed to radiate its own light, was a vision. Her hair cascaded down her back like a silken waterfall, framing a face lit with a smile that could melt glaciers. Lisa was mesmerized, her breath catching in her throat at the sheer beauty of her girlfriend. Robin caught her gaze and her smile widened, her eyes sparkling with delight.

She rushed towards Lisa, a joyful laugh escaping her lips. With a burst of energy, Robin embraced Lisa, the scent of jasmine and something distinctly Robin-esque filling Lisa's senses. She leaned in, her lips meeting Lisa's in a sweet, tender kiss.

Hand in hand, they stepped out onto the dance floor, moving seamlessly to the rhythm of the band, their bodies swaying in unison. Lost in the music and the moment, Lisa felt a surge of happiness, knowing this was exactly where she belonged, with Robin, in this beautiful world they were creating together.

* * *

The crisp autumn air whipped around Rose as she walked alongside Daron, the flickering streetlights casting long shadows on the sidewalk. A gust of wind, colder than the rest, swept through, sending a shiver down her spine. Daron, sensing her discomfort, swiftly removed his varsity jacket and draped it over her shoulders. "Thank you," Rose said, "You know, you're a real gentleman, Daron." He shrugged, a charmingly dismissive grin spreading across his face.

"Aw, I'm just doing what any man would do." Rose chuckled softly. "No, not all men. You'd be surprised how badly some men treat women." Daron's smile softened, his gaze earnest.

"My mama would kill me if I treated you anything less than a queen." Rose's smile widened, a hint of mischief in her eyes. "Go mom."

Daron paused, his gaze lingering on Rose for a moment longer than necessary. "It's such a beautiful night," he said, his voice low and husky. "What do you say to one more stop?" He extended his hand towards her, his palm open and inviting. Rose met his gaze, her heart skipping a beat. Taking his hand, she replied, "Lead the way."

The pulsating beat of the music thrummed through the room, a relentless rhythm that wrapped itself around Sandy's curvaceous figure as she swayed alone.

A seductive smile played upon her lips; her eyes closed as she reveled in the music. She stood amidst the swirling bodies on the dance floor, a solitary figure in a sea of couples.

Men, their eyes filled with lust, approached her, extending invitations to dance, but each offer was met with a polite refusal. Sandy wasn't looking for company, she was lost in her own private world.

Then, the air crackled with a sudden influx of energy as Zack walked in. The room shifted, the girls swooning over their arrival, their gazes glued to Zack like moths to a flame. But Maria, her own heart pounding with a mixture of jealousy and possessiveness, shoved the other girls aside, hissing at them to back off before grabbing Zack's hand and pulling them onto the dance floor.

"I was hoping you would show up," she said, her voice laced with a hint of triumph. "Have you seen Sandy?" Zack asked, their gaze sweeping the room, a flicker of concern crossing their features. "No, I haven't seen Sandy," Maria said, her voice strained, "Listen, how about we get out of here? I know you're not in here looking for love."

But Zack wasn't listening.

Their eyes had locked onto Sandy across the room, her beauty radiating like a beacon in the dimly lit space. She looked stunning, her smile a flicker of joy amidst the swirling chaos, and in that moment, everything else faded away. The music, the crowd, even Maria's presence, all dissolved into a backdrop as Zack focused entirely on the woman who stood bathed in the pulsing light of the dance floor.

Sandy locked eyes with Zack, and the world around them faded into a blur. Her feelings, dormant for so long, surged to the forefront, transforming her into a siren.

The music pulsed through her, and she swayed, a seductive dance of desire. Every movement was calculated, a weapon aimed at Zack's heart.

Zack, normally so grounded, was captivated, their eyes glued to her as if seeing her for the first time. Maria, left standing alone, became a fading memory as Zack was pulled further into Sandy's gravity.

Zack crossed the room… moving towards Sandy… their steps heavy with newfound desire… circling her like a predator drawn to its prey, absorbing the sight of her… their gaze tracing the lines of her body as she continued to move with an intoxicating rhythm.

The undeniable magnetism pulsed through her, weaving in and out like a live wire, drawing them in further; her every movement was a spell, casting enchantment that held them hostage in a reverie of longing.

She knew the power she wielded, offering Zack a tantalizing 360-degree view as she swayed and twirled seductively, deliberately maintaining her distance yet inviting them to imagine the warmth of her touch, the gentle embrace that promised to follow should they summon the courage to bridge the gap. Each motion was a seductive whisper, a silent challenge that begged them to pursue, to step closer and become lost in the whirlwind of her charms.

Zack had always cherished their friendship with Sandy, but tonight, under the shimmering lights of the crowded venue, they began to view her through a different lens. No longer was she just their best friend, but a captivating woman who drew them in with every twirl and smile.

Meanwhile, a group of rejected men watched from the sidelines, their expressions caught in a perplexing combination of shock and jealousy. They had each hoped for a chance with Sandy, always admiring her from a distance, but never once had they seen her exude such confidence. *"She's never moved like that before. She's never looked at anyone like that before,"* they thought, some clenching their fists in irritation. It was as if her transformation into this radiant woman was happening right before their eyes, leaving them uncertain and envious.

Zack closed the distant between them.

The men watching held their breath in unison, anticipating Sandy's next move. *Would she accept the invitation that Zack's approach seemed to offer?* Each partially hoping to see her retreat from Zack, but more secretly dreading the possibility of witnessing her drift further into the allure of a moment that they could only dream of.

As she spun gracefully within Zack's midst, her aura seemed to enchant the air around her, and Zack felt a magnetic pull that was impossible to resist. She slowly grinded her body against Zack's, their limbs intertwined in a silent conversation of passion that spoke volumes without uttering a single word. The way she swayed her hips, her gentle hands, so fluid in their movement, encircling her waist.

Yet, as the pair twirled through the crowd, the rejected men heartbreak was palpable on their faces, twisted expressions of envy and longing reflecting the raw intensity of what they had lost. Each glance from the sidelines told a story of desire unfulfilled, of moments that could have been, as they watched Sandy and Zack immerse themselves in their intoxicating ballet.

Sandy turned to face Zack, her eyes locked on theirs, drilling into the depth of their desire. Zack, captivated, leaned in, their lips poised to meet hers; a fleeting breath away from sealing their unspoken bond.

But Sandy, her voice a low murmur, stopped them short, asking, "Are you sure that's what you want?"

The question hung in the air, charged with unspoken desires and carefully laid traps.

Zack, their own emotions swirling, uttered, "You don't want to?" Sandy responded with a quiet confidence, "I want you to be sure. I don't play second fiddle to anyone." Her words were a declaration, a statement of her own worth. Zack, caught in the crossfire of their own conflicting desires, left without a word, leaving Sandy standing there, a beacon of unyielding self-assurance.

Over at Lover's Lane, Daron and Rose lay sprawled on the hood of his sleek convertible, their eyes fixed on the star-studded sky. "You were right," Rose sighed, her voice a soft whisper, "It is a beautiful night. The sky never looked so lit up with stars before." Daron nodded, his gaze lingering on her face. "Yeah, it's the kind of night that makes you appreciate the small things," he murmured, a hint of wistfulness in his tone. Rose, sensing his unspoken thought, echoed, "Yeah, the small things." She turned her head, her gaze meeting his. Daron shifted, breaking the silence, "What are your plans for after graduation?" he asked, his voice tinged with a touch of anticipation.

Rose responded with an equally playful snark, "You mean if the mayor doesn't force us to repeat our senior year again? Oh, gee, I don't know."

Daron chuckled, his eyes crinkling in the corners.

"Rose, you are a funny girl," he said, his voice laced with amusement. "What about you? What are your plans?"

"Oh, I'll be playing college football then going to the pros." Daron responded confidently.

A hint of admiration slipped into Rose's voice, "So, you must be really good?" she asked, almost incredulous. Daron, his face radiating pride, replied, "Yes, Rose, I have every major college scout wanting me to attend their college next year." Rose's eyes widened, "Wow, that must be exciting. You could go anywhere in the world."

Daron, a smile spreading across his face, said, "You have to come see me play, Rose." Rose, a touch of uncertainty in her voice, asked, "Am I allowed to?"

Daron, his brows rising in disbelief, replied, "Allowed too? There isn't any segregation in Queerville."

Rose was ecstatic to hear that.

"I should try out for the cheerleading squad." Her excitement was palpable, and she impulsively jumped up, her arms flailing in the air.

"You can cheer for me on the field at my next game." Rose, her voice brimming with enthusiasm, "Oh, I would be delighted to."

Daron, his heart pounding, leaned in for a kiss, but Rose, suddenly apprehensive, pulled away. "It's getting late," she said, her voice a little shaky, "I probably should be heading home now."

After the raucous singles bash had come to an end, Zack found themselves in a state of bewilderment, their thoughts swirling around the striking image of Sandy that lingered in their mind like a captivating melody they couldn't shake off. As they watched her from across the crowded room, she transformed in front of their eyes from the familiar friend they had known all their life into a breathtaking vision, an irresistible bombshell whose beauty seemed to light up any space.

It was as if a veil had finally been lifted, revealing a side of her that had always been there but had somehow gone unnoticed until that electrifying moment.

The realization sent a jolt of understanding through them—suddenly everything fell into place. Zack recalled all those times they had felt an inexplicable urge to chase away boys who dared to flirt with her, the barely suppressed rage that bubbled up within them whenever they sensed someone unworthy of her affections.

Could it be that beneath the surface, they had been guarding a heart that beat silently for her all along? This newly uncovered revelation opened up a floodgate of emotions—feelings they had buried and ignored were now surging forth, compelling them to confront the truth they had overlooked for so long. Faced with the undeniable fact that they had always considered her special in ways they had never acknowledged, they felt a mix of excitement and anxiety.

Zack couldn't shake the sense of urgency that washed over them; they realized they couldn't let another day go by without exploring this newfound connection. With a resolute heart and a mind racing with possibilities, Zack vowed to pursue Sandy, driven by a desire so profound it eclipsed all their previous hesitations. They knew they had to ask her out, to discover if this thrilling spark between them could ignite into something far more powerful and meaningful than either of them had ever imagined.

In the tenebrous embrace of a star-lit night, Val and her loyal band of accomplices orchestrated a daring heist on a secluded dirt road. As their roaring engines approached, the Bronxville Devil's drug-laden van careened off the asphalt under the force of their relentless assault. Brutally subduing the hapless occupants.

A brutal confrontation ensued, the air thick with the sound of fists connecting and bodies colliding. Val's crew seized control of the illicit cargo.

Val opened the cargo and triumphed ablaze in her eyes, as she addressed her eager followers, her voice a resonant echo in the darkness. "Gentlemen, it seems we're back in business. Load this onto our vehicles. I want a man in every nook and cranny of O Town – every dance hall, cinema, and skating rink. Let's not forget the Lovers' Lane clients. Tonight, we unleash a flood of euphoria upon the folks of O Town, propelling them into oblivion." Val spat with a greedy grin.

CHAPTER 4

Mississippi,
1957

Over at the College of Mississippi, the air crackled with a potent mix of defiance and determination, a palpable energy that surged through the crowd of protesters gathered on the university grounds.

Kelly, now a fierce advocate for women's rights, stood amidst this sea of fervent supporters, her heart racing in tune with the chants and slogans that called for equity and respect. The vibrant feminist signs, each adorned with powerful messages and bold artwork, formed a striking contrast to the traditional brick façade of the university, emphasizing the palpable shift in ideology that was taking place within these storied walls.

She clutched a stack of flyers; each one representing not only their collective struggle but also their unwavering demand for equality—an equality that transcended mere words and manifested in tangible change. The flyers spoke of a world where women weren't confined to the narrow expectations imposed by a patriarchal society, where their ambitions and dreams could flourish unimpeded by outdated norms. All around her, passionate voices echoed her sentiment, weaving a tapestry of hope and fight against injustice, as stories of resilience and courage filled the air like the sweet scent of blossoming spring.

In that moment, amidst the banners waving high and the rhythmic drums of solidarity, Kelly felt empowered, not just as an individual but as part of a larger movement—a movement that transcended geographical boundaries and history, promising a future where every woman could stand tall, free from the shackles of inequality, ready to carve her own path in the world.

Martin approached Kelly, his gaze fixed on the scene, "I just knew it was you causing all this chaos," he stated, a hint of accusation in his voice. Kelly, undeterred, met his gaze with an unwavering spirit.

"Well, no one has ever made a change quietly," she retorted, her voice carrying a quiet strength. Martin, intrigued by her resoluteness, sought to understand the heart of their protest. "So, what exactly are you guys protesting?" he asked.

"The wealthy donors and taxpayers don't see the necessity of a state women's college. So, they're trying to close it down once again," she stated, her voice laced with frustration. "And this is where you come in?" Martin asked, a flicker of confusion in his eyes, "You don't even go here."

"I'm trying to help my fellow sisters in need who just want to get an education," she said with conviction her words radiating empathy and solidarity.

Martin was caught off guard by Kelly's unwavering dedication. "Half of the women in this state attend college," he stated, seemingly oblivious to the systemic inequalities that limited access to higher education.

"Do you know just one point two percent of women attend college?" Kelly countered, her voice laden with disappointment, "The world has such narrow expectations for girls whose only destiny is to be married and let a man take care of her," she continued, her words a stark indictment of the societal constraints placed on women.

Martin, clinging to traditional notions of womanhood, responded with a prevailing patriarchal mindset, "Well, that is the goal, isn't it? Marriage, home, kids, that's the agenda," he stated, his words revealing a deep-seated belief in the inherent subservience of women. "Yeah, it's the male's agenda to keep women dependent on them. So, we don't think for ourselves and go out and start our own careers," she retorted, her words a powerful challenge to the established order.

Martin, taken aback by Kelly's fierce intellect and unwavering conviction, chuckled, his earlier skepticism replaced by a newfound respect.

"I have to say, Kelly Hamilton, I've never met any girl like you," he confessed, his voice tinged with admiration.

In that moment, a silent understanding passed between them. Martin, touched by Kelly's passion and the genuine plight of the women protesting, took a sign from the pile and held it up, joining the cause.

Kelly, witnessing his surprising shift in perspective, smiled. Her heart filled with hope, she knew that even in the face of seemingly insurmountable obstacles, change was possible, one step, one sign, one conversation at a time.

Present Day
Queerville, 1960

In the aftermath of the diner, Zack diligently worked to restore order amidst the shattered debris. As they swept away broken glass and scattered fragments, Charlotte, her heart heavy with sorrow, entered the establishment. Tears glistened in her eyes as she mourned the damage that had been inflicted upon her cherished diner. Zack extended their arms, embracing Charlotte in a comforting hug, offering solace amidst the turmoil.

"Don't worry," Zack reassured her, "With a fresh coat of paint and a bit of elbow grease, we can restore this place to its former glory." Charlotte, however, carried an unspoken weight upon her shoulders. "You know I won this diner in a poker game. Opened it with just one hundred dollars in groceries. I don't know about this Zack."

"We can't let it end like this. This diner is a safe haven to everyone in this community. We can rebuild it," Zack suggested. "Maybe if we rebuild it, Sandy will come back home," she suggested tentatively, her eyes searching Zack's for any sign of a spark—or perhaps desperation.

At the mention of Sandy, Zack's demeanor shifted; they looked away, clearly disturbed.

"You guys still haven't talked?" Charlotte pressed, feeling the tension in the air like a taut string ready to snap.

Zack hesitated, a mixture of pain and regret flashing in their eyes. "I haven't seen Sandy in two years… and I don't ever want to see her again." The weight of those words hung between them, an unspoken understanding that sometimes, even the strongest ties could fray and break, leaving behind only echoes of what once was.

Three years ago...
Queerville, 1957

The diner buzzed with the usual morning routine, filling the air with the familiar sounds of breakfast chaos: the clinking of dishes as servers deftly maneuvered between tables, the low murmur of conversations that ebbed and flowed like a gentle tide, and the insistent sizzle of bacon on the griddle that permeated the space with a mouthwatering aroma. In this orchestrated symphony of morning life, Zack stood out as a jarring note of raw nerves and excited anticipation.

They burst through the door like a whirlwind of energy, arms clutching a radiant bouquet of vibrant hibiscus flowers that seemed to almost glow against the dim ambiance of the diner. Sandy, standing behind the counter — looked up. The moment she spotted the flowers, a smile unfurled on her lips, warm and inviting as the morning sun spilling through the window beside her.

"Hey, Sandy," Zack breathed, a rush of exhilaration and anxiety coursing through them as they handed her the arrangement. "I got these for you."

The flowers, bursting with color, were a splendor unto themselves, and Sandy's delight seemed to light up the room, the sweet fragrance of hibiscus filling the air around her like an embrace.

"Hibiscus," she whispered, her voice rich with appreciation, and Zack felt a flicker of hope spark within them as they watched her eyes linger on the exquisite blossoms. "Zack, these are beautiful. You know these are my favorite," she continued, her gaze now locked onto theirs with a depth that was both reassuring and unnerving.

"Yeah, I... I know, I remember," Zack mumbled, their own nervousness suddenly palpable, causing them to fumble with their words like a child presenting a poorly illustrated drawing to a parent.

"Zack you can only get these three towns over."

"Yeah, I got up early."

"You got up early and took a drive, three towns over?" Sandy questioned, her brow furrowing in confusion, surprise etched across her features like a canvas of emotions.

"Yes."

"What for, Zack?" Sandy pressed, her eyes searching theirs with an intensity that made their stomach flip.

A heavy beat of silence hung in the air, thick and charged, before Zack took a deep breath, the moment feeling monumental.

"This is me asking my best friend... out on a date."

As soon as the words escaped their lips, the air shifted, and Sandy's smile faded, replaced by a look of sheer bewilderment that was almost palpable.

"Because you bought me flowers?" she questioned, a hint of disappointment lacing her tone like an uninvited guest.

"Well yeah," Zack mumbled, feeling their heart sink as what once felt like an audacious hope began to slip through their fingers like sand.

"Try harder, Zack," Sandy said, her voice gentle but firm, "The flowers are beautiful. Thank you."

A wave of dejection washed over Zack.

* * *

Over at Queerville High, Rose, with a nervous smile, watched the cheerleading squad rehearse.

The squad, a vibrant mix of black women with curves that moved with a natural rhythm, exuded confidence and energy. Rose felt a prickle of intimidation as she observed their fluid movements.

The head cheerleader, a tall, imposing figure with a fierce gaze, clapped her hands and announced, "Okay, girls, let's see what you can do."

As Rose stepped onto the floor, a wave of whispering and threatening stares washed over her. She fought the rising panic, determined to conquer this challenge. They started the routine. The head cheerleader watched Rose closely, her expression unreadable. Rose's moves were technically sound, she possessed a natural rhythm, but something was missing. She needed attitude, a fire in her eyes.

The routine ended, leaving an awkward silence in the air. The intensity in the room was palpable, every eye fixed on Rose. She started to feel uncomfortable, a tiny white girl surrounded by confident black and brown girls.

Then suddenly the head cheerleader spat, "Hey, red head," she addressed Rose, her voice firm, "You're in."

A collective cheer erupted from the girls; their earlier stares replaced with genuine smiles. Rose felt an overwhelming wave of relief wash over her.

"Really?" she exclaimed, her voice laced with surprise and joy. "Of course," the head cheerleader chuckled, "After all you and your friend did for this town, how could we not welcome you?" The girls enveloped Rose in a group hug, the tension dissipating. "Welcome to the Q squad," the head cheerleader declared, "We need to keep practicing for the prep rally tomorrow."

* * *

The diner buzzed with an unusual energy, the air filled with the scent of grease and something else, something faintly sweet and unfamiliar. Sandy attentively took the orders of two teenagers, whose eyes were bloodshot, pupils dilated, and their hunger seemed to be a bottomless pit.

The first boy in a garbled voice, requested an extensive feast of cheeseburgers, fries, a milkshake, and a slice of pie.

"Is this for both of you?" Sandy asked, her eyebrow raised in curiosity. The second boy, munching on a stray French fry, mumbled, "No, I'll have the ham and cheese, fries, Crème soda and a banana split."

Sandy, her mind struggling to keep pace with the unusual order, simply nodded and said, "Okay, I'll put these in for you guys." Sandy couldn't help but notice the peculiar behavior prevailing in the diner that afternoon. The patrons were noticeably euphoric, their laughter echoing through the air as they indulged in their meals with an almost frantic intensity.

As Sandy relayed the orders to Charlotte, who was diligently reviewing receipts, she couldn't resist expressing her observation. "Have you noticed anything different with people today?" Sandy asked, her voice laced with concern. Charlotte simply shrugged and said, "Different like what?"

Sandy, gesturing towards the room, "I mean...look."

Charlotte panned across the diner, observing the chaotic scene. Every patron, from the elderly couple to the young teens, was engulfed in a fit of uncontrollable laughter, their faces flushed and their appetites seemingly insatiable. They were all, undeniably, high.

Just then, Zack stormed in, holding out a pearl necklace, its glimmer catching the dim diner lights. Zack placed the necklace around Sandy's neck, "I saw this in the window, and I thought it would look better on you." Zack's voice tinged with a nervous excitement.

Sandy, taken aback, "This is beautiful, Zack, but I can't accept this." Zack, insistent and slightly desperate, pleaded, "Please Sandy, you've always been there for me. It's just a token of my appreciation," Zack paused, then added, "Just let me take you out on one date Sandy."

Sandy looked at Zack, their eyes brimming with desperation, and a hint of a smile played on her lips.

"You're getting closer," she said softly, patting them reassuringly on the chest. "Don't give up," taking a step behind Zack, she leaned in and whispered in their ear, "It's worth it, I promise."

As the sunbathed the Queerville High football field, casting a warm golden glow over the manicured grass and painted lines, Rose stood by the sidelines, bubbling with excitement and anticipation. The sound of cleats pounding against the turf and the rhythmic shouts of the football team practicing filled the air. She eagerly waited for Daron.

Her heart surged with pride about joining the cheerleading squad. She couldn't wait to share the news with Daron. Seeing him run off the field, his face lit up with a smile, she blurted out, "Daron, I made it! I made the squad!"

He swept her into a hug, lifting her off her feet, his joy mirroring her own. "I knew you could do it," he said, his voice full of pride. "I want to go out and celebrate," Rose declared, her enthusiasm bubbling over. "I have a workshop tonight," Daron replied, "how about tomorrow night?"

"Okay, that'll do," Rose agreed.

Suddenly, a voice cut through the air, "Is that Rose?" Rose's stomach twisted as she turned, and her eyes widened in horror. It was James, his smug grin widening as he took in the scene. "What are you doing here?" she asked, her voice trembling. "Finishing my senior year, just like you," he shot back, his eyes shifting to Daron.

"Who are you pretending to be for this guy?" he sneered, "A colored girl?"

Daron, his face hardening with anger, snapped, "Watch your mouth."

"No offense, but you don't have to buy the cow, she'll give you the milk for free," James said, reaching down and grabbing his crotch, his crude gesture fueling Daron's rage.

Daron, without hesitation, launched a punch that connected with James' jaw, sending him reeling backward. The team, alerted to the commotion, surged forward to separate the two.

"Who was that guy?" Daron asked, concern etched on his face. Rose, mumbled, "I'm sorry." Her face flushed with embarrassment and shame as she struggled to find the words to explain her past with James. Overwhelmed by guilt and humiliation, she turned and fled the field, leaving Daron alone with his unanswered questions.

Zack found themselves once again at the diner. As they burst through the doors, eyes desperately scanning for Sandy, the air crackled with the unspoken tension that had been building inside them ever since her rejection. It had been hours, but the memory of that moment still haunted Zack, leaving an ache within them that demanded to be addressed.

And there she was, perched on a stool at the counter, nonchalantly finishing her meal, completely unaware of the storm brewing in Zack's heart. Summoning every ounce of courage, Zack approached her, knowing that this was a pivotal moment.

"What are you doing, Sandy?" they blurted out, the intensity of their feelings spilling forth like a river breaking free of its dam. "Don't you feel what's happening between us?" The confusion that washed over her face felt like a blow straight to Zack's chest.

"What do you mean, Zack?" Her question was innocent yet piercing, prompting Zack's heart to race even faster as they tried in vain to articulate the complex web of unresolved emotions.

"You don't feel this chemistry between us? This longing that's driving me insane?" They could almost see the gears turning in Sandy's mind as she hesitated, her gaze flickering with uncertainty.

"I feel... a lot of things going on between us," she finally admitted, "But I'm not sure if it's what you think it is. Maybe we shouldn't risk ruining our friendship."

At that moment, Zack's heart plummeted, the weight of her words sinking deeply into their chest like a stone.

"We wouldn't ruin it," they insisted, their voice rising with conviction, "We can turn this into something special. Don't you want to give it a try?"

Sandy fell silent, her features unreadable as she weighed the gravity of Zack's plea. "It's not about what I want," she eventually replied, sadness lacing her tone, "It's about what you want, Zack."

Those words crashed over Zack like a wave.

"I want you," Zack declared, their gaze unwavering, every ounce of sincerity pouring into each word. But just as hope flickered, Sandy's challenge cut through the air like a knife.

"Prove it," she whispered, standing up slowly and leaving Zack with nothing but the stark reality of their solitude. Zack knew that they now had to embark on the unpredictable path of proving their love.

* * *

Rose and Daron's encounter unfolded in an emotional flurry. As Rose stormed down Main Street, her heart heavy with embarrassment, Daron caught up to her. His concern was evident in his voice, "Rose, there you are. I've been looking everywhere for you," he called out, his voice laced with concern.

Rose turned, her eyes red-rimmed, and a wave of sadness washed over her. "Hey, Daron," she mumbled, her voice barely above a whisper. "What's going on?" Daron pushed, his heart aching for her. "Talk to me, Rose."

She hesitated, then blurted out, "You deserve a better girl, Daron. I'm no good for you. You deserve a good, wholesome girl that's still a virgin."

"What are you talking about, Rose? What does any of that have to do with us?"

As if on cue, a group of white people passing by stopped to stare, their gaze lingered on Rose, making her feel like an exhibit in a zoo. She snapped, unable to contain her anger, "What are you all looking at? We are not a circus act. Keep it moving!" The white people shuffled away, but Rose's fury was far from extinguished.

Back in Daron's car, Rose finally broke down, overcome with shame. "I'm sorry, I should've been honest with you about my past," she confessed, her voice cracking.

"I should've told you everything."

Daron reached for her hand, his touch gentle and reassuring. "We all have a past, Rose. I don't care about any of that. My past doesn't define me, and yours shouldn't define you either," he said, his voice filled with sincerity.

A flicker of hope sparked in Rose's eyes.

"Do you mean that?" she asked, her voice trembling with uncertainty. Daron nodded, "Yeah, I have a past too. If you can forgive mine, I can forgive yours."

Rose's shoulders relaxed; a genuine smile finally graced her lips. "You know, no one's ever stood up for me before," she said, her voice thick with emotion.

Daron reached out, cupping her chin in his hand, his thumb gently stroking her cheek. "As long as you're my girl, no one will ever disrespect you again."

* * *

Dawn stepped into Max's home, the familiar scent of dust and the echo of past memories filling the air. It had been a long time since she'd been there, a time marked by the absence of Kelly, a constant reminder of the tragedy that had torn their family apart. Dawn, remembering the familiar comforts of the home, commented on the absence of the fine China, a stark reminder of how things had changed. "Yeah, my parents took all the good China so we're using paper plates."

"I don't mind it's kind of romantic," Dawn said, trying to lighten the mood, but the air felt heavy with unspoken sorrow. "How is Kelly?"

"Kelly is, well, Kelly."

Dawn sensed the underlying pain in his words, knowing that his sister's memory loss had created an unbridgeable chasm between them.

"Still no progress?" she asked gently.

Max shook his head. "Nope. My parents are thrilled she hasn't regained her memories. She's the perfect daughter they've always yearned for."

Dawn's lips tightened as she shared Max's bitter realization. "That's exactly what they wanted," she concurred.

"Before I left, I went to say goodbye to her. The person I was speaking to, had my sisters face, but it was someone else looking back at me."

"Losing that connection with your twin. That has to be hard for you. I still think she's going to come running through that door and raise hell."

"Oh, yeah, she would give my parents hell for what they did to her." "What about you Max? They sent you there too."

"It's different for me. I didn't lose someone I love." "Zack, boy did she love Zack. Her face would light up whenever she saw them. The love in her eyes when she would talk about Zack. It was sickening, I used to be so jealous of them. It's sad to know she'll never remember that."

As she spoke, the realization that Kelly would never remember Zack filled Dawn with a profound sense of sadness. A life stripped of cherished memories and moments that once brought her so much happiness.

How could something so beautiful be lost to the oblivion of forgetfulness? She would never grasp the essence of that love—a love that had blossomed like a flower in spring, only to be cruelly snatched away.

———————————————

The warehouse hummed with a tense energy as Val delivered her instructions to her crew. Her eyes, sharp and calculating, scanned the faces of Douglas, Lisa, Robin, and Maria, each one a cog in her ruthless machine.

"We have a big shipment, and we need to move quick," Val stated, her voice a low growl. "Every corner, every suburb, every hop, every skate rank – wherever there are square kids with sweaters, I want one of you dealing to them." She thrust a stash of heroin into each of their hands, a silent testament to their mission.

One by one, they filed out, leaving only Maria, whose gaze held an almost predatory admiration for Val.
"I love it when you take charge," Maria purred, a hint of a smile playing on her lips. "You're starting to come into your own, I see. Maybe I was wrong about you."
Val just shrugged, a small smirk playing on her lips. There was an unspoken understanding between them, a dark intimacy that pulsed beneath the surface.

Their exchange dissolved into a searing kiss, Val's hands pulling Maria's jacket off, her touch fierce and possessive. Maria, eager and responsive, lifted Val's shirt, her fingers tracing the soft contours of her body. The warehouse became a stage for their desire, the metal walls echoing with the sounds of their passion.

Val, consumed by the moment, lifted Maria onto the hood of her car, their bodies entwined in a desperate dance.

Outside, the crew were already in action. Teens, their faces pale and drawn, lined up outside an abandoned shop, their eyes fixed on the drugs being dealt with a detached, almost numb acceptance.

Douglas, his smile predatory, peddled his wares to unsuspecting housewives at their doorsteps.

Across town, Lisa and Robin worked their magic in the hotspots: paradise road, the cinema, the skating rink. Each deal, each transaction, fueled the insatiable machine that Val had created.

As the night fell, Douglas found himself at Lover's Lane, his usual haunt. A junkie, his eyes glazed over, approached his car, his need palpable.

"Hey man what you need?"

"A can," the junkie rasped, his voice barely a whisper.

Douglas, his face tight, shook his head. "I don't have that much on me right now. Those kids bought me out." The junkie, desperate, shifted his weight, his gaze pleading. "What do you have?" he asked, his voice a desperate plea.

"A few sticks," Douglas replied, offering his wares as a last resort. The junkie, rummaging through his pockets, realized he didn't have enough.

"I must've dropped some money," he mumbled, his voice laced with shame and desperation.

"Man, you trying to ice me?" Douglas asked, his voice laced with suspicion. "No, I really think I lost it. There has to be another way I can pay," the junkie pleaded, his eyes filled with desperation.

The air hung heavy with unspoken tension. Douglas, his face impassive, looked at the junkie, the question hanging between them: how could he possibly pay for his fix, knowing that his debt was far greater than just money?

* * *

Dawn and Max lay tangled in the sheets, their bodies intertwined, their breaths mingling. A fire built between them, fueled by desires that had been dormant for too long, until Dawn abruptly pulled back, her eyes wide with an intensity that Max couldn't quite decipher.

"Wait, Max," she whispered, her voice laced with a mixture of urgency and concern, "How does this feel for you? Is this exciting you?"

Max, caught off guard by the sudden shift in their momentum, answered simply, "Yeah," a confused expression clouding his face. Dawn pushed on, her voice quivering slightly, "So are you bi-sexual?"

Her question hung in the air, unanswered for a moment that stretched into an eternity. Max's brow furrowed in bewilderment. "What?" he finally managed, a hint of irritation edging into his tone.

"I just thought," Dawn stammered, "Because you were at the conversion camps..." The unspoken implication hung heavy between them.

Max took a deep breath, his voice calming as he explained, "Parents also sent their kids there to get them to behave, to follow their beliefs. They wanted to turn us into some square, conservative bots."

He paused, waiting for Dawn to understand. "So, you do like women?" she pressed. "Yes, Dawn." His answer seemed to break a dam within her, the tension she'd been holding draining away.

With a sigh of relief, Dawn leaned back into Max, and the fire reignited, hotter and more intense than before as they both surrendered to the moment.

Lover's Lane

In the dimly lit confines of Douglas' car, the Junkie's head bobbed thrusting frantically in Douglas' lap. Douglas' breathing grew ragged, reaching a climax as the Junkie lifted his head and wiped his mouth.

"I think that was worth two sticks," Douglas uttered, handing the Junkie the promised drugs. The Junkie took the drugs and vanished into the night.

* * *

Meanwhile, back in the warehouse, Val and Maria swiftly dressed. "You know if Zack finds out what you're doing..." Maria began cautiously. Val interrupted, "Zack ain't going to find out so keep your mouth shut." "How long do you really think you can hide it? Half of O Town look like zombies."

Val countered confidently, "Well, it's a good thing Zack has no more reason to go to O Town." "You're playing a dangerous game." Maria warned her. "So, what. I thought you liked gangsters."

Maria sighed, "See, that's where you and Zack are different. Zack never pretends to be something they're not."

Queerville, USA

As night enveloped Sandy's home, casting the world outside into shadows, Zack approached the curb outside. The dim light of the porch illuminated a tall man standing against the doorway. The sight knit their stomach into knots. The man's presence radiated confidence as Sandy opened the door, her face illuminated by the warm glow of the interior. With a radiant smile that Zack had always cherished, she ushered the stranger inside.

Zack's heart felt heavy, each beat echoing the hollow thud of disappointment as the realization washed over them like a cold wave. The box of chocolates they were holding became an anchor of despair as they felt its weight in their hands, a tangible reminder that they were merely an observer in a moment they longed to be part of.

With a bitter taste of unrequited love lingering in the air, they tossed the box aside, the sound of it hitting the ground muffled by the joyous laughter coming from inside—an ironic soundtrack to their heartbreak.

CHAPTER 5

Mississippi,
1957

The fluorescent lights of the Mississippi College study hall hummed overhead as Kelly hunched over her books, her brow furrowed in concentration. Martin approached her with a casual, almost conspiratorial smile.

"Hey, Miss Kelly, I knew I'd find you here with your nose in the book."

"Where else would I be? Barefoot in the kitchen cooking beef stroganoff."

Martin chuckled, a hint of admiration in his voice. "You are one sassy lady. Tell me, what are your plans for after graduation?" Kelly hesitated, her gaze drifting away from her textbook. "I don't know yet," she admitted, her voice soft. "I still haven't decided how I want to make a change." Martin's smile faltered, replaced by a look of confusion.

"A change? Like what? You're just a woman."

Kelly's eyes flashed with a spark of anger.

"Comments like that one is why more women are needed in the workforce." She slammed her books shut, her anger palpable, and stormed out of the study hall.

Martin, caught off guard, followed her out into the hallway. "Now, wait Miss Kelly I didn't mean anything by it." he called out, his voice laced with desperation.

Kelly stopped, her back to him, and replied with barely contained disdain, "Yeah, you never do." He pressed on, trying to salvage the situation. "It's just, I was thinking about settling down somewhere nice and starting my political career." Kelly turned; her eyes narrowed.

"You want to plant seeds, that's noble. I always had this crazy idea. I would travel the world with someone I love."

Martin's face held a look of disapproval, his voice tinged with patriarchal expectations.

"Oh, that's no life for a woman of your virtue."

Kelly's patience snapped.

"How would you know? You don't even know me." Martin, sensing his misstep, launched into a desperate attempt to redeem himself. "How about we change that? Let me take you out to dinner, Kelly. I promise to be on my best behavior." Kelly considered his offer a flicker of curiosity battling with her lingering resentment. The hallway buzzed with the echoes of their exchange, the unspoken tension hanging heavy in the air.

Queerville, 1957

Zack arrived at the diner with Maria and cozied up in a booth. Maria, draped over Zack like a possessive vine, was in full-on flirt mode, but Zack seemed more amused than anything else. Sandy, however, was not amused.

As she approached to take their order, she deliberately disregarded Maria's presence, her gaze locked on Zack.

The tense silence was broken only by the clinking of silverware and the hum of the diner's fluorescent lights.

"What can I get for you two?" Sandy finally asked, her voice clipped and unwelcoming. Zack, reveling in the tension, responded with a smirk, "Yeah, I'll take a vanilla shake."

Sandy's expression soured; disappointment etched on her face. Maria stammered, "I'll have my own…" intimidated by Sandy's icy stare, she trailed off, "I'll just have some of Zack's milk shake." Sandy's glare, a potent blend of anger and disgust, silenced Maria.

The air thickened further as Sandy, her eyes still locked on Zack, went to make the milkshake, her movements deliberate and slow. Maria, desperate for attention, began to grope Zack, each touch fueling Sandy's simmering fury.

Zack relished the drama, their gaze flitting between the two women, the tension between them seemingly a source of entertainment.

Sandy slammed and flung glasses punching the blender like a boxer before returning with the cold drink.

"Here's your milkshake, Zack," her expression fierce as she held the frosty milkshake above Zack's head, pouring it slowly until the cold liquid cascaded over them like a shower of white cream, "This one's on the house," her voice dripping with sarcasm.

Maria gasped, "Oh my gosh, Sandy."

"Here's a straw, maybe you can suck it out of Zack's ass," Sandy retorted, her voice laced with venom, before marching back to the counter.

Zack, wiping the milkshake off their face, followed behind her, "That was uncalled for."

"Uncalled for?" Sandy countered, her voice strained, "Zack, you're sitting there letting her grope you in front of me."

"So what? I'm single. I'm allowed to see who I want. You think you're the only one that can see other people."

Their faces were inches apart now, barely concealing the history of jealousy and unresolved tension. Sandy's expression faltered; "I'm not seeing anyone, Zack." "Yeah? So, who was your gentleman caller last night, huh?" Zack pressed, their tone accusatory, the atmosphere thickening further with every word.

Caught off guard, Sandy stammered, "What gentleman caller?" Zack's incredulous response echoed through the diner, "Oh, so now you're lying."

Nearby, a customer misread the scene, leaning over to Maria, whispering, "Those two have a lot of sexual energy." which made her startle and hiss at him, sending him scurrying back to his booth.

"What are you talking about?" Sandy demanded as her voice rose even higher, fueled by anger, "I didn't have a gentleman caller. And why were you outside my house last night?"

Zack's face softened, "I was bringing you your favorite chocolate. I know how you like to eat them when you watch your show," their voice tinged with sincerity.

A hint of sympathy crossed Sandy's face, "Zack, that was sweet."

"It doesn't matter, you probably were too busy to watch your show anyway," Zack muttered, their disappointment evident. "Thanks for the milkshake," they added before heading for the exit.

Maria, her hopes for a sex filled evening dwindling, trailed after them.

"Ugh, that was my landlord," Sandy sighed to herself, as she watched Zack and Maria sped off.

Zack's car pulled out of the diner parking lot, heading in the direction of Maria's house. "Wait, this is the way to my house," Maria protested, "I thought we were going back to your place." "I'm going home alone. I need a shower anyway." "Well, we can take a bubble bath together," Maria said, clinging to the last vestiges of her hope. Zack hesitated, "Maria, I've been using you and it's not right. I'm sorry if I've been giving you mixed signals, but I don't want to get back together."

"We don't have to be together to have sex, Zack."

"We should've never started having sex again," Zack said, their voice firm, "That can't happen anymore."

"Zack, it doesn't have to be this complicated."

"I know that's why I'm ending whatever this is," Zack replied, their voice emotionless, "I'm taking you home then I'm going home to take a shower."

"Fine," Maria said, defeated, taking a breath before continuing, her expression hardening with determination, "You know I've never seen you and Sandy fight before."

"Because that was our first fight," Zack said, the weight of their words hanging heavy in the air. "Sandy and I have never been mad at each other, ever. I need to set things right."

Mayor Lewis, his face a mask of forced calm, stepped into the wreckage that was once Machete Mike's unlicensed bar. Scars crisscrossed the walls, a testament to Frank Calhoun's violent visit. The few patrons huddled in the corner, their eyes wide and wary.

"Don't get your panties in a bunch folks. I come in peace," Mayor Lewis announced, attempting to project confidence.

As if on cue, Machete Mike, with a bloody machete in hand, emerged from the back, the sound of a man's screams trailing behind him.

"What do you want, mayor? You here to make a bet?" Mike rumbled, his voice hard as iron. Mayor Lewis responded with a practiced smile, "I make it a habit to only bet on myself. Is everything okay back there?"

Mike grunted, "Yes, everything is fine. Why are you here? You come to shut us down?" Mayor Lewis waved a hand dismissively, "Shut you down? Why, no. I need you in business, see, these folks make winnings with you, then they go give that money to my dealers. No, you stay open. In fact, let me know if there is anything I can do for you."

Mike, ever the suspicious one, chuckled, "Oh, I see another crooked politician aye?"

Mayor Lewis leaned in, his voice low and smooth, "Crooked? I'd like to think of myself as a straight crook. I give it to you straight, my money is always straight. And I expect the same from anyone I do business with. Shit, the only thing crooked is my dick, and even that is towards the right."

114

A genuine chuckle escaped Mike, a sign of grudging respect. "Okay crooked dick man, what can I do for you?"

Mayor Lewis, sensing an opening, pressed on, "Well word around town is you had a visitor. Who I'm assuming is responsible for this remodel. Frank Calhoun, where is he?"

The smile vanished from Mike's face, replaced by a steely glare. "Don't mention that name ever again."

"So, the rumors are true. He was here?"

Mike's voice was a low growl, "Yes, he was here. He shot the place to shit, killed my men and left."

"And what was a man like Frank Calhoun doing in this establishment?"

Mike looked at him, his eyes dark and unreadable, "Same as you. Looking for answers." Mayor Lewis, his voice laced with genuine curiosity, asked, "Answers to what?"

* * *

Amidst the hustle and bustle of the final preparations, for Queer House. Charlotte diligently oversaw every aspect of the space as it readied for the grand opening.

Lisa and Robin meticulously adorned the rooms with intricate wallpaper, while Val and Maria's bickering filled the air with tension. "What is your problem?" Maria asked. "Why were you with Zack at the diner?" Val retorted. "It's a diner." "Why are you always chasing after someone who doesn't want you," Val inquired.

"That doesn't seem to stop you," Maria shot back.

Lisa, unable to bear their constant feuding, interjected, "Could you two please stop and help us instead?"

Maria apologized, but Val stormed out in frustration.

As Charlotte entered the room to assess the progress, Robin, ever the efficient one, replied with a confident, "We're almost done, Charlotte." A wave of relief washed over her as she took in the scene.

The room, once bare and lifeless, had been transformed into a vibrant haven. Brightly colored walls, adorned with uplifting artwork, radiated a sense of joy. The space was filled with comfortable furniture, inviting teens to relax and unwind. "It looks wonderful, guys," she declared, her voice choked with emotion. "Thank you all again, for your help." Lisa, ever the supportive friend, beamed at Charlotte.

"Of course, Charlotte, what you're doing here is a beautiful thing. We're happy to help out."

Robin chimed in with a wistful sigh, "Yeah, I wish I had a place like this growing up."

"These teens are lucky to have you, but you'll always be our mother first, don't forget it." Maria added with a gentle smile. Charlotte, touched by their affection, could only manage a choked, "Awe, my babies," her voice thick with emotion. Overcome with emotion, she opened her arms, and they all gathered around, sharing a warm, comforting hug, surrounded by the love and shared purpose that filled the space they had created together.

* * *

As the sun beat down on Lover's Lane or the now druggie's lane, Douglas roamed from car to car, peddling narcotics to the vulnerable teenagers who sought escape and oblivion.

His car, a dented and faded jalopy, was a haven for those desperate for a fleeting high. As he sat behind the wheel, a young girl, her blonde hair a halo in the sun, approached, **seeking a fix. But she didn't have enough money.** Her desperation was visible in her wide, pleading eyes.

"How much do you have?" Douglas asked, his voice a smooth, deceptive whisper.

"Ten," she replied, her voice barely audible.

Douglas, his eyes raking over her youthful beauty, saw an opportunity. "Please, just give me one. I'll do anything," she begged.

A cruel smile twisted Douglas's lip.

"Get in," he said, unzipping his pants. He saw nothing but a means to an end, a fleeting moment of control over a lost soul.

Meanwhile, at Mama Zack's humble abode, Mayor Lewis, driven by curiosity, paid a visit. "Hello, Mrs. Calhoun," he greeted as she opened the door. Mama Zack, surprised and somewhat wary, responded, "Mayor Lewis?" "Yes. I was wondering if I might have a quick word with you."

As they settled into the kitchen for a cup of tea, Mayor Lewis delved into the mystery surrounding Frank's disappearance.

"That was the last time I seen Frank," Mama Zack recalled. "He hasn't ring you since?" the mayor inquired. "Well, no, I don't see why he would."

The mayor persisted, "Is there any place in Queerville that may have been sentimental to Frank?"

Mama Zack's mind wandered back to the hilltop, a place where Frank would often take the kids and push them on the swing. "The hilltop? He would take the kids up there and push them on the swing." The mayor's curiosity piqued, he asked, "Tell me, did Zack see Frank when he came to town?"

At the hilltop, Mayor Lewis surveyed the scene, a sense of unease creeping over him. He inspected the soil, searching for any signs of a hidden truth.

As police officers arrived on the scene, Mayor Lewis issued his command, "I want this entire hilltop dug up." "What are we looking for?" the officer asked. The mayor's voice hardened, "Well, a body, son." They searched for hours but found nothing.

* * *

Later, at Queerville High, a different kind of fever was brewing. A prep rally, fueled by the collective anger and pride of the school, crackled in the center of the football field.

A banner stretched across the top, *"Grill the Northerners."* The air was thick with the scent of burning wood and teenage rebellion. The crowd, a sea of faces, pulsated with an energy born of tribal loyalties and shared purpose. The cheerleaders, their voices high and clear, led the chants, their movements sharp and synchronized.

Rose stood amongst them; her face illuminated by the flickering flames. Her eyes met Daron's across the field, a silent exchange of love and shared ambition.

On stage, Coach Stevens, his booming voice echoing through the night, addressed the crowd.

"And we'll be expecting to see you all back out here after the game," he declared, "in the most joyous of Queerville customs, the burning of the North side mascot!"

Every word, every gesture, was a testament to the fierce pride of Queerville, a pride that seemed to be fueled by a deep-seated animosity towards the North side.

Cheerleaders, their faces painted with school colors, ran onto the field in a synchronized dance, their smiles unwavering, their movements precise.

As the band launched into the school's fight song, a wave of excitement swept through the crowd. Everyone was part of this, a collective organism pulsating with the rhythm of the drums, the energy of the crowd, the intoxicating scent of the burning fire. In the midst Lisa, Freddie, Val, Robin, Maria, tried to mimic the cheerleaders' routine. Their clumsiness was met with laughter, but their spirit was undeniable, a testament to the shared joy and belonging that the night offered.

In the midst of the bustling crowd, Rose's eyes lit up as she spotted Dawn. With a surge of excitement, she darted over and embraced her in a heartfelt hug that spoke volumes of their bond. Dawn's face beamed with warmth as she returned the affection, her eyes twinkling with a mixture of joy and surprise.

"Oh my god... Dawn!" Rose exclaimed; her voice filled with delight.

"Hi, Rosie. It's been ages!" Dawn replied, her tone equally elated. "You look absolutely radiant."

Rose's heart swelled with pride as she couldn't contain her happiness. "I've been on cloud nine, and I have a special reason I want to share with you," she said, her eyes twinkling with anticipation. Gesturing towards Daron who was standing nearby, "Daron, come meet my best friend, Dawn."

Daron approached with a confident stride, extending his hand to greet Dawn. "Dawn, meet Daron, my boyfriend."

"Boyfriend?" she echoed; her voice tinged with a hint of disbelief. "I don't think I've ever heard you use that word."

"He's the best," Rose whispered, her eyes shining with adoration.

"Hello, Dawn. It's a pleasure to finally meet the other half of the dynamic duo that saved Queerville," he said, a hint of admiration in his voice.

Dawn's eyes widened in surprise. "Dynamic duo? That's very flattering. Well, it's great to meet you, Daron. You must be quite special to have captured this one's heart," she remarked, a playful smile gracing her lips.

Daron chuckled in response. "That's what she keeps telling me." His gaze lingering on Rose with an unmistakable tenderness.

As he joined his team on the stage, Rose then turned to Dawn, her voice filled with genuine gratitude, "Dawn, isn't he just the sweetest?"

"Yes, he is," Dawn replied, her words carrying a weight of sincerity. "Happiness looks good on you, Rose."

With that, Rose pulled her friend into another embrace, their laughter mingling in the air as they celebrated their newfound joy and the unbreakable bond that had weathered the storms of life.

The night was young, and the flames of Queerville's passion were burning bright. But in the shadows, hidden from the light of the bonfire, Douglas continued his work, feeding the flames of another kind of addiction, one that promised oblivion but delivered only pain.

* * *

The phone buzzed on Mayor Lewis's desk, the insistent ring cutting through the quiet of his dimly lit office. He answered, his voice tight with fatigue, "This is Mayor Lewis." The voice on the other end, a woman's voice, chirped, "Yes, Mayor Lewis, I'm returning your call about the John Doe we have."

The mayor's face tightened, a glimmer of hope flickering in his eyes. He was desperate. He'd been scouring the city, every police station and hospital, for any sign of the man he'd been looking for. He immediately hopped in his car, heading for the city's hospice, a place he'd never been before but had suddenly become his only hope.

He found the nurse, a woman with kind eyes and a weary smile, who confirmed that they had a John Doe who matched the description he'd sent.

"Poor guy," she sighed, "He washed up on the beach with no ID. No clue as to who he is. You're the only one who ever came looking."

She led the mayor down the dimly lit hallway, the air thick with the scent of antiseptic and unspoken worry. They arrived at a room, the door slightly ajar.

"Is this the man you're looking for?" the nurse asked, barely above a whisper.

The mayor's face lit up in recognition, and he eagerly inquired, "What's wrong with him?"

The nurse, her face somber, explained, "He was shot in the face. The bullet went through his cheek and out the back of his head. He suffered severe brain trauma." Mayor Lewis felt a chill run down his spine.

"So, he's a vegetable?"

"No," the nurse replied, "He's in a coma."

The mayor's face fell. "A coma? So, he'll never wake up?" he asked, his voice thick with despair.

"We don't know," the nurse replied, "Only time will tell. But with no one paying for his stay here, the state will soon order to cut off his breathing machine."

"That would kill him!" the mayor exclaimed, his voice rising in urgency. "No, I need him alive. I'll take care of his stay here."

The nurse, curious, asked, "Who is this fella?"

The mayor took a deep breath, his gaze hardening.

"He's the future of Queerville," he said, his voice firm, "And the key to it all."

———————————

The diner was closing, an empty husk of its bustling self, with not a customer in sight and all the staff having long departed. Outside, the neon sign flickered in the twilight, casting a muted glow that danced across the deserted space, illuminating the remnants of a day that had slipped unnoticed into night.

Sandy, having just emerged from the back where she had been carrying out the tedious tasks of cleaning and restocking, paused as she caught sight of Zack at the entrance. They were locking the door, the sound of the bolt sliding home echoing in the otherwise silent diner, a final barrier against the outside world.

As they extinguished the last of the overhead lights with a flick of the switch, the stark contrast of darkness enveloped her like a heavy blanket, making the neon glow outside seem all the more vivid and inviting.

Zack looked different in the dimness, their features sharpened, their jawline more defined – sexier than usual... Sandy's throat tightened.

Her heart skipped a beat as Zack took slow steps toward her with an air of deliberate seduction. Their piercing gaze met hers, holding her captive in a moment of unspoken intimacy. The silence was deafening, their hearts pounding in unison.

"Wow. I thought you would be heading home with Maria," Sandy remarked.

"I don't want Maria."

Sandy, feeling the pull of Zacks' gaze, asked, "What do you want, Zack?"

They moved closer toward her, slowly and deliberately, each step a measured seduction.

Zack stopped mere inches away, their breath mingling in the close space.

"How many times do I have to tell you..." their voice low and husky, leaning in Zack whispered, "I want you."

Sandy, feeling the heat rise in her cheeks, took a step back, bumping against the soda machine. The moment stretched, an eternity in the quiet diner.

Zack's lips were a whisper away, their eyes locked in an unspoken promise.

Their fingers brushing against her cheek, and she felt her entire body tremble with heat. But just as their lips were about to touch hers, she stopped them, her voice barely a whisper, "I don't think we should do this."

Zack's eyes narrowed, their lips curving into a seductive smile. "Then tell me to stop." The words hung between them, a challenge and a plea.

Sandy was paralyzed, her tongue unable to form the words. Zack leaned in again, their lips grazing her ear, their breath hot on her skin.

"I can't hear you," Zack whispered, their voice a dangerous seduction, while kissing Sandy behind her ear; her knees buckled. Zack wrapping their arms around her, left soft kisses down her neck, sending shivers down her spine.

She tried to pull back, her voice a choked plea, "Zack, don't." Her heart fluttered as Zack's lips traced a path back up to her ear, drawing a trail of fire in its wake.

"Tell me to stop," they repeated, their voice a husky murmur, their eyes burning into hers. She didn't speak, her body trembling with a mixture of fear and desire.

In a moment of desperation, she dropped everything she held in her hands, her heart racing like a wild stallion as she reached for Zack, grasping their collar with a force that caught them both off guard. Their lips met in a rush, a passionate kiss that ignited a fire deep within her, one that had been smoldering for far too long. Her fingers tangled in their hair, a physical manifestation of her desire, as she drew them closer, igniting a fire that both exhilarated and consumed them. Their lips locked in an intoxicating kiss, tugging Zack closer as if she were trying to meld their very beings into one. The diner serving as a witness to their undeniable chemistry, a whirlwind of heat and passion.

Zack tore open her dress, the silky fabric falling to the floor, lifting her onto the counter, where their desire raged unabated.

As Zack's skilled hands explored Sandy's body. Her inhibitions melted away-- with every kiss, Sandy felt a surge of ecstasy that consumed her entirely. Zack's hands cupping her breasts, their lips finding her neck, their fingers playing with the delicate lace of her bra. Her breaths quick and ragged, unable to contain the pleasure that surged through her. They teased her nipple with their tongue, sending a wave of sensation through her.

Zack lifted her legs, kneeling between them, their head lowering to devour her. The heat of the moment enveloped them, creating an electric atmosphere filled with raw desire. She moaned softly, her hands instinctively gripping Zack's hair, anchoring herself as they savored her warm, sweet juice. Each flick of their tongue ignited fire within her, her body arching toward them in a desperate need that surged through her veins.

Her breath hitched in her throat, a gasp escaping her lips as she let herself succumb to the waves of pleasure washing over her. "Oh, Zack," she breathed, her voice coming out in a broken whisper, filled with disbelief and exhilaration.

Could it really be? Zack, her best friend and protector, was delivering this intoxicating wave of ecstasy. It felt so right, yet so wrong, a delicious contradiction that heightened her excitement—the thrill of crossing an invisible line. The pleasure, however, was undeniable; it was overwhelming, building toward a crescendo that threatened to push her over the edge.

Zack stood up, the smooth fabric of their pants sliding down to their ankles, pooling around their feet. The sudden revelation of their powerful frame was enough to take her breath away. They exuded a strength and confidence that was magnetic, drawing her in even further.

Caught in a trance, she found herself captivated by the sight before her—the way Zack's athletic form seemed to command the space around them, the confidence radiating from them like a powerful aura. It was as if every inch of them held an invitation, a daring challenge that made her pulse quicken. She couldn't tear her gaze away, entranced by the raw magnetism they projected, the way it sparked a sense of yearning deep within her.

Zack spat on their hand, using the warm moisture as an improvised lubricant before entering her.

She gasped, her eyes widening in surprise.

"Compliments to the surgeon," she whispered teasingly, a playful smile curving her lips like a secret shared between lovers. Her fingers tightened around their back, anchoring herself as they began to thrust into her with relentless strokes.

Each powerful movement sent ripples of delight coursing through her body, compelling her to surrender to the euphoric rhythm they established together.

Moans of pleasure escaped her increasingly parted lips, louder and more fervent with each passionate thrust.

Her arms instinctively wrapped around them, pulling them closer, as if to merge their bodies into one entity. The heat between them intensified, her body moving in perfect harmony with theirs, responding to each thrust that sent waves of ecstasy crashing over her like a tidal wave. The pleasure mounted, deeper and more intense with every movement, leaving them both breathless and craving more.

Zack lifted her effortlessly into the air, cradling her body in their strong arms. In that moment, their movements were bold and primal, a dance of unrestrained passion that spoke volumes of their connection. Her body became a canvas for their exploration, each touch and shift igniting a fire that surged between them.

As Zack thrust her up and down, they became lost in the rhythm of their united energy. With each thrust, they climbed higher and higher, inching closer to that exquisite peak where pleasure and ecstasy intertwined.

Afterwards, they laid on the floor, entangled limbs, their breaths ragged, their bodies still trembling from the intoxicating aftershocks of their union. The room was quiet, save for the soft sounds of their labored breathing.

Zack turned their gaze towards her, their eyes locking in a moment that felt suspended in time, each searching for answers within the depths of the other's soul.

"Any regrets?" they whispered, the words barely escaping their lips, laced with a sense of vulnerability. Their voice was hoarse, a testament to the intensity of their performance and the emotional weight that hung in the air.

It was a question that held more than just curiosity; it was an invitation to reflect on the whirlwind they had just experienced, an opportunity to face the uncharted territory of their feelings and desires.

Sandy, her eyes filled with a mixture of longing and regret. "Zack, as amazing as that was," her voice barely above a whisper, "It can never happen again."

Zack frowned, confusion etching deeper lines across their forehead. "Why not?" They searched her face for answers, longing for clarity amidst the swirling storm of feelings around them.

She let out a deep, weary sigh, a wave of sadness crashing over her like a relentless tide. "I told you already." With a mixture of determination and vulnerability, she pushed herself up, fingers fidgeting nervously with the hem of her torn dress.

Each tug felt like an attempt to reel in the chaos within her, emotions swirling like leaves caught in a fierce autumn wind, leaving her feeling raw and exposed in front of them.

"Wait, Sandy," Zack pleaded, their voice laced with concern, "Talk to me. What's wrong?"

Looking at Zack, tears gathered precariously at the corners of her eyes, threatening to spill over. "There's nothing wrong, Zack," she choked out, though the tremble in her voice betrayed her.

Zack, moved closer, their hand reaching out to touch her arm, "Sandy, clearly, you're upset. Just talk to me." Zack was earnest, desperate to find the words that would unlock the door to her heart, the door she seemed intent on keeping shut.

Taking a deep breath, she struggled to gather her thoughts, the sting of their earlier connection still fresh, a bittersweet reminder of how fragile emotions could be.

"I didn't want to give you my body before I gave you, my heart. You took that away from me," she confessed, her voice breaking with the weight of unshed tears.

"Sandy, I told you I want to be with you," Zack murmured; the depth of their intention laid bare in the hope shimmering in their eyes.

She shook her head, an ache of disappointment settling heavily in her chest.

"You don't want to be with me, Zack. You just wanted to fuck me, like all the rest," she replied, her words sharp and laden with hurt, as if every syllable was a small cut that added to her growing wound.

Zack reached for her again, their hand hovering uncertainly above hers, yearning to break through her walls. "Sandy, I've been trying to win you over for weeks now. You won't let me in." There was sincerity in their plea, a quiet desperation that resonated within her.

But she pulled away, eyes filled with a tumultuous blend of sadness and simmering anger.
"Stop trying to win me over. Lord knows you already have me. I wanted you to win my heart, Zack," she said, her voice a bitter echo of the truth that hung in the air between them like a dark shadow.

The weight of her words hung heavily, suffocating the space that had once felt electric and alive.

With that, she turned away, each step taking her further from Zack, her heart aching and heavy, feeling shattered and heartbroken.

The door to her heart closed silently behind her, leaving Zack standing in the wake of a storm, grappling with the reality that sometimes, sex was insufficient to heal the chasms caused by miscommunication and unfulfilled aspirations.

CHAPTER 6

Mississippi,
1957

As Kelly and Martin sat across from each other at the dimly lit restaurant, an air of anticipation mingled with the scent of rich Italian cuisine, not just from the novelty of a first date, but also from the contrasting ideas that each held about life and relationships. Martin leaned in, a hint of surprise in his voice as he remarked, "I was surprised you actually agreed to go out with me." His genuine curiosity hung in the air, prompting Kelly to raise an eyebrow and ask, "Why is that?" Laughter could barely temper the tension as Martin pointed out, "We have a different matter of opinions."

"You can still have a difference in opinions and eat," she replied with an assertiveness that revealed a layer of her personality he had not witnessed before. It was at that moment that Martin decided to delve deeper, asking, "What do you see in your future? What is it that you want?"

Kelly paused before saying, "I want a husband and kids. I just want a happy family that goes to church every Sunday," she said almost repetitiously. Martin seemed taken aback, a frown crossing his face as he parsed her words. "So, you do want to get married and have kids?" he clarified, trying to reconcile this with the spirited woman seated before him. "Yes, Of course I do. What else is there for me to do?" Kelly said but Martin couldn't tell if she was being sarcastic.

"I swear sometimes you are as different as night and day. You are special, Ms. Kelly Hamilton," he said, the compliment, a bridge over the gulf that separated their worlds. Kelly smirked at the acknowledgment, feeling a flicker of warmth.

As the conversation shifted, Martin leaned closer, curious to explore her emotional landscape. "Tell me, Kelly, have you ever been in love?"

The question lingered, an invitation into the depths of her soul, and Kelly found herself pausing, her thoughts cascading like a series of delicate ripples across a still pond. In that fleeting moment, her mind wandered to Zack—It puzzled her why they emerged so easily in response to such a simple inquiry, a figure summoning both warmth and regret from the depths of her soul.

Nervously, she replied, "No, not that I can remember."

The words fell between them, a fragile truth that displayed both her vulnerability and the invisible barriers she had carefully constructed. This admission hung in the air, heavy with unspoken emotions. It was more than just a simple "no"; it was a window to her guarded heart; a revelation of the tender hopes she had left unexamined.

In that shared silence, there was an unexpected intimacy, a recognition of their mutual need for connection, however tentative. Facing the honesty of her own feelings, she realized that perhaps love was not merely a destination but a journey that began with understanding oneself, and maybe, just maybe, she was ready to explore that path with another.

Queerville, 1957

The morning sun streamed through the large glass windows of the diner, casting a warm glow on the stainless-steel tables and red vinyl booths. Zack strode in, their eyes scanning the space, but instead of the warm smile they longed to see from Sandy, they were met with the presence of Charlotte behind the counter, wiping down the surfaces with practiced ease.

The brief moment of anticipation quickly morphed into disappointment as they approached Charlotte, trying to mask their gloom.

"Hey, Charlotte, where's Sandy?" they inquired, hopeful yet apprehensive. Charlotte looked up from her task, "Oh, she took the day off." The weight of her words settled heavily on them, intertwining with their frustration as they sat down. "What's going on with you two?" Charlotte pressed gently. Zack sighed, running a hand through their hair as they opened up about their struggle to communicate their feelings to Sandy.

"I've been trying to show Sandy that I want something more. But she just keeps telling me to try harder."

Charlotte nodded knowingly, her voice steady as she replied, "Baby, flowers and jewelry are not going to cut it with a woman like Sandy. These men come in here every day with gifts. You need to show her something different."

"I don't know what she wants from me."

"You have to come from the heart. No more with all these material things. When did you ever do any of that for Miss Kelly? Everything you did to win that girl came from the heart." Zack's brows furrowed in thought, grappling with Charlotte's insights.

"Tell me what to do and I'll do it. I'll do whatever I have to do to show Sandy that I'm serious about us," they stated with determination. Charlotte's expression shifted; she saw a spark in Zack's eyes that hadn't been there before.

"Well, for starters, you can come in tomorrow and pick up a shift. She could use the help."

Zack chuckled at the absurdity of the suggestion, "Me? Work here?" But Charlotte's serious demeanor silenced their amusement.

"Yeah."

Zack couldn't help but smile at the thought, willing to put in the effort if it meant getting closer to Sandy.

"Okay, I'll do it. Now, I need you to do something for me, but I need it by tonight." With their plan brewing, Zack knew the next step was crucial, prompting them to visit Mayor Lewis to discuss the event that would hopefully show Sandy just how serious they were about them.

As they arrived at the mayor's office, Mayor Lewis greeted them with a mix of surprise and curiosity.

"Zack Calhoun in the flesh. Do my eyes deceive me," the mayor exclaimed as he invited Zack to sit.

"Please come in, have a seat. Tell me you're here about my proposal."

Zack wasted no time, their urgency evident as they replied, "I need a favor." Tossing a booklet onto the mayor's desk. "What exactly are you asking me to do here?" Mayor Lewis examined the papers before him, brows knit in confusion. Zack took a deep breath, stating their request firmly. "I need it set for tonight at the Town Park."

The mayor's eyes widened at such a short notice, his hesitation clear. "Tonight? Zack, that's a hell of an ask..." Zack stood up and headed for the door, feeling a flicker of doubt creeping in when the mayor called after them.

"Woo... now hold on a second. I didn't say I couldn't get it done. I can make a few calls and have everything available to you. I assume you'll have some of your people help with this?"

Relief washed over Zack as they recognized the opening. This was it—a chance to craft something meaningful for Sandy, something that would show her their true commitment and feelings.

* * *

Mark was bent over the chassis of a vintage car, absorbed in his work, while Freddie casually sipped on a beer, basking in the morning sun streaming through the open garage door. Suddenly, the atmosphere shifted as Zack stormed in, their presence commanding immediate attention. "Stop what you're doing!" they exclaimed, urgency in their voice.

"I need you guys' help, but we got to move quick." Freddie, unfazed, raised an eyebrow and quipped, "I got a shovel in the car." The unexpected suggestion drew a puzzled look from Zack, who quickly retorted, "Not that kind of help, Freddie." Confusion washed over Freddie's face as he asked, "Then what?"

The scene transitioned promptly back to the diner. Zack whistled sharply, and like clockwork, Val, Maria, Lisa, Robin, and the rest of the gangs rushed out, their faces a mix of curiosity and excitement.

The narrative unfolded further as they all marched to the town park, where crews were seen hammering stakes into the ground, assembling what appeared to be a festive tent.

Freddie stood off to the side, eyes wide in disbelief, "Okay, this is not what I was expecting. Don't you just want me to hide a body?"

Maria, clearly unimpressed, chimed in, directing her attention to Zack with a hint of sarcasm, "Zack, how come you never did anything like this for me, huh?" Zack responded without missing a beat, "Maria, you know why. You hate romance." A small fire ignited as Maria quickly retorted, "No, that's not true." "Maria, I brought you flowers once, and you set them on fire."

"I'm allergic," she replied to which Zack humorously countered, "Yeah, to romance."

Just then, Val interjected, her brow creased in concern, "Hey, Zack, you think we're going to have this all up by tonight?" Zack reassured her, "Yeah, we have enough people."

Lisa, with a dreamy look, remarked, "Zack, this is really sweet. I wish I had a date for tonight." She cleared her throat to get Robin's attention. Robin remarked, "You can come with me... I mean, I don't have anyone to go with either so." The two exchanged a playful kiss.

Charlotte, asked, "Zack, what's my job in all this?"

Zack met her gaze with a mischievous glint in their eyes, teasingly, "You're the main event." Horror and indignation flickered across Charlotte's face, "See, no, I don't like that look."

The scene encapsulated a day threaded with camaraderie, humor, and the hint of a special event brewing in the air, all under the watchful eye of Zack, the orchestrator of this peculiar gathering, a mix of adventure and romantic mischief brewing just beneath the surface.

As the evening air settled around them, Zack found themself standing at Sandy's front door, anxiety bubbling in their chest. They weren't sure how she would react—would she be angry, or worse, would she slam the door in their face? but when Sandy opened the door, her shocked expression immediately caused their heart to race.

A concoction of happiness and frustration danced in her eyes, "Zack, what are you doing here?" she managed to ask, her tone masking the genuine joy of seeing them again. They took a deep breath, mustering every ounce of courage they had. "Just hear me out, please."

As Sandy stepped outside, the warm evening air wrapped around them. "I've been such a fool. You've been telling me all this time what you wanted, and I didn't listen. I'm sorry," Zack confessed, seeing a flicker of softness in her expression. They continued, "But you were wrong. Sex is not all I want... I want to stay up looking at the stars with you. I want to cuddle up on the couch watching flicks, bubble baths together, our first fight, our first breakup to make up. I want it all with you, Sandy."

A smile broke across her face, warming them from the inside out. "There it is. I miss that smile."

Skepticism clouded her eyes as she replied, "Zack, I don't know..." Sensing her hesitation, they quickly urged, "Hold that thought. Will you come with me somewhere, just for a minute, please?"

"Where?"

"Just trust me."

Zack reached out their hand, and despite her initial reservations, she couldn't resist the pull of those alluring eyes. Taking Zack's hand, they set off together.

Before they arrived at the Town Park, Zack gently placed a blindfold over her eyes, leading her through the familiar pathways adorned by twinkling lights.

"Zack, what is this? Where are we?" she asked, confusion lacing her voice as excitement tinged the air.

"Sandy, trust me," they replied, guiding her carefully.

When they reached their destination, there was an electric energy coursing through the air as Zack asked, "Are you ready?" With a swift motion, they removed the blindfold, revealing a carnival in full swing—colors shimmering, laughter echoing, and her favorite rides spinning under the starlit sky.

The disbelief washed over Sandy as she gasped, "Oh my god! Zack! How did you do all of this?" Her eyes filled with astonishment as laughter bubbled within her; her initial frustration forgotten.

"With a lot of help," Zack replied.

Just then, Charlotte, decked out in a ringmaster's outfit, greeted them with a flourish. "Step right up this way! Welcome to Zack's Carnival of love! We have games, rides, and all that your heart desires."

Sandy's heart fluttered at the sight of her friends gathered around her, vibrant smiles lit up their faces. She spotted Freddie, always the jokester, ready to make her laugh with his silly antics.

Lisa stood nearby, her warm demeanor radiated kindness, while Robin bounced with excitement, bubbling with anticipation. Val handed out balloons.

Halle was the quiet support in the background, offering a reassuring smile, while Patty, with her infectious energy, was already preparing the next fun activity. Dee, the organizer of the night, had taken charge of making sure everything ran smoothly, and even Maria, who had surprised her joining the festivities, was there. Each of them had taken on a special role at the carnival, embracing their tasks with enthusiasm, all working together to help Zack create a magical and unforgettable night for Sandy.

"Zack, how did you pull this off?" Her heart overwhelmed with joy.

"I called in a favor."

"A favor to who?" Sandy pressed, her curiosity burning.

"The mayor," Zack answered nonchalantly.

"The mayor!" she exclaimed; disbelief mixed with amusement. Sandy was enchanted as Zack extended their hand towards her, and after a moment of contemplation, she took it, their laughter echoing amidst the joyous chaos of the carnival.

Each game they played, every ride they boarded, further stitched the fabric of a possible new romance, from the delighted teasing at the corn hole game to the cozy intimacy of the Ferris wheel. Bumper cars that pitted couples against couples and the merry go round that somehow ended in a race.

As Zack drove Sandy back home, the warmth between them deepened, Sandy couldn't help but reflect on the effort Zack had put in to make her feel special.

As they reached her front porch, Sandy turned to face them, her heart fluttering in her chest as she spoke softly, "Zack, tonight was really fun, thank you. I still can't believe you did all of that for me. You remembered how much I love carnivals." Her eyes sparkled, reflecting the joy that had filled the evening.

Zack's gaze held hers with a warm intensity that made her pulse quicken. They leaned in slightly, their voice steady and sincere as they replied, "I remember everything about you. What you like, what you don't like, your favorite color, your biggest fear, your biggest turn on."

There was a teasing hint in their tone, making her cheeks flush as they leaned in closer, the space between them charged with an electric energy. The moment felt suspended in time.

As their lips almost met, a thrill shot through her, exciting and terrifying all at once. It was a whirlwind of emotions that left her breathless and yearning for more. But the reality of the moment suddenly crashed down on her. "I have to get up early in the morning, so I'm going to go," she said hastily, her voice laced with urgency as she rushed inside, her heart racing.

Sandy pressed her back against the door, attempting to steady her breath, overwhelmed by both the sweet memories of the night and the intensity of her feelings for Zack. There was no denying them anymore.

The next morning, Sandy rushed into the diner, her heart still fluttering from the beautiful time she had with Zack the night before, the memories replaying in her mind like a favorite song. The bell above the door jingled as she entered, and she immediately felt the warmth of the diner wash over her. She glanced at the clock on the wall, panic flooding her as she realized how late she was for her shift.

"Sorry I'm late; I overslept," she exclaimed breathlessly, hoping her breathlessness wouldn't betray the whirlwind of emotions she was feeling.

Charlotte looked up with a knowing smile and waved her off. "It's okay; the new server was covering for you," she replied. Confusion washed over Sandy.

"What new server?" she asked, raising an eyebrow, her curiosity piqued as she scanned the diner for any unfamiliar faces. That's when her eyes landed on Zack, adorned in a full diner uniform that made them look adorably out of place, complete with a hat that sat slightly askew on their head.

Shock bubbled within her, prompting an uncontrollable laugh to escape her lips. "Why do you have Zack in full uniform? No one wears that!" she exclaimed, sharing a glance with Charlotte, who only shrugged further, her own smile indicating there was more to this than just a costume. "I wanted Zack to get the full experience," Charlotte replied with a wink, before continuing, "Zack wanted to show you they would do anything to be near you."

Sandy felt her cheeks flush with warmth, a smile breaking across her face that was all too revealing.

Zack's first shift at the diner unfolded like a disastrous comedy sketch, and they couldn't help but feel the sweat bead on their forehead as they desperately tried to keep up with the chaotic flow of orders. They had just dropped off two vanilla milkshakes at a table full of teenagers, only to be met with correction.

"Um, I ordered a chocolate milkshake," the teen scolded.

"It's the same thing, just without the melanin," Zack mocked, but the laughter that followed was not in solidarity; the sharp glances revealed they were on thin ice.

A rapid montage of mishaps throughout their shift. Zack delivered a cheeseburger accidentally when the customer had specifically requested a plain burger, a momentary brain lapse. "Just remove the cheese don't be a douche." Zack remarked.

An embarrassing moment when they fumbled a burger bun, allowing it to drop to the floor before picking it up and casually placing it back on the sandwich as if nothing had happened.

As the door swung open and familiar faces spilled into the diner, Zack couldn't help but feel a flicker of comfort wash over them, despite the chaotic scene unfolding around them. The laughter of their friends— Freddie, Mark, Val, Maria, Robin, and Lisa—filled the air, their playful jeers echoing off the laminate tables and retro booth seats.

They wasted no time in poking fun at their lackluster service skills, declaring exaggeratedly that they should be demoted for the burnt fries they had just served Freddie and Mark, who were faking outrage as they threatened to complain to the manager. With a playful spark in their eye, Zack shot back, "I will spit in your food," half-joking yet somehow serious as the words left their mouth, which elicited an uproar of laughter from the gathered crowd, a natural rhythm of camaraderie.

Maria seized the opportunity to flirt shamelessly, leaning over the counter with a mischievous grin.

"You look handsome in your little uniform," she said in a light, teasing whisper, her eyes sparkling with playful intent. In an audacious move that took everyone by surprise, she reached out and took a handful of Zack's backside, a brazen gesture that drew an audible gasp from Val and sent the rest of their group into fits of laughter.

However, the laughter quickly morphed into a tension-drenched silence as Sandy, who had been observing from a distance, suddenly seethed with protective jealousy. Her eyes narrowed like a hawk spotting its prey, and with firmness in her tone, she declared, "That is no longer on the menu." Without hesitation, she reached across the counter, her fingers latching onto Maria's offending hand and yanking it away from Zack with a mix of irritation and possessiveness that left everyone momentarily speechless. The assertiveness in her action bore unmistakable evidence of her feelings.

Zack's heart soared; the way Sandy stood up for them only confirmed what they had been feeling all along, that there was something deeper brewing between them.

In the midst of this dramatic exchange, Zack made their way to deliver a burger to Lisa, who had been waiting with a mix of impatience and hunger. But when she saw what they had placed before her, her reaction was immediate and vocal. "Zack, what is this?" Lisa exclaimed, holding up a plate that looked more like a culinary disaster than a meal.

"Is it even cooked. His heart still beating," Robin sneered.

"I'll get you another one," Zack offered.

Each time they returned to the kitchen, the sound of laughter followed them, a constant reminder that they were the punchline for the day.

Burning food and smashing plates became the melody of their shift as the kitchen erupted in chaos, their lack of experience only fueling the mischief.

Finally, they stumbled back to the front with new orders that only managed to land them in more trouble.

"This is burnt!" Lisa declared, laughter erupted as Zack, unable to comprehend the hostility, turned around to find everyone laughing, including Sandy, it was all a playful setup orchestrated by her, who wanted to serve them a taste of humble pie, while in her heart, she knew it wouldn't take long for them to win her over for real.

Zack finally caught on, with Sandy slowly approaching them, they asked, "Will you go out with me now?" their eyes wide with hope. Sandy, unable to suppress the smile that crept across her face, pulled Zack in for a passionate kiss, making the laughter around them fade into a warm glow that felt a lot like love. "Yes," she chuckled against their lips, knowing in that moment that all the craziness was worth it—after all, every misstep had brought them to this perfect moment.

The sunlight streamed through the curtains, illuminating the cozy scene of Zack and Sandy, still tangled in the sheets, the next morning, snugly wrapped in the remnants of their clothes from the night before.

The calm of the morning was abruptly shattered by the shrill ring of Sandy's phone, slicing through the stillness like a knife. Sandy groggily fumbled for her phone, barely managing to bring it to her ear. "Hello? Yeah... Okay, I'll tell them," she murmured before hanging up, the urgency of the call jolting her back to reality. "Charlotte said don't be late today," she informed Zack, who stretched like a cat waking from a long slumber, groaning as they pulled themself out of the comforting cocoon of the bed.

The two of them sat at the cozy kitchen table, a breakfast of toast and scrambled eggs laid out in front of them. As they ate, a lighthearted atmosphere filled the space, broken only by the soft clinking of forks on plates.

"I can't believe we fell asleep in our clothes," Sandy laughed, shaking her head in disbelief, the shared memory evoking a playful nostalgia.

"Yeah, we haven't stayed up all night talking since we were twelve," Zack replied, a grin stretching across their face. Sandy's eyes sparkled as she reminisced, "Oh my god, I remember my parents would take the phone and lock it up so I wouldn't call you." Their laughter filled the air like a sweet melody, underlined by the unbreakable bond they've cultivated over the years.

But as the laughter subsided, a more serious tone emerged, creating a delicate tension between them.

Zack looked directly at Sandy, sincerity etched across their features, "I want to apologize to you Sandy, for playing with your emotions, for making you give me your body too soon. I should've listened to you."

Sandy's expression softened, reflecting understanding as she responded, "I wanted it just as bad as you did. I was just mad at myself for giving in." The air grew thick with honesty; Zack took a deep breath and declared, "I want to take sex off the table. I want to show you that I'm serious about us. That this is not just sex for me." Their words hung in the air, heavy with implication. Sandy, momentarily confused, tilted her head, "What?"

"Sex isn't everything, and it doesn't keep a relationship solid." Sandy's laughter was laced with bitterness as she countered, "Boy, do I know that. Every man I ever dated cheated on me. Doesn't matter how much sex we have or how attractive they find me. They still cheat."

The weight of her words resonated in the space between them, and Zack reached over, and caressed her face with tender conviction. "I would never hurt you like that, Sandy," Zack assured her, their voice strong yet gentle. "Yeah, they said that too," she murmured, skepticism creeping into her tone.

Unfazed, Zack responded, "Well, I'm not them." Sandy could hear the sincerity in Zack's tone, evident in their eyes. "You're serious? Zack, we don't have to."

"I know, but I want to focus on connecting with you first. I know Sandy the best friend, but I want to get to know Sandy the lover."

Her heart swelled; cheeks flushed. With a softer tone, Zack asked, "So, will you be my girl?" Sandy's smile beamed, radiating joy, "I thought I already was," she whispered with a teasing glint in her eyes, "Can we still kiss? Is that allowed?" "Yeah, kissing is cool," Zack replied.

In that moment, the kitchen bloomed with warmth as Sandy wrapped her arms around Zack, pulling them close and sealing their newfound connection with a sweet, lingering kiss.

Now that Zack had started dating Sandy, a new set of challenges emerged that neither of them had anticipated. Zack found themselves grappling with the incessant attention that Sandy attracted wherever they went. Zack would sit and watch Sandy at the diner, her radiant smile lighting up the room and effortlessly drawing the attention of every man present. They could see their eyes glistening with a lustful appraisal that sent a jolt of irritation through Zack. It felt as if they were dissecting every inch of her, and Zack's fists clenched involuntarily, struggling with the unfamiliar surge of insecurity.

They could hear the thoughts streaming through the men heads—thoughts laced with desire, entitlement, and an all-too-obvious lack of respect for her as a person. This reaction made Zack's skin crawl, and they felt an uncomfortable wave of possessiveness wash over them. It all became too much for Zack.

In an outburst fueled by frustration and protectiveness, they yelled at the group of men who were openly gawking at Sandy. In a fit of rage, they stormed across the diner, forcefully yanking several of them out of their seats, and shoving them towards the door as if they were unruly children. Their startled faces reflected a mix of confusion and anger, but Zack barely noticed; they were hyper-focused on what they perceived as defending Sandy's honor.

Sandy, however, was infuriated by Zack's explosive reaction. She stood up, her face flushed with anger, and shouted, "What the hell are you doing?" Zack's defensive instinct overridden their rational thought: "I'm just trying to protect you, Sandy! You shouldn't have to deal with this kind of attention!"

But Sandy wasn't having it. With fire in her eyes, she reminded them, "Those men support the diner financially, they also leave generous tips.

They're harmless. Let them be." she implored, her voice rising in intensity.

Zack stood frozen, grappling with their emotions. They felt a whirlpool of fear and jealousy coiling in their stomach at the thought of losing Sandy, but they also recognized her right to make her own choices.

Slowly, the fire in Sandy's eyes softened, revealing vulnerability beneath her anger. She stepped closer, wrapping her arms around Zack before saying, "They can look all they want; it doesn't mean anything. I'm with you—my heart is yours, and no one else matters."

In that moment, Zack realized that they had to confront their own insecurities if their relationship was going to thrive. Finally, they took a deep breath and nodded, the heat of the moment deflating as they muttered an apology.

"I'm sorry, Sandy. I guess I just got carried away."

"It's okay, now go find you something to do while I go fix this." Sandy kissed Zack, playfully shoving them out.

The news spread like wildfire through town, igniting a reaction that was as instantaneous as it was intense: Sandy is with Zack, the two biggest heartthrobs in the state now an item; leaving a trail of shattered hearts in their wake.

Men, who had nurtured secret crushes on Sandy, felt the sharp sting of disappointment slicing through their optimism, their fantasies shattered like glass.

Meanwhile, women who had been waiting for their chance to win over Zack now wore expressions of barely concealed envy, their hopes dashed and transformed into bitterness as the reality of their unattainable dreams settled in.

The local diner, once a buzzing hotspot filled with laughter and lively banter, began to dull in energy, as many of Sandy's regulars—those who had come in with spirited anticipation of flirtation—started to trickle away, unable to bear the sight of the couple together.

A few loyal patrons remained, clinging to the frail thread of hope that Zack would falter in their commitment, that the glamorous facade of their relationship would crumble under the weight of reality. These lingering souls occupied their usual booths, nursing their coffee and exchanging furtive glances filled with a mix of longing and resignation, convinced that perhaps the tides would turn in their favor, and they would have another shot at love.

The atmosphere was charged with energy and a sense of belonging as the Queer Youth House buzzed with excited chatter of teens finding solace in each other's company.

In the heart of the room, Mark stood confidently, sharing his harrowing yet empowering story of survival from the P.G.A. conversion camp. His voice echoed through the crowded space, filled with faces of various expressions—some curious, others empathetic, but all captivated by his honesty. "You know it wasn't the Bible mumbo jumbo," Mark asserted, his determination evident.

"It was the fight for my soul. Who I am. That's what they were attacking." His words resonated deeply, each syllable steeped in a painful truth that had once held him captive; for years, he struggled silently, grappling with shame and fear, convinced that divine love was meant for someone else, someone who fit a predetermined mold.

"But it wasn't until they tried to get me to hate myself that I refused to," he continued passionately, eyes aflame with defiance against a backdrop of dark memories.

The torment he endured, palpable as he described the nightmares triggered by the indoctrination, sending shivers through the attentive audience.

Though Zack stood nearby, absorbing every word, they eventually walked out, as the weight of their shared torment loomed too heavily for them to bear, their own unprocessed trauma bubbling just below the surface.

This moment of vulnerability and strength pulsed throughout the room, as Freddie watched Mark with admiration, his heart swelling with pride for his boyfriend's bravery, recognizing the profound impact of his words in a space that welcomes and protects them.

* * *

In stark contrast, a different scenario unfolded in the diner, where Daron and Rose sat across from each other, indulging in a shared milkshake that symbolized their budding relationship, filled with sweetness and the innocent hope of young love.

Daron, with a mix of nervous excitement and a dash of playful bravado, leaned forward, breaking the bubble of their flirtation with a proposal. "Rose, will you wear my pin?" he asked, eager for her acceptance. Rose's eyes sparkled with excitement at the idea, yet an undercurrent of hesitation tinged her response as she stirred the milkshake.

"Your pin?" she echoed, and the warmth in her voice was undeniable, but it was accompanied by a flicker of uncertainty. "Yeah, you wear my pin, and everyone knows you're my girl," he quipped lightly, hoping to ease any hesitance.

However, Rose raised a valid concern, one that dug into the raw reality of their lives— "Are you sure you want that? Once people find out who your girl is, they'll have a lot to say." Daron's heart sank slightly; he felt trapped in the shadows of secrecy, and his mind begun to race, "Or maybe your friends will have a lot to say," he retorted, the playful banter shifting into a deeper, more uncomfortable territory.

Her confusion only amplified the tension as Daron pushed back, "I keep trying to fool myself, but I can't keep pretending like you're really into me," he stated, his confidence faltering to reveal vulnerability.

"But you're not Rose. You keep saying people will talk but it's me you're afraid they'll talk about. That's why you meet with me in secret. That's why you didn't want to kiss me. I'm done wasting my time," his voice thick with emotion as he got up. With each stride away from the booth, he took with him a piece of Rose's heart, leaving her feeling the sting of loss as she desperately called after him, "Daron, that's not true!" as she sprinted after him, her heart pounding not just with urgency but with a fear of what it would mean if he walked out of her life.

* * *

Back at the Queer youth house, the air was thick with anticipation as Zack prepared to share their insights with a group of eager teens. With a mix of bravado and authenticity, they stepped forward, embodying the essence of someone who's frequently walked the road less traveled.

Standing tall, they looked intently at the diverse group resting on bright chairs, each teen grappling with their own identities and struggles.

"I was a hothead," Zack began, a hint of self-deprecating humor lacing their voice. "Some might tell you I'm still a hothead. I've always had a problem with authority, and I thought it was just because I hated being told what to do. But then I realized – it's because I believe I know a better way."

The room fell silent as their words sunk in, resonating with many seated there who had felt the weight of others' expectations pressing down upon them.

"No one can dictate how you should live your life," they continued, their passion burning brightly. "It's your life! People will always project their fears onto you, but don't let that steer you off course. Discover what lights you up, what brings you joy; that's how you'll uncover your purpose."

There was a connection in the air; their message ignited something within the teens.

A hand shot up from the back—an earnest face eager to understand. "How do you find your purpose?" a teen asked, the vulnerability in their voice softening Zack in an instant.

"Keep an open mind," they replied, their demeanor shifting into that of a mentor. "Try new things, learn new skills, and don't be afraid to step out of your comfort zone."

The weight of their words hung in the air like a shared secret as Josephine, an attractive single mother, listened closely, her interest piqued as she admired the way Zack lit up the room.

Another teen asked, "You own the car shop in town, right?" "Yes, Zack Auto Shop."

"You think you could hook up our rides, for free?"

"Sure! Every teen who brings me at least a B report card can get a hot rod upgrade!" Cheers erupted, the energy in the room transformed into infectious excitement.

Afterwards, amidst the vibrant chaos of laughter and shared stories, Zack noticed an adorable toddler sitting quietly alone, lost in a world of colorful blocks. They approached the boy, kneeling down to meet his gaze.

"Hey, what are you doing all by yourself? I see you like blocks. Let me show you something cool."

Demonstrating their playful side, Zack crafted a dinosaur, watching as the boy's face broke into a radiant smile, sparking joy in Zack's heart that they couldn't quite articulate.

The moment was tender and pure, and just as they were relishing the interaction, they heard a voice from behind.

"Wow, he hasn't smiled in months." It was Josephine, her presence radiant as she leaned against the wall, an enchanting smile playing on her lips.

Zack, momentarily caught off guard by her beauty, stood and brushed off the remnants of their artistic endeavor.

"Really?" Zack asked, genuine surprised. "He seems like such a happy kid." "Yeah, he doesn't look like what he's been through," Josephine replied softly, her eyes reflecting a profound understanding.

A lull settled in as Zack turned their gaze back to the child, remembering the resilience found in vulnerability.

"The strong ones never do."

"I'm Josephine, by the way," she offered, extending her hand. "Zack," they replied, their handshake a silent promise of connection.

"I heard your speech; it was really inspiring." Flushed with a blend of modesty and pride, Zack replied, "You thought so? Good to know someone enjoyed it."

"I'm sure I wasn't the only one."

Their eyes locked, Josephine asked, "Would you like to join us for some ice cream? I'm sure Anthony would love for you to join us."

Zack was startled, taken aback for a moment. The name "Anthony" struck a chord deep within them, evoking a rush of memories of their own brother, buried beneath years of pain and longing. "What did you say?" they asked, their voice a mix of surprise and curiosity.

Josephine clarified, "Anthony. His name is Anthony." In that moment, as Zack looked at the small boy, now beaming with excitement, they felt an inexplicable bond forming, a thread pulling them toward something larger than themself, something that felt like fate.

* * *

Rose sprinted after Daron, her heart racing and her mind swirling with a tumult of emotions as she called out, "Daron, wait please!" Desperation laced her voice, and she could see him hesitating, though he quickly turned to face her with a hint of skepticism still lingering in his expression.

"For what, Rose?" he asked, the challenge evident in his tone. "So, I can talk to you. Please!" Rose pleaded, all the while trying to muster the courage to reveal her vulnerabilities.

When Daron finally stopped, she took a deep breath, her heart aching as she confessed, "You have it all wrong. I'm not ashamed of you. I'm ashamed of my past. I don't want my past to affect you." Each word felt heavy but necessary, spilling out her fears for Daron, who was inherently different from anyone else she had ever met.

"You're the first boy that ever mattered to me," she continued earnestly, "And I'm terrified of screwing it up."

A glimmer of sincerity flickered in Daron's eyes as he listened intently; he could see how deeply her words resonated within her.

As unshed tears glistened in her eyes, she owned up to her reservation about the other night, revealing, "I didn't kiss you because I was afraid it would lead to sex, and I didn't want to ruin it. I never had anything as special as this." "Why didn't you tell me any of this?"

With a chuckle, Rose half-heartedly replied, "Because I was pretending to have it all together, but really, I don't." Daron's laughter intermingled with hers, a shared moment of vulnerability enveloping them.

"Rose," he said gently, "You don't have to be perfect for me. I don't want perfect. Perfect is boring; I want scars to kiss, wounds to watch heal. Because all of that makes you, Rose. And I kind of like her." With those soothing words hanging in the air, Rose felt a rush of emotions, she suddenly grabbed him and kissed him, sealing their newfound understanding in a moment that felt both terrifying and exhilarating.

Meanwhile, Josephine, Anthony, and Zack sat together in the parlor, their ice cream bowls slowly melting as they savored the moment. Josephine smiled warmly at Zack, gratitude radiating from her, "Thank you for coming with us. I haven't seen my son light up over someone in a long time." Zack returned her smile, their eyes sparkling as they replied, "It was my pleasure; he's such a sweet boy. I couldn't say no to that face."

The atmosphere softened with laughter as Josephine teased, "He has you under his spell now. You're doomed." With a chuckle, Zack felt Anthony climb onto their lap, drawing them even deeper into their shared warmth. Josephine looked on, amused, as Zack playfully addressed Anthony, "Hey, little ankle biter."

Anthony's request for Zack to feed him some ice cream led to Zack scooping up a bit of ice cream and bringing it to Anthony's eager mouth. The delight in the boy's eyes mirrored the satisfaction written across Zack's face.

"Look at that smile," Zack said, glancing at Josephine. "He's not going to sleep anytime soon," she chuckled in response. "Just let him run around a bit; he'll get tired."

As Zack continued to take delight in feeding Anthony, a deeper conversation unfolded about parenthood, with Josephine gently nudging Zack to consider the idea of having kids, "You'd make a great dad."

Zack pondered her words, a contemplative look crossing their face, "You think so? I don't know about that. I didn't have much of an example of what a great father is supposed to be."

Josephine's reassuring voice cut through their self-doubt, "Well, for someone that didn't have an example, you sure are doing a great job. Someone wise would say if you don't have an example, you should be the example."

A chuckle escaped Zack, a mix of amusement and disbelief, "Oh, someone wise, huh? That's great advice; however, I lack the proper organs to reproduce."

The shy response lingered in the air, a hint of anxiety dancing in their thoughts as they questioned whether Josephine understood that they were trans. The moment teetered between vulnerability and humor, but Josephine sidestepped the tension effortlessly.

"You might not have the organs, but you still have the means," she said, winking at them.

In that instant, surrounded by Anthony's bright laughter and Josephine's playful spirit, Zack found themself reevaluating their definition of family and what that could mean in the warmth of innocent, joyful moments shared with Anthony and Josephine.

* * *

Zack snuck up on Sandy from behind, wrapping their arms around her in a warm embrace that felt familiar and comforting, a gesture so inherently theirs that Sandy knew it was them without even turning her head. No one else dared to touch her with such affection; it was a privilege that only Zack had.

A radiant smile spread across her lips the moment she felt Zacks' presence, that electric thrill of joy coursing through her veins just as it always did. "Zack, I've missed you," she exclaimed, her voice filled with genuine delight as she spun around to face them, their lips meeting in a soft, lingering kiss that spoke volumes of the connection they shared. The world around them faded away as they lost themselves in each other.

"I missed you too," Zack replied with a warmth that seemed to envelop them both, and with that, they glided over to the counter, where they could sit and catch up in the evening light filtering through the window. Sandy leaned in; her excitement evident. "So, how did it go?" she asked, her curiosity dancing in her eyes.

"Well, no one left crying, so I guess it went okay," Zack replied modestly, a humble grin tugging at the corners of their mouth. "Stop speaking down on yourself; I'm sure you did great," she reassured them.

With a hint of embarrassment, Zack revealed, "They asked a lot of questions."

"Questions are good," Sandy encouraged, her eyes sparkling as she leaned in closer, eager to hear about their day. "I told all the teens if they bring me a B report card, I'd give them a free upgrade on a hot rod."

Sandy couldn't help but laugh, "That's amazing! You know they'll probably start forging their report cards now, right?"

Zack's eyes widened in realization, "I didn't think of that," they responded with an innocent charm that only heightened her affection for them. "You're so cute," she said fondly, leaning in for another kiss. "Oh, and I met this young mother today; she had this adorable little boy with her who took a liking to me, so that was pretty cool," Zack added, a boyish pride shining through.

"Awe, that's cute, Uncle Zack," Sandy teased, but Zack protested jokingly in mock disbelief. "You joshing? I'm leaving," they said, getting up and making a show of heading for the door.

"Wait! My shift is over. Just let me get my purse," Sandy called out, reaching for it under the counter, her movements teasingly exaggerated.

As she bent over, poking out her backside. Zack watched with a playful smirk, humorously misinterpreting her innocent gesture. "Oh, you're playing dirty," they laughed.

"What?" a hint of confusion lacing her voice.

"Why do you have to poke your butt out like that? You know what you're doing. You know I'm trying to stay off sex, and you're trying to seduce me," Zack insisted playfully, gaining confidence with each playful jab.

Sandy, with a melodic laugh, replied, "Are you serious?"

"Yes, you're using your curves as a weapon," Zack declared, their tone flirty yet sincere.

"Oh, yeah? Is it working?" Sandy shot back; her sarcasm layered with a teasing tone.

"Yeah, it's working. You're smoking hot," they replied, their gaze warming her from the inside out.

"I don't think you're going to last very long if I can't reach for things," she countered, a daring glint in her eye.

"You can reach; just don't poke your butt out." Their playful banter bringing a brightness to their easy camaraderie, as they lost themselves in witty repartee.

CHAPTER 7

Mississippi,
1957

The warm afternoon light flooded the small room, casting a golden hue over the furniture and walls, amplifying the intimacy of the moment as Kelly and Martin were lost in each other's presence. The air thick with passion as they made out, their bodies moving closer, hearts racing in sync.

However, as things began to escalate, Kelly pulled back abruptly, her expression a mix of surprise and determination. "Down boy, that's not happening," she declared, her voice steady yet fraught with a hint of defiance.

Martin's eyebrows raised in playful astonishment, his teasing remark cutting through the charged atmosphere.

"Didn't take you for the virgin type," he quipped, unaware of the offense his words would evoke.

Kelly, caught off guard, straightened up—her indignation palpable. "Excuse me?" she retorted, astonished that he would presume to label her so narrowly.

Realizing he had stepped over the line, Martin's demeanor softened; his apologetic tone washed over her like a gentle tide. "I mean I just thought. I'm sorry, my words are coming out all wrong. I guess you have that effect on me," he confessed, his eyes revealing both his sincerity and the undeniable charm that made her find it hard to stay mad.

Curiosity flickered in her eyes as she pressed him further, "What effect is that?" she asked, her voice challenging yet intrigued. "You make me nervous," he admitted, vulnerability creeping into his tone, laying raw his feelings in a way that caught her off guard.

Kelly, her heart thumping wildly, adopted a more serious tone, declaring, "Nerves or not. I'm saving myself for marriage." The weight of her commitment lingered in the air as Martin considered his next move, a flicker of stubborn determination lighting up his features.

"Come home with me, Kelly. I want you to meet my folks; I just know they will love you." Despite the warmth radiating from his words, an uncertain cloud passed over her face as she hesitated. "I don't know," she sighed, a mingling of curiosity and apprehension reflecting her thoughts.

Martin leaned in, his voice dropping to a sincere plea.

"Please, Kelly, I really want them to meet you." The simplicity of the request, coupled with the intensity of his gaze, left her breathless—a moment of clarity amidst her conflicting emotions as she weighed the gravity of his invitation against the steadfastness of her own convictions.

Queerville, 1957

In the heart of the bustling police station, the sheriff stood before a group of officers gathered for an impromptu training session. The severity of recent overdoses among teenagers—had compelled him to address an urgent issue that had intertwined with their investigation.

Although the source of the overdoses remained shrouded in uncertainty, the police had narrowed their focus onto recreational drug use, particularly targeting marijuana smokers.

The sheriff, began his lesson with a firm reach into his pocket, producing a joint that seemed almost to glimmer under the fluorescent lights of the station.

"Now, you can see the difference," he instructed, holding the joint aloft for all to see, "Between a real cigarette and marijuana. And there will be no mistaking the texture or contents if you were to handle it." he emphasized the distinction, "The darker one has been rolled in wheat-straw paper. In most of the reefers a double thickness of paper is used."

The officers leaned in closer, some taking notes, others exchanging glances of concern. "Take a long look," the sheriff continued, his voice a mix of authority and exasperation.

"If you see any teen smoking one of these, it is, in fact, a reefer, and you should confiscate it and arrest them."

One of the younger officers hesitantly raised a hand, his brow furrowed in confusion.

"Is that what's making all the kids O.D.?" he asked, the weight of their task palpable in his voice.

The sheriff's expression softened slightly, though his eyes remained steely. "We don't know," he replied, the honesty hanging heavy in the air. "We're still running tests on the drugs found in the kids' systems."

In that moment, the room was filled with a sense of urgency, the gravity of their mission settling over them like a thick fog; it became clear that while they were focused on the immediate threat of marijuana, a far more insidious danger lurked beneath the surface, eluding their grasp like the very smoke that dissipated from the joints they were now tasked with identifying.

Lover's Lane

As Max and Dawn pulled into Lover's Lane, a place that once held the promise of young love and innocent make-out sessions beneath the stars, now a jarring sight that shattered their expectations.

The idyllic spot had transformed into a grim tableau; the bright beam of the sun was overshadowed by the harsh reality of a drug den, strewn with discarded needles and crinkled baggies that hinted at the vices taking hold of the youth.

Cars, once mere vessels of romance, now served as makeshift cocoons for teens who appeared to be lost in a haze of intoxication, their heads lolling, and eyes glazed over in an odyssey of oblivion.

The serene atmosphere that once enveloped the lane was now thick with the stench of desperation and loss. Dawn's heart raced with horror as she surveyed the chaos; it was as if a dark cloud had descended upon a cherished sanctuary.

"Can you believe this?" she gasped, disbelief etching lines of concern on her face. Max, equally shaken, echoed her sentiment, "What happened to this place?" Dawn's thoughts raced back to the warnings she had heard—the sheriff's grim reports of overdoses that plagued the town, two lives extinguished each week by the very substances that now tainted the air around them.

"I told you something was going on," she insisted, her resolve hardening. "The sheriff said there's an O.D. twice a week." Faced with the grim reality, Max's voice trembled with urgency, "What are they on?" yet it was ultimately Dawn's fierce determination that emerged, "I don't know, but I'm going to find out before this town is destroyed."

Steeling herself, she approached one of the high teens, her heart pounding as she attempted to draw out the truth, desperate for answers.

"Hey, what are you on? Where did you get this?" she implored, hoping to peel back layers of despair surrounding the boy. His response, a vague murmur, hinted at deeper connections—"Uh…" he stammered, lost in the fog of his reality. "Where did you get this? Who gave this to you?" Dawn pressed, her frustration mounting.

"Dougie… Douglas," he finally muttered, and the name ignited a flicker of recognition within her.

"Douglas, that douche that's always hanging in the bleachers smoking reefer," she muttered, anger and determination intertwining as she remembered the young man she once dismissed as a mere nuisance.

"We should call for help; these teens could O.D."
Dawn nodded, the urgency of their situation
crystallizing in her mind. "Yeah," she agreed, "Let's go
get help then we find Douglas." Time was of the essence,
as they set in motion a plan to combat the darkness
overtaking their town.

* * *

Zack and Mark were deep in the throes of their work
at the auto shop, surrounded by the scents of oil, metal,
and the faint whir of machinery, when the door swung
open, and in walked Josephine, a cheerful spark of
energy, with Anthony at her side.

The moment Zack spotted Josephine, their heart
lifted, and they felt a rush of warmth that dispelled the
fatigue of the day.

"Josephine, you came to check out the shop?" they
exclaimed, a wide smile breaking across their face. She
nodded enthusiastically, "Yea, I thought Anthony might
like to see a car shop. Maybe even sit in a hot rod."

"Oh, you came to the right place," Zack assured her,
before introducing her, "This is my mechanic, Mark.
Mark, this Josephine."

Mark was sizing Josephine up with a curious glance,
seemingly trying to decipher her vibe. Mark extended a
hand with a casual wave, greeting her with a polite,
"Hello," and Josephine responded warmly, her bright
smile lighting up her face.

"I think I can make that happen. I was headed over to
Queer house for Charlotte's announcement."

"So were we! That's perfect," Josephine replied.

"Let me go change and we can take off."

Moments later, they were on the road, Zack gripping the wheel with one hand while they held Anthony on their lap with the other, letting the little boy help steer in a way that made him giggle uncontrollably.

The car was filled with laughter and warmth, and as Josephine watched Zack interact with Anthony, she felt a subtle flicker in her heart, realizing she was starting to fall for Zack, captivated by their effortless charm and the joy they brought to her son.

The day was unfolding in a way that felt serendipitous, as the three of them cruise through the streets toward their destination, the promise of the day lingering in the air like the scent of gasoline and the thrill of adventure.

* * *

The sun hung low in the sky, casting a warm glow over Queerville High School, where the sound of laughter and chatter filled the air, yet there lingered an undercurrent of tension that was impossible to ignore. Dawn and Max, their hearts racing, sat perched on the bleachers, eyes locked on Douglas.

He appeared nonchalant, leaning casually against the metal railing as he exchanged whispered words and small packages with a series of anxious teens, each transaction coated in a thin layer of secrecy.

It was a scene that unfolded too easily amidst the innocence of school life, a stark contrast to the bright uniforms and spirited discussions about homework and weekend plans surrounding them. Max furrowed his brows, the gears in his mind turning. However, they both knew that they couldn't just sit there and watch;

they had to follow him. As Douglas finished his last deal, a sense of urgency propelled them from the safety of the bleachers.

They slipped down the steps, moving swiftly but stealthily, careful not to draw attention to themselves but unable to shake the feeling that they were stepping into something far deeper than they had anticipated. The afternoon sun framed Douglas as he made his way to an old, beaten-up car—its faded paint a testament to years of neglect, but it was his sanctuary, one that harbored secrets and shadows.

With each step, the gravity of their decision settled heavily on their shoulders; Max exchanged a glance with Dawn, a silent agreement passing between them as they ducked behind a nearby tree, peering out at the unfolding drama.

As Douglas finally took off, the engine roaring to life like a dormant beast awakening from its slumber, Dawn and Max wasted no time; adrenaline coursed through their veins as they hopped into their own car, the tires crunching on gravel, hearts syncing to the rhythm of the pursuit, and they followed behind him, cloaked in the excitement and tension of the impending unknown.

Each twist and turn brought them deeper into a narrative they never intended to be a part of, yet felt inexorably drawn to, as the afternoon sun slipped lower in the sky, painting the world with hues of orange and red, foreshadowing the intensity of what lay ahead.

* * *

The atmosphere inside the Queer House buzzed with anticipation as the diverse gangs gathered in the vibrant and welcoming space, each person eager for Charlotte's announcement that promised to steer the direction of their community.

Zack, typically more reserved and positioned behind the scenes, stood at the center of the room, their presence commanding attention while raising a hand in greeting.

"It's good to see you all here today," they began, a hint of nervousness underlying their tone.

"I know I'm not usually the one to have the floor, but Charlotte asked me to step up more so she can focus on all of her new endeavors…"

As they spoke, a wave of admiration swept from the audience, particularly from Maria, whose gaze fixed on Zack with unabashed longing. Josephine, ever the observant one, caught the spark of desire in Maria's eyes and couldn't help but raise an eyebrow, a smirk creeping onto her face.

Zack, momentarily letting their eyes drift to Maria's hopeful expression, pushed deeper into their agenda, quickly transitioning to updates that had everyone leaning forward with interest.

"First on the agenda is our third annual Queer off contest," they announced, their enthusiasm building, "Coming up soon. I, along with Maria and Sandy, will be participating in it. I hope you all can come out to support. We'll be raising funds for Queer House so we can keep these teens sheltered, fed, and clothed."

Just then, Charlotte's voice resonated from off-screen, playfully demanding, "I better see every one of your queer faces in attendance."

With a confident stride, Charlotte stepped into the spotlight, the room shifting as Zack took a seat next to Maria, who wasted no time throwing herself into them. Zack, slightly flustered, managed to maintain their composure as they politely distanced themself, a feat made increasingly difficult by Val's intense stare of disapproval.

Meanwhile, Charlotte continued, "Thank you, Zack honey. Please, if you need anything or have any questions, see Zack or Maria." Her words floated through the air as Josephine observed the comedic push and pull between Maria's obvious advances and Zack's awkward attempts to decline them.

The laughter and side-eye glances were palpable in the atmosphere, sparking amusement among the crew. Shifting away from the lighthearted banter, Charlotte adjusted her tone, drawing the group's collective attention.

"Now, the moment you've all been waiting for. Why I gathered you all here today," she stated, her gaze steady and purposeful. "Since the events that took part in O Town, it's left a lot of openings to some very influential doors…" Intrigued and attentive, the crowd leaned in closer, the air thick with curiosity.

"I am putting my name in for deputy mayor." The ripple of applause that followed reverberated through the room as cheers erupted, a tangible excitement surging among everyone present. Charlotte beamed at the support before continuing, "I'm in the running with one other person, and the vote is this Monday. So, I need you guys to make some signs and post them around, maybe do a little campaign run and get people to vote for me. Ah, I'm so excited! Grab some flyers off the table, and we're taking it to the streets in an hour."

The energy in the Queer House shifted dramatically, igniting a collective sense of purpose as the crew sprang into action, ready to champion their leader and ensure that Charlotte's aspirations ascended beyond the community hall and into the heart of their city.

In the vibrant chaos of the queer house, a space adorned with glittering Queerville pride flags and the scent of markers, Zack, Josephine, Val, and Maria were sprawled across a table covered in cardboard and colorful paints, focusing intently on crafting signs for Charlotte's campaign.

"I can't believe we're here making signs," Val scoffed, disbelief evident in her voice, as she slaps a catchy slogan on a bright piece of poster board, her brow furrowing with annoyance about how they reached this point.

Maria, always the peacemaker, shrugs with a grin, casually questioning, "So what, what's the big deal?" but Val is quick to unveil her underlying tension, "We need to be doing something about these O Town people mixing in with our people."

Zack interjected, their tone a blend of exasperation and pragmatism, "There is no more O Town," a statement that weighed heavy in the air—and in that moment, the group's simmering grievances came to the surface.

Val, attempting to provoke Zack with a jab, "Yeah, you made sure of that Zack. You took down a whole damn city just to come home to lose your girl and make a sign."

"You want to say that again?" Zack said with a harsh glare.

The tension building in the air as Val tread cautiously, "I'm saying where is the old Zack? The Zack that was always ready to crack heads. Now you are cracking glue bottles and making signs."

Maria rolled her eyes, and intervened to defend Zack, ~~insisting~~, "Why are you always getting at Zack?" proving how tangled their friendships and vendettas have become.

Josephine found herself stealing glances at Zack, who was the center of attention thanks to Maria's mischievous advances.

"Save it Maria," Val blurted, adding, "she only wants you now to get to me." "That's not true. I love getting screwed by Zack. It has nothing to do with you."

The tension shifted as they were interrupted by Josephine, who offered a lighthearted commentary, "I think I'm at the wrong table." "Josephine don't mind these two. That's Val and this is Maria." Zack introduced them, Josephine and Maria exchanged phony smiles.

"I'm out this drag. Zack if want to start handling business again come see the crew," Val said before storming off.

"You created a monster," Zack retorted to Maria, who sat there grinning, enjoying the playful chaos they've cultivated.

"She wanted to be you so obliged her."

"That's gross."

Josephine was finding the banter amusing.

"How about we get out of here and go back to my place."

Maria proposed with flirtatious audacity, the words hanging in the air as if challenging Zack's loyalty. Josephine watched intently as Zack, ever the gentleman, quickly dashed down the proposition with a smile that seemed forced, "Maria, you know I'm with Sandy now."

"A girls got to try," Maria said before kissing Zack on the cheek and taking off with her sign.

Josephine, taking note of the subtle power dynamics, probed Zack, "Aren't you the popular one."

"Not at all, Maria is my ex."

"Oh, that explains a lot."

"Yeah, she's really harmless." _After a pause!_ Disappointed

"So, you do have a girlfriend?"

"Yeah, her name is Sandy, she's great."

"Of course, you have a girlfriend. And how does she feel about Maria," her voice betraying a hint of jealousy. She leaned in closer, wanting to capture Zack's response as if it held the secret to their heart.

"She knows how to handle her." Zack smirked.

* * *

Dawn and Max lingered outside the worn, graffiti-laden exterior of the warehouse, their bodies low in the cramped confines of their vehicle as the afternoon sun casts long shadows across the pavement. The smoldering tension in the air ~~mixed of anxiety and anticipation~~ as they waited any signs of activity.

Max's impatience bubbled to the surface as he pivots to Dawn, "How long are we going to sit out here? I'm steaming hot like some apple pie in the window."

"Until we see something. Douglas didn't drive all the way out here to take a nap in an abandoned warehouse."

"Do you think this is his drug house? Where he keeps the drugs?"

"I don't know. But he's been in there a long time. He might be waiting for something or someone."

"Maybe we should call the sheriff."

"And say what? We have to wait and see what he does."

The sound of tires crunching against gravel pulled them from their thoughts, prompting a rush of adrenaline as they ducked instinctively, watching a new arrival. The tension was building—who could it be? Dawn and Max held their breaths in anticipation, the air thick with uncertainty. The car door opened, and the sunlight gleamed off the polished surface of the vehicle, casting elongated shadows on the ground. As a figure stepped out, the tight knot in their stomachs began to loosen just slightly, yet the unease lingered like a specter in the back of their minds.

"It's Val," Dawn murmured, her voice a blend of relief and caution. Max narrowed his eyes, "Who is Val?"

"She's a part of the Red Dragons."

"Red Dragons? You mean Zack's crew?"

"Yes. Do you think Zack is involved?"

The notion sent a wave of unease washing over them, but Max shook his head firmly. "No, there's no way. Kelly told me Zack doesn't even smoke cigs. They're like some spiritual guru," he reassured her, but doubts still danced between them like flickering candlelight in a dark room.

Suddenly, Val opened her trunk and handed Douglas bags of marijuana, and a chill ran down Max's spine. "Look, what is that?" "I think it's reefer," Dawn responded, though her tone betrayed her uncertainty.

"Reefer? Is that what the kids are on these days?" Max couldn't help but question, though the gravity of the situation weighed heavily on him.

"Reefer doesn't put kids in the morgue. No, there has to be something else going on," she asserted, her instincts screaming that the night was unraveling into something much darker. "Okay, can we get out of here now before someone sees us?" Max urged, his heart racing as they decided to retreat.

They scrambled into Dawn's car, adrenaline still coursing through their veins as they buckled in, not daring to look back. "What now?" Max asked, stealing a furtive glance in the rearview mirror. "Is there a bash happening this week or a hop?" Dawn replied, trying to keep her mind focused amid the chaos. "Yeah, there is actually. Douglas is throwing a secret bash tonight," Max responded, his voice thick with anticipation.

Dawn's expression hardened, a determined glint igniting in her eyes. "That's when we'll get him."

* * *

The late afternoon sun cast a warm glow over Main Street, illuminating the faces of Zack, Josephine, Maria, and their crew as they energetically passed out flyers urging the community to vote for Charlotte. The atmosphere was vibrant, filled with the sound of laughter and spirited conversations, as people stopped to engage and learn more about the campaign. Amid the bustling activity, Josephine turned to Zack, her eyes sparkling with admiration, "You know I heard about what you did up at the conversion camp," she said, her voice tinged with both curiosity and respect.

Zack, ever humble, shrugged and replied, "Yeah?" With a smile that radiated warmth, Josephine continued, "You saved a lot of people." "That's what they say." The moment lingered between them, "Humble and sexy—you are hard to resist, Zack."

Just then, the unmistakable sound of a horn erupted through the air, drawing their attention to Charlotte, who was cruising down the street in her campaign-inspired convertible. The energy shifted as Charlotte's voice boomed from her blowhorn, rallying the citizens.

"Vote for Charlotte for your next chairperson!" she shouted enthusiastically; her passion contagious. "I will be the voice for all the Queer folks in this community. Let's stand together and make them see us!" The sight ignited a sense of unity among the crew, reaffirming their shared mission.

Back at their strategic post, Zack checked their watch.

"I have to go pick up Sandy from work."

Josephine felt a tinge of disappointment yet masked it with enthusiasm, ~~for their next assembly,~~ "Will I see you tomorrow?" she asked, her hopes rising. "Yeah, we still have a lot of voters to sign up. See you back here tomorrow," Zack assured her, their smile bright against the backdrop of the setting sun. "I look forward to it, Zack," she replied, her heart warm. "Have a good night." "Good night, Zack," Josephine echoed, watching as they walked away, already anticipating the next day.

* * *

Later that night, the atmosphere inside Douglas's bash was chaotic, a swirling tempest of noise, laughter, and the eerie calm of detachment that often accompanies substance abuse. The loud music thumped like a heart struggling to keep time as pairs of teenagers swayed and stumbled across the dimly lit space, some nodding off on couches and floors, their bodies a testament to the overwhelming consumption of not just alcohol, but the illicit substances permeating the party.

In one corner, Val was perched like a hawk, hocking small bags of weed to eager hands, while Douglas, the mastermind behind the evening's event, prowled the scene with the sinister air of a drug lord, his focus primarily on the more potent heroin he was pushing to those willing to pay the price. The reckless mixture of youth and drugs had reached a critical point when a teen, barely comprehensible and twitching on the ground, drew gasps from onlookers—his body betraying him in the depths of an overdose

Then, amidst the swirling chaos, the dreadful spectacle caught Dawn and Max off guard as they stumbled into the scene, their expressions morphing from curiosity to horror. They exchanged glances, eyes widening as they took in the drooping figures and the unmistakable signs of a crisis brewing within the revelry.

She discreetly slipped away from the unsettling scene, her heart racing as she found refuge in a nearby bedroom, where the muffled bass could barely drown out the panic rising in her chest. Her fingers trembling as she dialed emergency services, her voice barely a whisper as she relayed the gravity of the situation.

"Hello, yeah, I'd like to report an illegal party going on right now," she managed, her urgency climbing along with the dread, "There are people taking drugs and overdosing on the floor. Send the police now."

Each word felt like a lifeline, a desperate plea for help in a world where the boundaries between youth and peril had become blurred, and the consequences of reckless abandon loomed over them like a dark cloud, ready to unleash its fury.

* * *

The atmosphere at Queerville High was electric, with the lights illuminating the field like a stage set for a grand performance, bringing a sense of anticipation that buzzed in the air. Daron, clad in his football gear, stood on the cusp of entering the battlefield, but not before he took a moment to share a special interaction with Rose, "Hey, beautiful." The smile that blossomed on Rose's face was radiant, a sign of the connection they shared.

"Save me a victory kiss," he suggested. And with a playful glint in her eye, she shot back, "Why wait?" With that bold affirmation, she pulled him close and pressed her lips against his in a kiss that instantly filled him with a surge of confidence and joy.

Once he donned his helmet, Daron made his way to the field, his heart racing not just for the game ahead, but also for the moments waiting after it with Rose.

As he gathered his teammates, fire ignited in his eyes, and he rallied them with motivation, "Alright fellas, let's give these boys a quick and painful ass-whopping.

I got a date with my girl later and I'm not trying to be late. Let's show them what Queerville is all about."

The team responded with a rallying chant, a blend of adrenaline and camaraderie echoing across the turf.

The game commenced, a series of dynamic shots capturing Daron as he navigated the field with agility and skill, dodging tackles.

Each sprint, each tackle, each cheer wove together an unforgettable tapestry of youth, ambition, and the thrill of love intertwined with the spirit of competition; it was here, beneath the bright lights and the watchful stars, that Daron played for victory.

On the sidelines, Rose cheered him on, her heart swelling with pride and exhilaration with each yard he gained, fully aware that beyond the camaraderie of the game, it was this boy who made her life sing brighter than any victory in the sport could.

───────────────

As the vibrant atmosphere of the bash reached an exhilarating peak, the living room pulsed with the energy of teenagers packed in, laughter mingling with the thumping bass of the music that echoed through the house. The dim lights flickered, illuminating dancing bodies swaying to the rhythm of the night, while others soaked in the revelry in small clusters, drinks in hand, sharing secrets and dreams amid the chaos.

Just as Douglas and Val felt the night couldn't get any better, their joyous bubble burst with the sudden, jarring jangle of police sirens piercing through the laughter. Panic erupted as partygoers scrambled, the joyful ambiance instantly transforming into chaos.

Seizing the moment, Douglas and Val, desperate to escape the encroaching law, darted through the house and made a beeline for the backyard, adrenaline pumping through their veins.

However, fate had other plans; as they burst into the moonlit yard, they collided head-on with a waiting patrol car, its lights flashing a daunting blue and red. Douglas and Val had nowhere to run, their hearts racing not just from the thrill of the party, but now from fear and impending consequences. "What do we do now?" Doulgas asked.

"Don't say anything. We'll be out within the hour."

"I have a can on me." Doulgas remarked.

"Doesn't matter. We'll be going home soon. Trust me."

Before they knew it, they were ushered into the back of the cruiser, the weight of the handcuffs a stark reminder of how quickly the night had turned from carefree exuberance to grim reality.

They found themselves in a drab cell, a fluorescent light buzzing overhead as the reality of their situation sank in.

Douglas, feeling the weight of his choices, leaned back against the cold metal of the bars separating him from Val, who sat on the adjoining female side. The two still reeling from the arrest, sat in silence, their backs pressed against one another, united despite the steel separating them.

"What do we do now?" Douglas whispers, his voice trembling slightly, the gravity of the situation dawning on him.

Val, attempted to maintain a modicum of hope amidst despair, responded with quiet conviction, "Don't say anything," Val, refusing to let despair take hold, reassured him, "We'll be going home soon. Trust me." Her words a fragile thread of hope in the sterile, unforgiving walls of the jail, as they brace themselves to confront whatever awaited them in the hours to come.

* * *

Sandy was perched playfully in Zack's lap, the tension in the air heated as their lips collided in fervent kisses, deepening the connection they both ardently craved.

Zack fought valiantly against the waves of desire crashing over them, determined to uphold the promise they had made to each other—a promise to abstain from sex. With every flutter of Sandy's tongue and every teasing caress, it became increasingly difficult for Zack to remain steadfast. "Wait, Sandy, stop," they managed to whisper breathily, their voice laden with both longing and restraint.

But Sandy, with a mischievous glint in her eyes, brushed aside their plea, her lips continuing their delightful assault on theirs, igniting an inferno of passion in Zack that they couldn't easily extinguish. "I don't want to stop," she murmured softly, her breath warm against their skin, further stirring the conflict within them. Zack felt near their breaking point; they lifted her gently off their lap, desperate to create a physical barrier to combat the desires overwhelming their senses. "Please, you're making it so hard for me," they confessed, grappling with the intensity of what was unfolding. "Well, I can help you with that if you'd let me," Sandy teased, her eyes sparkling with flirtation, but beneath the playful banter, Zack saw the seriousness in her demeanor—a mixture of affection and mischief that only added to their dilemma.

"Sandy," Zack murmured, their voice firm yet softened by affection, which prompted her to tuck her knees into her chest, retreating slightly into the corner of the couch as if she were contemplating the unspoken boundaries they had set. "What now?" she asked, the challenge evident in her tone as an awkward silence loomed over them, though a playful smirk danced on her lips, clearly amused at their predicament.

"We can talk," Zack suggested, their attempt at normalcy feeling almost absurd in the moment, but a part of them held onto the hope of navigating this delicate situation. "How was your day, today?" they asked, trying to steer the conversation to safer waters.

"It was great," Sandy replied, a cheerful tone coloring her words. "What did you do?" Zack inquired further, desperate to fill the silence with mundane topics. She responded, "I worked." They could sense that her mind wasn't entirely on the conversation. "And how was work?"

Her playful retort caught them off guard. "Zack, we can talk and have sex," she declared, without hesitation, she leaned back into Zack, pressing her lips against theirs once more, pulling them into the whirlwind of desire they both fought to contain.

Under the stormy night sky, the atmosphere crackled not just with electricity from the thunder and lightning but also with the palpable tension of a tied game that seemed to hang in the balance, each second stretching out like an eternity.

The crowd was a sea of anticipation, their breath collectively held as Queerville took its time-out, players huddled tight together like a pack of wolves strategizing their next move, every voice a mixture of adrenaline and strategy, the stakes higher than ever.

As the whistle blew and the huddle broke, the plan was in motion, and energy surged through the air, electrifying each player as they took their positions on the field. The quarterback, with an intensity that cut through the chaos of the dreary night, gripped the ball tightly, his eyes scanning the field for the break that could change everything.

With a swift motion, he unleashed the ball, sending it spiraling through the tempestuous night air as Daron dashed down the field, his feet pounding rhythmically against the wet turf, each step igniting a fire within him to push harder, run faster. The rain poured down in sheets, a curtain of silver that blurred the lines of the gridiron, but in this moment, it sharpened Daron's focus as his heart raced with adrenaline.

He could hear the pounding of his own heartbeat mixed with the roar of the crowd; a sound that somehow became distant as he focused solely on the ball arcing toward him. Time seemed to slow as he extended his hands, feeling the leather slip seamlessly into his grasp. In that miraculous instant, the chaos around him faded away, and amidst the cacophony of the storm, the end zone glowed like a beacon of hope, a sanctuary just within reach.

As he crossed the goal line, a breathtaking moment unfolded, suspended in time—his body surging forward with pure exhilaration, the thrill of triumph coursing through every vein as the crowd erupted in a euphoric wave of cheers and disbelief.

The eruption of joy from his teammates swirled around him like a wild dance, their cheers mixing with the thunder, a triumph forged under pressure.

In that ecstatic, chaotic moment, Daron's eyes found Rose, her face radiant with pride and happiness.

As his team hoisted him high above their heads, he caught Rose's gaze, and leaned down to kiss her, sealing the night with a promise amidst the chaos. "That was for you," he whispered, his heart racing from both the thrill of the win and the warmth of her presence.

Rose's teasing smile sparkled brighter than any lightning flash around them as she playfully responded, "You're so getting laid tonight." leaving Daron momentarily speechless, lost in the joy of the game and the moment, before his teammates, brimming with energy and camaraderie, swept him away, their exuberance echoing through the now electric night.

* * *

The relentless patter of rain against the windows created a cozy soundtrack for a night sizzled with temptation but redirected toward playful intimacy. Sandy and Zack endeavor to channel their sexual energy into a spirited montage of fun activities that transform the mundane into a magical evening. The kitchen became their playground; laughter erupted as flour flew into the air, creating a delightful mess while they attempted to whip up cookies.

Amidst the chaos, a spontaneous dance break ignited their spirits, each twirl and spin were an electric connection, their chuckles harmonizing with the rhythm of the storm outside.

The mood shifted to a competitive showdown over a game of cards, where the stakes rose with every hand Sandy lost, her laughter ringing out as she playfully peeled away a layer of clothing, the lighthearted teasing fueling an unspoken tension.

As the scene transitioned, Zack strummed their guitar, and serenaded Sandy who danced freely, the flickering candlelight casting shadows that accentuated their joyful night.

Afterwards they settled into the plush living room, cuddled close together, an array of popcorn scattered about as the flickering screen showcased a spine-chilling horror movie.

"This is my favorite way to spend time with you," Sandy confessed, her eyes sparkling with affection. Zack responded, their voice tender, "Yeah? Anytime I get to spend with you is my favorite." Their words wrapped around them like a warm blanket, each moment steeped in an unbreakable bond.

Sandy's affectionately uttered, "Awe, baby." Zack caught off guard, murmured, "That's the first time you've ever called me baby." Sandy paused for a brief moment, her eyes filled with a mischievous glint as she replied, "Is it?"

They shared a knowing smile, and Zack felt a rush of warmth at her playful teasing.

"Yeah, I like it," they admitted, leaning in to kiss her passionately, igniting a spark that crackled between them. Sandy responded eagerly, pulling Zack in tighter, her heart racing with excitement and desire as their lips interlocked.

But, just as quickly, Zack drew back slightly, trying to maintain a balance between passion and restraint.

"So, we're really not going to have sex?" Sandy asked, disappointment lacing her tone, as if the fire they had just ignited had dimmed in an instant.

"No, Sandy," they replied gently, their expression serious but warm, trying to soothe her disappointment, their eyes searching hers as if to convey all the affection they felt without words.

She sighed wistfully but nodded, understanding that they were in a moment more profound than mere physical connection.

"Fine then," she replied with a playful huff, giving in gracefully as she nestled closer to Zack, enveloping herself in their warmth. They settled into a comfortable silence, wrapped in each other's arms, understanding that intimacy comes in many forms, and tonight, their connection is as rich and fulfilling as the warmth of each other's presence.

Later, while trying to keep their hormones at bay. Zack and Sandy decided to share the joyous news of their relationship with Mama Zack.

The couple made their way to her cozy home, their excitement tinged with a hint of nervousness about how she might react. As they approached the front door, the lovely aroma of Mama Zack's cooking wafted through the air, instantly putting them at ease.

Upon entering, they were greeted with her beaming smile, the kind that always made them feel welcome, followed by a delightful dinner filled with love and laughter. They sat together at the table, surrounded by the comfort of home, but the weight of their secret lingered in the air.

After some light conversation and a few teasing comments, Zack finally cleared their throat, their heart racing. "Mama, we have something to tell you." Glancing at Sandy, who took their hand in encouragement. They exchanged a determined look, the kind that spoke volumes of their bond, before Zack continued, "We're together. Sandy and I are in a relationship."

In that moment, Mama Zack's eyes widened with astonishment, and a wide grin spread across her face, lighting up the room as she leaned in closer to them.

"You two? Are you two really together?" she asked with an unmistakable blend of disbelief and excitement. "Yes, Mama," they both replied, their voices synchronized and filled with the thrill of being open about their love. "Well, about time!" she exclaimed, bursting into joyous laughter as she stood up to wrap them both in a tight embrace.

In that heartwarming moment, the love in the room enveloped them like a blanket, and the acceptance they felt from Mama Zack made their hearts swell. It was a beautiful confirmation that their relationship, was not only a cherished part of their lives but would also be celebrated and embraced by the people they loved most.

_____

The room was drenched in harsh fluorescent light, depicting an atmosphere heavy with tension and uncertainty. Officer Whitey leaned casually against the metal bars, a slight smirk creeping onto his face as he unlocked the cell. "You two are free to go," he announced, his voice echoing in the sterile environment, which had seemed both claustrophobic and suffocating.

Douglas blinked in disbelief, his heart racing as he searched Val's face for confirmation of this unexpected news. "Really?" he stammered, a mix of hope and skepticism dancing in his eyes. Val leaned back, her signature swagger momentarily at bay as she shot Douglas a reassuring look. "Told you, Dougie boy," she replied, her voice calm, like a seasoned gambler who had just played a daring card.

As they pushed through the heavy door and into the night air, Douglas felt a mix of elation and dread wash over him. "I was scared shitless," he confessed, the shadow of the jailhouse looming behind him, a stark reminder of the choices that had led him there.

Val shook her head, a knowing smirk creeping across her lips. "You can't be scared in this game; it will get you killed," she replied, her eyes glinting with the playful menace of someone who had navigated darker paths.

"Now what?" Douglas asked, anxiety creeping back into his tone, wondering what lay ahead beyond the freedom they had just been granted.

In that moment, a sleek, black ford pulled up to the curb, its windows tinted and ominous, almost like a predator waiting to pounce on its prey. "Just get in," Val instructed, urgency wrapping around her words as she motioned for Douglas to follow her into the car.

As they slid into the plush interior, the air felt thicker, each breath laden with unspoken expectations. Douglas's heart pounded as he caught sight of Mayor Lewis seated in the back, the man who held the strings of power and consequences. "Mayor Lewis?" he questioned, barely concealing the tremor in his voice as reality set in.

Val, the composed one, leaned with a relaxed confidence, eyes fixed on the mayor. "You wanted to meet the man in charge; now you have," she said, as though they were engaging in an intricate dance of power dynamics.

Mayor Lewis expression hardened, his brow furrowing with irritation. "How did you two fuck this up so poorly?" he shot back, his voice heavy with disappointment.

The air grew tense, the atmosphere charged with a mix of danger and opportunity, as Douglas and Val exchanged glances, their expressions a blend of defiance and fear. The night had only just begun, and they were about to navigate a labyrinthine world of politics, loyalty, and survival, where one misstep could lead them back to the very place, they had fought so hard to escape.

CHAPTER 8

Mississippi,
1957

As Kelly and Martin approached his parents' home, a swirl of nerves churned in Kelly's stomach, making her fidget with her vibrant poodle skirt and the snug fit of her top. She had never met anyone's parents in such a lavish setting, and despite Martin's encouraging words, she couldn't shake the feeling that perhaps she should change.

"Aw, Kelly, you look just dandy," Martin assured her, but that did little to quell her worries.

"Maybe I should've worn something different to meet your folks," she murmured, looking down at her attire, feeling out of place in the opulence that surrounded them.

"No. No, they will like you as you are Kelly. Just be yourself."

As they stepped through the ornate door, it swung open to reveal Mrs. Campbell—a picture of Southern elegance with her pristine, conservative attire and perfectly coiffed hair. "Martin, my dear boy. How are you?" she chimed, her voice dripping with the kind of warmth that felt barely genuine to Kelly.

"Hello, Mother, I want to finally introduce you to my girlfriend, Kelly Hamilton."

"Oh, that's right dear. You did say that you were bringing a friend. Well do come in."

The Campbell home was nothing short of a mansion, reeking of old money and showcasing a lifestyle that made Kelly's own wealthy upbringing seem minimal in comparison. The opulent decor and extravagant backyard lawn party made Kelly feel like she had stepped into a world she barely recognized.

It struck her as almost surreal that she was witnessing such a scene, one that starkly contrasted with her previous experiences in her own hometown; the presence of black servants operating seamlessly in the background was a culture shock, an unsettling reminder of the differences in their worlds.

As she took a seat at the meticulously set table—exquisite silverware gleaming in the soft sunlight—the nerves twisted tighter in her stomach. The whole scene seemed excessive for the mere six guests around the lavishly set table.

There sat Martin's brother and sister—Julie and Kevin—whose laughter filled the air as they quizzed Kelly with eager curiosity. "So, what do you do, Kelly?" Mr. Campbell asked, while everyone sat quietly.

"I attend the university?" Kelly replied.

Mrs. Campbell, with a condescending tone, sneered at the very thought of women getting higher education.

"University? Dear god, what for?" she chuckled, leading to awkward laughter from the table. But Kelly stood her ground, feeling the weight of their assumptions and judgments bearing down on her.

"Well, Mrs. Cambell to get an education."

"Kelly wants to make a difference in the world. She wants to make the world see women as a force to be reckon with." Martin spoke proudly about her ambitions, igniting a flicker of confidence within her.

"Are you thee Kelly Hamilton, the one from O Town?" Julie asked, shockingly. "No way," Kevin whispered.

"Now what's that son, do you know Kelly?" Mr. Campbell inquired. "Yeah, she's like famous," Kevin exclaimed.

"She was one of those teens that were at that conversion camp," Julie added.

"Conversion camp? The one from last year?" Mrs. Campbell asked, appalled.

Kelly's heart sank. Uncomfortable memories rushed back as tension enveloped them, even as Mrs. Campbell pried deeper.

"Oh, those folks were just trying to help them teens become better Christians. The news blew things all out of proportion," Mr. Campbell passively remarked. Which only enraged Kelly further.

"Excuse me?" Kelly said defensively.

"Didn't the news say that you were involved with one of those Queerville kids that burned the place down?" Mrs. Campbell posed, as the atmosphere turned heavy with scrutiny.

Kelly could only shake her head, the anger within her bubbling up like a volcano ready to erupt with every dismissive comment.

"Yes, I was," she replied bluntly, setting the stage for an awkward silence to settle uncomfortably among them.

When Mr. Campbell clumsily probed, "Burned it down? Well, good lord, why would he do such a thing?"

"Because I was being tortured inside and nearly died," she shot back.

As she spoke, her voice trembled not only with anger but with a lifetime of struggles. The awkward silence that followed was stifling, as if the laughter had sucked all the air out of the space, and Kelly realized, in that vulnerable moment, that her truth was a heavy burden in a world so far removed from the authenticity she valued.

Abruptly, she stood up from the table, her heart racing, feeling the weight of their judgment bearing down on her and desperate to flee the suffocating charm of Martin's privileged world.

Queerville, 1957

Sandy watched as Zack slept peacefully in bed, their chest rising and falling gently with each breath, the morning light streaming through the curtains casting a warm glow over them. As Zack turned on their stomach, she felt a swirl of emotions looking at them, a mix of affection and admiration, prompting her to lean closer and caress Zack's back, hoping to rouse them from their slumber.

However, as her fingers glided over their skin, her attention was drawn to the scars that adorned Zack's back. Each mark told a story, an undeniable testament to the lengths Zack would go to for the one they love. Sandy didn't view these scars with disgust; rather, they filled her with a profound respect for Zack's resilience and loyalty.

Overcome with adoration, Sandy pressed gentle kisses to each scar, feeling an overwhelming connection to Zack's past struggles and triumphs. Just as she placed the last kiss, she noticed Zack's eyes flutter open, meeting her gaze with a sleepy smile. Grinning, she leaned in and captured their lips in a soft, tender kiss. In a playful turn of events, Zack rolled over, bringing Sandy on top, and their kiss deepened, igniting a spark of passion between them.

In a moment of eager spontaneity, Zack slipped off Sandy's nightgown, their hands exploring each other, causing sighs and gasps to escape their lips as Zack cupped Sandy's breast, igniting a fire of desire that spread between them. Sandy began to leave hickeys along Zack's neck.

Their bodies intertwining in a passionate embrace, lips melding together in an overwhelming rush of affection. The atmosphere thickened with desire as Zack's mouth found its way to Sandy's nipples, drawing soft moans from her as pleasure coursed through her body.

With a playful smile lingering on her lips, Sandy pushed Zack on their back, making sure to leave a trail of soft, lingering kisses down from their neck, savoring every inch of their skin as she moved lower. She relished the taste of Zack, tracing her kisses down towards their abs, pausing to pay extra attention to each defined muscle, her tongue dancing across all six of them in a teasing manner.

Zack could hardly catch their breath, the sensations sending waves of warmth coursing through them. Sandy looked up at them, locking her gaze with theirs. With a teasing smile, she licked her lips and lowered herself further.

Her inquisitive mouth found its way as she enveloped them, her warmth welcoming against them. Zack gasped, feeling a delicious rush of pleasure as Sandy gently took them into her mouth. Zack wasn't used to this type of pleasure; this was a first. Sandy licked the tip of Zack's erection; as they gaped down at her, savoring them, like a pop sickle on a summer day.

With a teasing spat, she slicked it with a sheen of heat, a precursor to the eager passion that was about to unfold. As she thrust Zack into her mouth, the world around them faded, leaving only the intoxicating connection they shared. Each devouring movement was met with soft, breathy moans that escaped her lips, revealing the sheer delight that coursed through her. Zack, caught in the throes of this electric exchange, felt every ripple of pleasure resonate within them, the warmth of Sandy's mouth sucking them, the sensations aligning seamlessly to create an experience unlike any other.

The air around them was thick with anticipation, every breath charged with unfulfilled desires as Sandy's tongue swirled around, teasingly exploring every inch of Zack's hard cock.

Zack was trying desperately to hold back the tide of pleasure building inside, but the exquisite warmth and wetness of Sandy's mouth was nearly overwhelming, causing their toes to curl the sheets as they gripped the headboard.

The urgency of the moment propelled Sandy to reach for the lube, her fingers deftly applying it as she teased Zack.

Sandy gently grasped their erection, guiding it inside of her as she slowly sank down onto it. She gasped at the fullness as Zack groaned at how tight she felt.

She grinded her hips and peered into their alluring eyes, continuing to sway her hips gently and seductively. Her mouth agape she couldn't believe how good Zack felt inside of her.

She loved the way Zack's body responded to her, how they faltered when she brushed against them, pushing boundaries, testing limits. Each sway of her hips left a mark on their resolve, and she pushed further into the depths of their connection.

The intensity of their connection surged around them, enveloping them like the warm summer air. Zack found themself captivated as they gazed up at Sandy, who moved with an effortless grace and a sensuality that was uniquely her own. Her fingers gently caressed her breast, each touch a soft invitation that stirred something deep within them, riding Zack with an allure that left them breathless.

Her tightness gripping them, igniting a flood of overwhelming emotions that surged to the surface. It was a tension that demanded release, and with a voice that quivered between longing and awe, Zack moaned the words that had been lodged in their heart for far too long..."I love you." Sandy savored the truth in their words as if they were a secret she had longed to hear but never dared to hope for.

In that moment, she saw a reflection of her own feelings the depth they'd both been too nervous to explore until now, a well of vulnerability and desire that shimmered just beneath the surface of their playful banter and fleeting glances.

Sandy's lips curled into a teasing smile as she met Zack's gaze with an intensity that matched the heat swelling between them. "I told you it was worth it," she murmured, her voice sultry and smooth like velvet, wrapping around each word. They were no longer merely dancing around the edges of something profound. Instead, they were taking the plunge into uncharted waters, ready to explore the depths of what could be, a union forged in sincerity that mirrored the undeniable chemistry crackling between them.

Zack grasped her hips, as she rode them like only Sandy could. Feeling the warmth of her body against them, they realized that every longing glance and every moment spent watching her sway by the jukebox was leading to this electric encounter. Sandy was a force of nature, effortlessly commanding the attention of those around her, her hips swaying with a hypnotic grace that drove the men wild and fueled their fantasies. But now, in this intimate moment, Zack was the one lucky enough to experience the power of those hips firsthand.

A spark surged between the rhythm of their movements synchronized flawlessly, each thrust a testament to the deep chemistry they shared, an unspoken bond that tightened around them like an electric current.

Sandy reveled in the power she possessed; a coiled spring of desire that drew Zack even closer. With each controlled thrust, she could feel the barriers around Zack's heart melting, exposing vulnerability like petals unfurling under the morning sun.

Sandy rode faster, grinding her hips while thrusting herself down onto Zack's rock-hard shaft...

Zack eyes grew big... head arched back... throat wide, a huge gasp as they lost themself in the sensations that consumed them. "I LOVE YOU SANDY," they exclaimed, as if declaring it to the universe itself.

Her laughter danced around them, sweet and infectious, amplifying the ecstasy that wrapped itself around their bodies. Pleasure was a language, one she spoke fluently, and she loved the way Zack responded to her, opening up in ways they hadn't even known they could.

"Do you? Do you love me, baby?" she asked teasingly, her eyes sparkling with mischief as she rode Zack harder.

Zack, unable to contain their emotions, nodded their head vigorously as they repeated emphatically, "Yes, I love you, Sandy," their voice filled with a mix of eagerness and longing. The sheer joy in Zack's voice made Sandy beam with happiness.

The way she peered deeply into their eyes stirred something primal within them, with a swift maneuver, Zack rolled Sandy on her stomach, penetrating her from behind. Sandy arched her back, a wave of pleasure coursing through her as she thrust her hips backward, letting out a low, satisfied groan. The feeling of Zack's hands firmly wrapping around her waist sent shivers down her spine. Their touch was both commanding and tender, a perfect mix of strength and sensuality that ignited her senses. With each stroke, they applied just the right amount of pressure, connecting them on a deeper level—hard yet infused with a sensual rhythm, deeper, blending intensity with tenderness.

Sandy turned her head slightly to gaze back at Zack, her eyes wide with disbelief and excitement. She was completely taken aback by the raw passion that seemed to consume Zack. It was surreal how her best friend was bringing her into an experience that felt so over-the-top, like something straight out of a steamy movie. The thrill of it all was exhilarating, and yet, she couldn't help but question how she had missed out on this before.

In that instant, a wave of jealousy washed over her as she thought about Kelly, Maria, and all the other girls who had seemingly enjoyed this kind of connection. How had they been allowed this pleasure, while she had remained in the dark? It stung more than she expected, a bitter taste of envy filling her as she realized the depth of what she had been missing all this time.

Her mouth wide, but she couldn't speak nor moan. Zack was hitting her spot; leaving her paralyzed with ecstasy.

Zack's hand connected with a light smack against Sandy's backside, the sound echoing in the sunny room. A rush of excitement coursed through Sandy as she felt the sting of their palm mixed with exhilaration. Zack confidently wrapped their fingers in her hair, pulling it back just enough to tilt her head, exposing her neck leaving sweet kisses. This bold, dominant side of Zack was intoxicating. Sandy surrendered to the sensations overwhelming her. With each thrust, she felt herself teetering on the edge, a breathless scream escaping her lips as waves of pleasure crashed over her. The thrill of losing control pushed her further into the moment, and she responded by pressing back against Zack with fervor, eager to feel them closer, almost desperate in her need for them. Zack's intensity surged to unparalleled levels as they skillfully maneuvered Sandy onto her back, transitioning her into the missionary position.

Their eyes locked in a potent gaze; Zack took a moment to appreciate the beauty of Sandy. Her face was a captivating blend of anticipation and surrender, emotions intertwining to form an alluring tapestry of vulnerability and trust. Each subtle nuance in her features spoke volumes, inviting them to explore further.

With a gentle but firm embrace, Zack once again entered Sandy, causing a soft gasp to escape her lips. It was a sweet, breathy sound.

Zack was a master of rhythm, their movements fluid and intentional as they grinded their hips, they seemed to weave a spell that enveloped her senses, drawing her deeper into a world of pleasure and intensity. The fluidity of their actions created a mesmerizing rhythm, each beat resonating with the very core of her being. As the energy between them surged, Sandy found herself lost in the moment, surrendering fully to the overwhelming sensations that Zack's mastery evoked. It was a beautiful interplay of skill and emotion that transcended the physical, leaving her breathless and yearning for more.

In a whirlwind of passion, as her fingers gripped tightly onto Zack's broad shoulders, she felt the heat radiating from their body. Her nails dug in just enough to ground her amidst the crashing waves of pleasure that engulfed her, offering a tether to reality while simultaneously amplifying her connection to them.

The sounds spilling from her lips became a beautiful melody, a breathy mix of gasps and moans, punctuated by mumbled words that flowed like an incantation—

almost as if she were invoking an ancient language spoken only in the throes of ecstasy. Each thrust sent shivers racing down her spine, igniting a fire deep within that she never knew existed. Zack, fully attuned to her rhythm, responded by lifting Sandy's leg, allowing them to delve deeper, long, hard strokes, exploring the depths of Sandy. Their breaths came in ragged bursts, growing more frantic as they both approached the pinnacle of their desires.

As they found their crescendo, a euphoric wave surged through Sandy, pulling Zack along with her as they both climaxed together, their bodies arching in harmony, suspended in the blissful aftermath, where the world softened into a dreamlike haze and all that remained was the echo of their shared pleasure.

Zack and Sandy lay spent on the bed, completely satisfied and exhausted, their bodies entangled in a lazy embrace that spoke of both intimacy and comfort.

"That was better than the first time. How is that possible? How are you so good at this?" she said, her voice a mix of disbelief and admiration as she caught her breath, her heart still racing from the exquisite moments they had just shared. The sensations that coursed through her were overwhelming, leaving her both stunned and thrilled, making her wish she had taken the plunge sooner.

She couldn't shake the feeling of pure euphoria; it was by far the best she ever had. Every fiber of her being seemed to hum with a delightful energy that enveloped her like a warm embrace. In that moment, floating in blissful afterglow, she felt a delightful vulnerability blossom within her. It was more than just the physical connection; it was the emotional intimacy that hit her like a warm wave, washing over her and leaving her breathless. No one had ever made love to her like that, with such intensity and passion. The way Zack had expertly navigated her desires, attuning to her every reaction, had her hooked—they were unlike anyone she had encountered before.

Watching Zack, she noted the slight blush that tinted their cheeks, a playful smile dancing on their lips as they seemed almost unfazed by her praise, "A lot of porn," they sneered, winking at her as they picked at the sheets nervously. Sandy let out a melodious laugh, a sound that echoed in the quiet room and filled it with warmth.

As she reached out, her hand found Zack's, fingers intertwining in a silent promise. The warmth of their skin against hers sent a familiar thrill cascading through her, awakening all the feelings she had tried to suppress. It was a moment suspended in time, a reckless leap into the depths of what could be—a chance to taste the passion that had once flared between them but was kept at bay by fear and uncertainty.

"I can't believe we waited so long to do this," she murmured. "You wanted to stay friends," Zack reminded her, a gentle smile softening their features. Their presence was intoxicating, and she felt alive in a way she hadn't for far too long.

Sandy, now emboldened by their newfound connection, gazed into Zack's eyes, an unreadable intensity shimmered there, and before she knew it, her desire was rekindled.

Her heart raced, pounding fiercely against her ribcage as she leaned in, her breath mingling with theirs, her voice barely a whisper but laden with lust and urgency.

"One more time," she urged, each word laced with the yearning she could no longer contain.

Sandy strolled into the diner like a ray of sunlight breaking through the clouds, her smile radiating warmth and happiness as she waved enthusiastically to the regulars scattered throughout the bustling space. Patrons turned their heads, drawn by her infectious energy.

Charlotte, perched at the counter with a coffee cup in hand, shot Sandy a look that could cut through glass.

"Bitch, you late," she snapped, punctuating her words with an exaggerated eye roll that screamed exasperation.

Unfazed, Sandy's smile only widened, her innocent demeanor shining through as she replied, "Am I? I'm sorry; I must've overslept." The sweet naiveté in her voice only prompted a snarkier retort from Charlotte, who leaned over the counter, a mischievous glint dancing in her eyes.

"You ain't oversleep, ho. You were getting that back blown out. I know that look."

Sandy gasped in pretend confusion, "What look?" she asked, prompting Charlotte to elaborate with a wink, "Zack blew that back out."

The pride in Charlotte's voice was evident, almost maternal, as if she were recounting a heroic feat.

Sandy, momentarily caught up in the memory, closed her eyes and shook her head as if shaking off the remnants of a dream; laughter spilled from her lips as she confessed, "Sorry, flashbacks," as if the very memory sent delightful shivers down her spine.

"Just nasty!" Charlotte shot back, unable to contain her own laughter as she stirred her coffee.

The laughter from both women filled the diner, melding with the sounds of plates hitting tables and the sizzling of burgers, creating a harmonious backdrop to their teasing repartee.

* * *

As the afternoon light streamed through the dusty windows of the old warehouse, Mayor Lewis stood at the center, a map sprawled across a wooden table before him, his eyes gleaming with a mixture of ambition and desperation.

"Listen up, this Bronxville crew are complete morons," he declared, throwing his hands in the air as if to dismiss their incompetence, "They don't even have an escort for this shipment. That's where you guys come in, ram them off the road, pin them down and take it."

Val leaned against the grimy wall, her brow furrowed in thought, clearly skeptical as she interjected, "Are you sure they don't have an escort?"

Meanwhile, Douglas, arms folded and posture tense, chimed in warily, "It's not like them to not have an escort. We would be outnumbered; we don't have as many guns as they do." Ignoring their hesitations, Mayor Lewis's voice intensified, "I said, they won't have an escort. I got it from a reliable source. Now, I want this on the streets as soon as you get it in your hands."

The urgency in his tone hung heavy in the air and as he paced back and forth, Val felt a shiver of unease that had nothing to do with the sweltering environment.

"Why the rush?" she asked with a hint of confusion, to which Mayor Lewis replied, "There's a storm coming – I need to be prepared."

Val's disappointment seeped through as she questioned, "What storm?" and the mayor's tone shifted, darkening with ominous forewarning, "Why, Zack, of course."

Val rolled her eyes dismissively, her tone laced with sarcasm as she said, "Zack? You don't have to worry about Zack." However, Mayor Lewis wasn't convinced by her nonchalant attitude. Instead, he leaned in closer, his expression becoming more serious, and escalated the tension brewing in the room by asking, "Do you know who Zack really is? Do you have any idea what the Calhoun family is all about?"

"Wow, Zack is a Calhoun?" Douglas exclaimed incredulously, his eyes widening in disbelief. The skepticism he had initially harbored began to morph into a dawning realization as he grasped the rising stakes of their conversation. The name 'Calhoun' carried with it a legacy, an echo of whispered fear and respect within the community.

Val, still somewhat detached from the gravity of the discussion, merely shrugged and replied, "Okay, Zack is a Calhoun." It was a statement that, while true, failed to convey the significant implications that came with it. But Douglas, now fully engaged and caught up in the unfolding drama, couldn't contain his excitement.

"Not just a Calhoun. The Calhoun family." With that single phrase, the room's atmosphere shifted palpably, thick with the weight of history and power.

Mayor Lewis, sensing the shift, continued on, his voice dropping to a conspiratorial whisper, as if he were sharing a deeply buried secret. "The Calhoun family is one of the most powerful mob families in the Midwest. Anthony Calhoun was next in line to lead it—now Zack is to take his place. Do you know why so many people in this town treat Zack with such respect? It's because Zack is untouchable in ways you can hardly comprehend."

Douglas let out a gasp, "Holy shit! I knew Zack was a badass but a made man?"

This explosive revelation laid bare the underpinning fear that had fueled Mayor Lewis's urgent warnings. "With Anthony being killed and Frank missing in action, Zack must now take control of the business," Mayor Lewis continued, his tone shifting to one of grave concern, "The Calhoun mob family will be coming, and I want a seat at the table," he declared, his resolve now unyielding and filled with an unsettling mix of ambition and dread.

The stakes had risen to an alarming level, and it was in that pivotal moment that the realization struck each of them: the world they had known was on the brink of drastic transformation.

"This is how we do it: money and territory. The world as you know it is about to change," he concluded with a stark warning that resonated throughout the eerie expanse of the warehouse, leaving Val and Douglas in a gripping silence, grappling with the implications of their next moves in a game that had grown infinitely dangerous.

As the sun dipped low in the sky, casting warm golden hues over the bustling streets of Queerville, Zack and Josephine stood at their booth on Main Street, animatedly engaging with the crowd while handing out buttons and flyers emblazoned with the bold slogan...

"VOTE CHARLOTTE."

A sense of excitement filled the air, peppered with laughter and playful banter as Josephine leaned in, her curiosity piqued, asking, "So, Zack what are you most looking forward to at the Queer Off?"

"A lot of naked queer boys and girls and a shit load of glitter." Eliciting a spark of amusement from Josephine. She quipped back, "Glitter? Really?"

"Are you coming? It's going to be a lot of fun," Zack asked almost teasingly. Josephine, ever the flirt, slyly asked, "Is that an invite?"

Zack shrugged, "Sure, why not."

"Will you be participating?"

"Yeah, I'm competing for dream boat of the year and best masculine body."

"Well, you have my vote in both categories," Josephine said with a wink causing Zack to blush.

* * *

Meanwhile, across town at Rose's home, the atmosphere was warm and welcoming as Daron arrived, greeted by Rose's exuberant embrace. Her infectious enthusiasm provided him with just the encouragement he needed, as he admitted to feeling nervous about meeting her parents for the first time.

Inside the well-furnished family home, Mr. and Mrs. Thomas provided a polite yet probing welcome. "Mom and Dad this is my friend Daron." Rose said with glee. "Friend huh? Do you have a last name son?" Mr. Thomas inquired while giving Daron a firm handshake. "Greene, sir. Daron Greene," Daron replied, eliciting a smile from Mrs. Thomas, who embraced him with warmth that made the moment feel a little less daunting. "Pleasure to meet you, Daron. Rose has told us so much about you. Please have a seat."

As they gathered around the living room, the conversation flowed seamlessly, "So, you're the star running back at Queerville High School."

"Yes sir, three years running."

"Do you have plans for the future?" Mrs. Thomas inquiry caused Rose to be annoyed, "Mom and Dad, are you writing a book?"

"We're just making sure he has a good head on his shoulders."

"It's okay Rose. Um, I plan to play college football then go the pros."

"There's a lot of talent at that Queerville high school. You think you can make the cut?"

"Yes, I do."

"Of course, he can. Daron is the best running back in all the Midwest," Rose added, beaming with pride.

———————————

Sandy and Patty stood behind the counter at the diner, the hum of nearby conversations and the clatter of dishes creating a familiar backdrop for their afternoon heart-to-heart. Patty leaned back; her brows furrowed as she vented her frustrations about her latest fling.

"This guy I've been seeing is just a rag," she scoffed, her voice thick with exasperation, "He doesn't do anything for me; all he wants is sex and expects me to go above and beyond for him. He didn't even remember my birthday! How can you expect so much when you treat a person so little?"

Sandy nodded in sympathy, recalling her own past experiences, and battles with self-worth, "I spent so much time having to tell a man my worth and watching him fail tremendously," she replied quietly, a flicker of vulnerability in her eyes, "I've never thought about making them happy or doing things for them. But now that I'm with someone who knows my worth and treats me better than any man ever has. I find myself obsessing over ways to make them happy."

Her words hung in the air, heavy with the weight of transformation that love could bring. Patty chimed in, her tone shifting to one of revelation, "Yeah, because they deserve it. It's mind-blowing how automatic it is. Once you've been loved correctly, it all falls into place. You find yourself doing things you never did before."

The conversation had shifted from an expression of disappointment to a celebration of love's redemptive power, a shared acknowledgment that when someone genuinely respects and appreciates you, it sparks a natural desire to reciprocate that affection.

"You flip your lid," Sandy teased, her mischievous grin igniting laughter from Patty, who couldn't help but roll her eyes as she bemoaned her current lover's complete ineptitude in the bedroom.

"Yeah, it would be one thing if the sex was worth it. But this guy is like a damn jackhammer, just drilling a hole to China. What is it with men?" Her frustration resonated through her words, each syllable punctuated by a mix of humor and exasperation.

Sandy, smirking, "Oh, no, Zack doesn't do that. Zack is a stroker, not a poker."

The distinction drew a giggle from Patty, who, in a moment of playful desperation, quipped, "Well, can Zack give him some pointers?"

"Get you a transman; they're not afraid to put their hips into it," Sandy teased as she swayed her hips playfully, making Patty erupt in a fit of laughter, "Maybe I should. There's a fine line between confidence and delusion, and he hasn't quite grasped it. He has the nerve to brag like he did something revolutionary. I manage to let out one little moan, and suddenly he thinks he's a super dick."

The two women burst into laughter, the sound filling the cozy diner and transforming awkward moments into shared solidarity, a moment of genuine connection amidst the trials of modern dating. Sandy leaned back, a smile playing on her lips, "I actually stopped dating a guy because he made fun of me for moaning once. Seriously, I went silent after that. He never heard another peep from me." Patty's laughter turned to a dramatic choking fit, and Sandy added with a twinkle in her eye, "I was a silent movie."

"Ugh, such a wet rag," Patty said, rolling her eyes dramatically, but Sandy continued her heartfelt praise for Zack, emphasizing the difference of being with someone who held space for her emotions and vulnerability.

"One of the things I love about Zack. They never brag, never throw anything back in my face. Zack makes me feel so comfortable and safe. I can be vulnerable and allow my body to express what I'm feeling. I can scream, moan, let out my wild side. And never feel embarrassed or have to hide my face afterwards. Zack just holds me and never says a word," she confessed, her eyes sparkling with affection.

Patty, playful yet intrigued, teased, "Maybe I do need a transman. Wait, what's the package size?" Sandy, taking hold of a cucumber from a nearby plate, held it up proudly, drawing an exaggerated gasp from Patty, who clutched her chest in mock horror. "Oh, Zack! Dear Lord," she exclaimed, both of them laughing uncontrollably.

* * *

The vibrant atmosphere of Main Street in the afternoon buzzed with energy as Zack, Josephine, Anthony, and Charlotte campaigned passionately, on a mission to encourage the colorful and diverse community around them to exercise their right to vote.

The street was a celebration of life, filled with a kaleidoscope of intersectional identities, predominantly Queer individuals, who moved between laughter and cheers, their voices intertwining in a harmonious chorus of solidarity.

Charlotte took center stage, her charisma undeniable as she engaged the crowd, "Vote for me darling I will host the first ever Queer parade right here on Main Street, an event I promised to be a joyous manifestation of pride and community celebration."

As Zack and Josephine energetically distributed flyers, they exchanged stories, "So, how did you and your girlfriend meet?" she asked, genuinely interested.

Zack's face lit up with a warm smile, a beacon of joy that reflected their fondness for the memories.

"I met Sandy when I was eight years old. Our parents would take us to the same park," they began, their voice brimming with nostalgia.

"We would play together, just a couple of kids running wild. It wasn't long before our families started arranging playdates for us." As Zack recounted those innocent, carefree days, it was clear they cherished every moment of their childhood bond.

"Wow, so you're basically dating your best friend."

"Yeah, I am," Zack replied, a sense of pride swelling within them. The love they felt for Sandy was rooted as deep as their shared memories, and it was heartwarming to see it flourish from playful days at the park to the meaningful partnership they now enjoyed.

In that fleeting moment, as they continued to hand out flyers, Zack realized how lucky they were to have found love in such an unexpected place, with the person who had known them through it all.

"How is it dating your best friend?" Josephine asked, hoping to find signs of cracks in their relationship.

"It's great, takes a lot of the pressure off. She basically knows everything about me. There's nothing to hide. I don't have to pretend. She accepts me for who I am."

"That's beautiful. I wish I would've tried the friend route. But men only want one thing from women and a friendship isn't one."

"Maybe you should change the type of men that you date." "I wish I would've met you sooner," Josephine sighed and the two shared a moment of connection that suggested a deeper understanding—one perhaps tinged with unspoken attraction.

Just then, interrupting their camaraderie, young Anthony sprinted over, his face lighting up with the innocent excitement that only one thing could inspire.

"Can we go get ice cream?" he asked excitedly.

"Ice Cream? That's all you eat boy," Zack remarked.

"Did I hear that someone wants ice cream," Charlotte said as she approached.

Anthony turned and nodded his head yes.

"Well little one, I just so happen to own the shop with the best ice cream in town," she confessed, sparking joy in Anthony that was palpable.

* * *

The scene shifted to the diner where they all gathered after their hardworking day—Charlotte treating them to ice cream, a sweet reward for their efforts.

"Thank you, guys, for all your hard work today." Charlotte placed three big ice cream boats in front of the trio, topped with all the sweet essentials. Anthony's eyes grew big. "Oh, wow!" he drooled, walking over to Zack.

"You guys enjoy this it's on the house. There's more where that came from."

"Thanks, Charlotte," Zack said as Anthony reached up for them, his tiny hands grasping for Zack. With a gentle smile, Zack scooped him up, settling the little boy on their lap, the bond between them radiating warmth and comfort.

From behind the counter, Sandy and Patty watched the scene unfold, amusement sparkling in their eyes.

Patty, slightly entranced, still lost in her daydreams about Zack's package, blurted out, "Hi, Zack," with a shy wave. Sandy couldn't resist a playful nudge at Patty as she sauntered over to Zack's table with her signature broad smile, radiating confidence.

Josephine looked up and was captivated by Sandy's beauty, feeling as though she were in the presence of a goddess. Every dainty feature and confident stride made Josephine's heart sink a little deeper, an insidious thought creeping in—she could never compete with someone as stunning as Sandy.

"Well, hello, there."

"Hey, baby," Zack greeted Sandy as they stood up to meet her, pulling her in for a soft, tender kiss that left Josephine's throat dry, and her eyes narrowed with jealousy. Turning back to the table, Zack introduced them, "Babe, this is Josephine. Josephine, this is my girlfriend, Sandy."

The moment was charged; Josephine's voice came out in a nervous blur, "Oh, wow, you're gorgeous."
Sandy graciously accepted the compliment, her smile widening, "Thank you, so are you. Nice to meet you."
"And this little guy right here is Anthony."
Sandy's brow briefly furrowed—a flicker of suspicion crossing her features—as she echoed his name, "Anthony?" The pause hung in the air, tension building as the coincidence couldn't be ignored.
"Yeah, right? What a coincidence."

She shook off her suspicion, "Well, Hello Anthony, I'm Sandy," she offered, her voice turning sweet and playful. "Sandy," Anthony murmured. "Oh, wow he hasn't even said my name," Zack said with a hint of disappointment, their voice tinged with playful jealousy that elicited a soft laugh from Sandy.

"They say kids can see angels; he probably just sees my halo," she mocked lightly, her playful tone attempting to mask the slight pang of suspicion that lay just beneath the surface.

"Oh yeah? You're my angel," Zack whispered before leaning in to kiss her again, the sweet spontaneity melting away any fleeting tensions in the air.

Josephine couldn't help but admire this vulnerable side of Zack, the warmth radiating from their interaction like a gentle glow that contrasted sharply with her own feelings of inadequacy.

"I'll bring you guys over some more napkins," Sandy offered, her voice bright as she slipped behind the counter, though it was clear her attention was entirely focused on them, observing their every exchanged glance and tender moment with an almost too-watchful eye.

Amid the laughter and light-hearted banter, a flicker of jealousy simmered beneath Sandy's observant gaze as she noticed Josephine's lustful glances toward Zack.

"Um, who is that?" Patty inquired suspiciously.

"That's, Josephine," Sandy replied, trying to keep her tone casual, though the slight tightening of her jaw revealed her inner thoughts. "Um, keep an eye on that one. Only hoes are named Josephine," Patty quipped, the sharpness of her comment slicing through the air like a chilly breeze. Sandy suppressed a smile at Patty's bluntness, but her exhaustion threatened to override her humor. "Zack and I will be heading home shortly.

Do you think you can handle the night shift all alone?"
"Yeah, I'll be fine. Go home and enjoy your night."

The soft glow of the setting sun filtered through the sheer curtains, casting a warm, golden hue over Rose's bedroom, where Daron and Rose were entwined, lost in a world of their own as they made out on her bed. Their laughter blended with soft whispers, creating a delicate atmosphere of intimacy.

"Slow down, sailor," Rose playfully teased as she pulled back slightly, her cheeks flushed not just from the heat of the moment but also from the flutter of her heart.

"Do you think your parents liked me?" Daron's voice was laced with a hint of vulnerability, seeking affirmation in the uncertainty of teenage love.

With a flicker of her bright eyes, Rose reassured him, "Of course, they do. They know how special you are to me. You are the only boy I ever brought home." Daron's eyebrows shot up in surprise, realizing the significance of his presence in her life. "Really?" he asked, curiosity etched on his face. "Yeah, well, I wasn't really the 'meet my parents' type of girl," Rose admitted, a wry smile playing on her lips as she reflected on past relationships that never reached this level of seriousness. Daron, sensing the depth of her feelings, probed further, "So why did you want me to meet them?"

The air around them seemed to thicken with anticipation as she replied, "Because... I love you, silly." Rose words felt a weight lift off her shoulders. She had never uttered those words before to any boy.

His heart swelled at her admission, and a bright smile spread across his face as he reciprocated, "I love you too, Rose." The exhilaration of their young love ignited a surge of emotions, prompting Rose to grab Daron and pull him in for a passionate kiss that sealed their shared confessions, enveloping them in a cocoon of warmth and connection, a promise of the many firsts that lie ahead for both of them.

Meanwhile, in another corner of the world, Sandy and Zack were settled comfortably on the couch, the faint glow of the television reflecting their easy camaraderie as they waited for their pizza to arrive—a moment of shared anticipation punctuated by Sandy's occasional sneezes.

"Bless you. You've been sneezing all night. Are you coming down with something?" Zack's concern was immediate, their eyes darting towards her with genuine care. "No, probably just dust," Sandy assured them, brushing it off as she tried to stifle another sneeze.

Zack, pivoted to the more important question at hand. "Okay, you want horror or funny?"

"You know I love watching horror flicks with you," she enthuses, her voice brightening at the thought.

"Horror it is." Zack put on the flick, just as anticipation boiled, the doorbell rang, signaling the arrival of their much-awaited pizza.

Settled back on the couch, the delicious smell of pizza filled the air as Zack and Sandy shared slices, laughter punctuating their conversation, and yet, Sandy's dove into a more serious topic.

"Zack, how well do you know Josephine?" she asked suddenly, her tone shifting from playful to contemplative.

"Not well at all. Why do you ask?"

The mention of Josephine introduced a tantalizing hint of tension into their cozy evening.

"I don't know. I just don't trust her," Sandy admitted, shadows of doubt dancing behind her eyes.

"Why not?" Zack questioned, bewildered by her sudden suspicion, and Sandy's cheeks flush with the heat of worry as she asked, "Where did she come from? And her son's name just happens to be, Anthony."

Zack looked at her incredulously, "You don't trust her because her son's name is Anthony?" The absurdity of the accusation triggered a small chuckle from Zack, but Sandy's earnest expression remained unwavering.

"Somethings not right, baby. Be careful with her," she insisted, her voice steady, filled with a protective instinct that tugged at Zack's heart.

"You don't trust me?" Zack probed. Sandy laughed softly, "Oh, baby, I trust you just fine. You're not crazy, but you know I am."

Their eyes locked, a silent understanding passing between them as the weight of their connection deepened with a kiss.

———————————————

The dimly lit warehouse buzzed with tension as Val stood at the center of a makeshift command post, a dry erase board plastered with hastily drawn diagrams and notes outlining the audacious plan to ambush the Bronxville Devil's gang.

Surrounding her was Douglas, Lisa, Robin, and Maria, each of them visibly anxious but resolute, their eyes trained on Val as she detailed the operation's nuances with a fervor that demanded their complete concentration.

"The Bronxville Devil's will be taken the back road, which means no oncoming traffic and no witnesses," Val asserted, her voice steady, yet carrying an undercurrent of urgency that sent chills down their spines.

Robin, fidgeting slightly, broke the silence first, hurriedly asking, "How many cars do we need?" Val calculated quickly and replied, "Three should be fine," before Lisa chimed in confidently, "I'll take mine."

Maria followed suit, declaring her intention to ride with Val, her loyalty evident, while Douglas added with a smirk, "I have a custom grill. So, I can rear-end him off the road," provoking a chuckle among the group that momentarily alleviated the tension.

But Val pivoted back to the gravity of the situation, her eyes narrowing as she questioned, "Guns? Who has the guns?" Robin shrugged, revealing, "I grabbed what I could from the club, but you know Zack has most of them locked up somewhere." Maria interjected, recalling vividly, "Yeah, a whole arsenal. I've seen it."

Val awaited her confirmation and pressed, "Do you remember where it is?" to which Maria replied with a hint of defeat, "No, Zack blindfolded me. You know, trust no one." With a slight nod, Val decided, "Alright, well these will have to do. We're going to hit them and hit them hard. Let's get with it."

The weight of their mission hung heavily in the air, as the crew mentally prepared themselves for the violent confrontation that awaited them.

* * *

As night fell over Bronxville, the crew followed the van transporting the drugs, the adrenaline fueling their determination.

Douglas, with a fierce look, hit the gas and rear-ended the van with a violent jolt, throwing the occupants within into a frenzied panic.

Val seized the moment, barreling up on the left side and slamming into the van with a forceful crash.

Lisa, showcasing her driving prowess, darted across Val's vehicle, cutting off the van, while Douglas viciously rammed it again, managing to knock the van off the road entirely—a pivotal move that instigated chaos.

As the men emerged from the van, guns blazing, Val and Robin retaliated, returning fire in a frenzied exchange that echoed through the night.

With grit and authority, Val shouted above the gunfire, "Leave the van and leave with your life!" But the men kept shooting. "Okay, have it your way," Val barked, signaling to Lisa to maneuver around the van.

In a dramatic twist, one of the Bronxville men took aim at Lisa, but Robin, sharp-eyed and quick on the draw, intercepted him, firing her weapon with precision.

As the smoke clouded the air, Val closed in on the remaining men, a smirk of grim satisfaction tugging at her lips. The acrid scent of gunpowder mixed with the debris swirling around her, creating an atmosphere thick with tension. Her heart raced, but her hands remained steady, fingers poised over the trigger. She had them point-blank in her scope, she addressed them with a chilling nonchalance, "Sorry boys. I promise I'll make this quick."

One of the Bronxville Devil's, eyes filled with fury, hissed, "You know this will mean war, right?" He tried to inject a sense of finality into his words, but Val merely chuckled, unfazed by his threats. The absurdity of his bravado only fueled her amusement. "I guess we're winning," she countered coldly, the very embodiment of defiance. With that, she pulled the trigger, the sharp crack of gunfire slicing through the tense atmosphere. Each shot was executed with ruthless efficiency, silencing the threats around her and leaving the smoke to writhe in the wake of her wrath.

CHAPTER 9

The Town Hall buzzed with excitement as Mayor Lewis stepped up to the podium, the energy thick in the air as friends, families, and supporters gathered to witness a historic moment in Queerville. The crowd was a tapestry of diverse faces, all united in their enthusiasm for the new chair member, Mrs. Charlotte, whose journey had been one of resilience and dedication.

As Mayor Lewis announce, "To the great people of Queerville, please join me in welcoming your new deputy mayor, Ms. Charlotte Brown," the applause thundered through the hall, echoing the sentiment that hope was alive and well within the community.

Charlotte, adorned with a warm smile, ascended the stage to embrace the mayor in a heartfelt hug, a symbolic gesture of gratitude and solidarity. Taking her place at the podium, she gazed out at the sea of familiar faces—Zack, Sandy, Freddie, Mark, Dawn, Rose, Max, and the rest of her loyal crew—all there to support her on what was clearly a momentous occasion.

"Thank you to everyone that voted for me," she began, her voice brimming with passion and sincerity.

"I promise to turn Queerville back to the people and make the city safe again for all." When she finished speaking, the cheers erupted, drowning out any lingering doubt that her vision could unify the town. But Charlotte wasn't done; she had another important message.

"I want to see you all tonight at our third annual Queer Off Bash! We will be raising money for the Queer Youth House. So come out to support!" The crowd erupted once more in a fervent display of solidarity, their voices mingling into a hopeful chorus that signified the dawning of a new era for Queerville, one filled with anticipation for change, celebration, and the promise of a safer, more inclusive community for everyone.

* * *

As the afternoon sun streamed through the dusty windows of Zack's shop, illuminating the scattered tools and half-finished projects, the atmosphere buzzed with the sounds of hard work and rock and roll. Zack was deep into the engine of an old Ford, their hands deftly navigating the intricate components, while Mark was meticulously tuning up another vehicle across the room, the clinking of metal and the rumbling of machinery blending into a familiar symphony of the workshop.

"Are you participating in tonight's Queer Off?" Zack's voice broke through the focus. Mark glanced up, a hint of reluctance in his eyes, "Freddie wants me to," he replied, weighing the prospect. Zack urged him on with enthusiasm, "You should! It's a lot of fun, and it's for a good cause."

Despite the excitement radiating from Zack, Mark remained uncertain, "I don't' know. What should I compete in?" "Whatever you think your best attribute is. Start with that you can't go wrong."

"It's that simple huh?" "Yeah, we mostly just have fun no one takes it too seriously."

"I'll throw on some threads and hit the floor."

"Oh, just a heads up. I'm taking Sandy on a vacation, so I'll be gone for a few days. You'll be in charge of the shop." "Wow, where are you guys going?"

"Miami." The very mention of Miami painted vivid images of sun-soaked days and palm-lined beaches in Mark's imagination.

"Miami? Wow that's so rad. I always read about people going to Miami. It always looks so sunny. They have the most beautiful beaches. I've always wanted to go. I hope you have a blast. Sandy is going to love it."

"I hope so. I really want to do something nice for her. She's always working so hard. She never takes a break and relax." "She's going to love it, Zack."

Just then, the sound of footsteps interrupted their conversation, and Josephine appeared at the doorway, her arms full of beers, a bright smile illuminating her face. "Hello, Zack, Mark," she greeted cheerfully, and Zack appeared surprised but pleasantly so at her arrival.

"Hey, what are you doing here?"

"I thought you guys could use something to drink. I know how hot it can get in here." With that, she hands them each a chilled beer, the crisp sound of tops popping open ringing in the air like a little celebration of spontaneity. "Thank you," Zack said appreciatively, and they all took a moment to soak in the refreshing pause, the cool drinks providing a welcome relief from the relentless heat.

* * *

Dawn paced nervously, a storm of thoughts swirling in her mind. She had just returned from the police station, her heart racing as she relayed the shocking news to Max; "Val and Douglas were set free."

The incredulity in Max's voice mirrored the disbelief that had settled in her own stomach when she first heard it. "What? Are you serious?" He could hardly process the implications of what he was hearing.

Dawn confirmed, "Yes, I went up to the station and they said they were bailed out. The Officer says the drugs mysteriously disappeared."

Max's skepticism erupted as he questioned, "How does evidence disappear from a police station?" It was a question that weighed heavily on both of their minds, indicating a depth of corruption or incompetence that was unsettling.

As Max grappled with the idea, Dawn's determination hardened; they needed to take action. "They want drugs. We'll give them drugs," she declared, the resolve in her voice cutting through the air, electrified with danger. "This time it will be too much to just disappear." "Are you sure you don't want to get Zack involved?" "No, we don't know if Zack is behind this." "There's no way Zack is a part of this. My sister would never fall for someone who was capable of this. We need to tell Zack." Max insisted, desperate for clarity and confronting the imbalance that had invaded their lives.

Dawn held her ground, her voice calm yet resolute.

"Just wait, please. We need to see who else is involved," she reasoned, their fates tethered together as they stood on the brink of a dangerous gambit, the dynamic between them pulsating with an unspoken understanding that the stakes had never been higher.

———————————

Josephine leaned casually against the workbench, a playful smile dancing on her lips as she chatted with Zack, who despite their casual demeanor, was visibly flustered by her attention. "I can't wait to see you tonight at this Queer Off," she declared, her eyes sparkling with mischief.

Zack chuckled, trying to downplay their nerves, "Don't make me nervous, 'cause I won't hit the stage." Josephine's response was instant, playful yet pointed, "Well, if you're not going then I'm not," bringing a forced pout to her face, which made Zack roll their eyes in mock exasperation.

"No, I'm definitely going. Sandy is competing, so I have to show and support her," they insisted, earnestness creeping back into their tone. The mention of Sandy's name brought a hint of jealousy to Josephine's expression, though she masked it well beneath her sultry bravado.

"Awe, how sweet. What are you doing after the bash?"

At that moment, just as the words left her lips, Sandy entered the scene like a fierce storm, her confidence unmistakable. She had sensed something about Josephine and wasn't about to let it go unchecked. The slight shift in her posture and the narrowing of her eyes told everyone that this was her territory.

Mark, leaned against a nearby tool shelf, an amused smirk playing on his lips as he observed the unfolding drama.

Sandy's voice came out sharp as she greeted Josephine, "Hello, Josephine, I didn't know you were going to be here."

Zack, seemingly oblivious to Sandy's possessiveness, greeted her affectionately, "Hey, baby." Their kiss was brief but loaded with undertones—Sandy's territorial claim on Zack was clear. Josephine stepped back; her earlier boldness slightly dimmed but not extinguished. Her forced nonchalance stung just a little inside; stating, "I just came to wish Zack good luck for tonight, not that they'll need it," her tone a mix of sarcasm and genuine goodwill.

Sandy, picking up on the underlying tension, smirked and replied, "That's sweet of you."

An awkward silence enveloped the trio, thick with unspoken chemistry and rivalry before Josephine cleared her throat. "I guess I'll see you both later tonight," she said, forcing a cheerful note in her voice as she turned to leave. Zack's parting words—"Thanks for the beer"—were almost an afterthought, swallowed by Sandy's intense gaze as she shot daggers at Josephine's retreating figure.

* * *

Val and Mayor Lewis found themselves on the outskirts of town, the weight of their clandestine undertakings hung heavily in the air. The mayor's voice was laced with irritation as he disclosed, "Those Bronxville cats are fishing around trying to find who hit their shipment," a clear acknowledgment of the precarious situation they both faced.

Val, feeling a sense of betrayal at the unfolding chaos, shot back, "You said no one would find out."

The mayor snapped defensively, "No one was supposed to find out, but shit hit the fan okay," underscoring the urgency of the matter as the implications of their actions began to spiral out of control. Val, her mind racing with the potential fallout, demanded, "Well, what do we do now?" showing a blend of frustration and authority.

In response, the mayor probed her loyalty, asking, "Has anyone in your crew been talking?" to which Val, with a fierce pride in her community, retorted, "You mean snitch? Ain't no snitches in Queerville, okay."

His reply was frank and dire, "Well, keep it that way. As long as your people stay quiet, they can only speculate who they think robbed them." "Speculate? These are gang members; we kill each other for less."

The reality of their situation was becoming clearer, the stakes higher. Mayor Lewis, thumbing through his own tension, shot back, "Okay what's your bright idea, tough guy?" he snapped, half in jest but wholly serious. He was met with a response that was as calm as it was outrageous.

"I'm going to the Queer off bash. You need to relax." For a moment, Lewis couldn't fathom how anyone could think of a party when they were standing on the precipice of chaos. The mayor's sarcasm, "Oh, okay so you're going to a party that's great," contrasted sharply with Val's resolve as she handed him a joint, "Here, calm down. You worry too much," she implored just before getting into her car, revving the engine loudly as she accelerated away into the veil of night, leaving the mayor alone with the heavy burden of their secrets and the looming danger that hovered over their heads like a storm ready to break.

The atmosphere in the Queer Off Contest was electric, a vibrant tapestry of eclectic styles and exuberant energy that brought the spirit of community and creativity to life. The crowd, adorned in outlandishly colorful outfits and dazzling costumes, embodied the very essence of the queer experience, as each person showcased their unique flair as they filled the dance floor with infectious enthusiasm.

With a nod to the past, silhouettes sway and twirl to the lively drums of the doo-wop tunes, an era that seemed profoundly influential in the fabric of queer culture.

Spectators, each clutching a *VOTE* sign emblazoned with their chosen contestant's name, cheer wildly, turning the space into a raucous celebration where self-expression reigns supreme.

Patty, alongside three other drag judges, sat off to the side of the runway, their expressions a mix of excitement and mischief as they prepared to witness the dazzling performances ahead.

Charlotte, ~~the captivating host~~, stepped onto the stage, her presence commanding the room as she welcomed everyone to the third annual Queer Off Contest with a cheeky grin and a bold declaration: "Where you bitches battle it out to see who's the Queerist of them all."

The cheers from the audience erupted like fireworks,

Meanwhile, backstage, the energy shifted as Maria fidgets nervously, her excitement dampened by anxiety as she prepares to take the stage. Val tried to calm her nerves, facing the fierce determination and worry swirling within her. "Don't tell me to calm down," her frustration palpable. "You got me doing all kind of crazy dangerous stunts. My nerves are all wrecked and now I have to go out there and face that crowd," she replied sharply, her nerves threatening to unravel her.

Val, in an attempt to soothe her friend's racing heart, offered a makeshift remedy— "Here, smoke this it'll help you calm down."- a smoky blend that promises to take the edge off. Caught between anxiety and the exhilarating promise of the stage.

"Is this mary jane?" Maria inquired.

"Theres mary jane in it," Val replied ominously. Maria took a tentative drag from the joint, inhaling deeply as the world of the contest outside pulsates with life, and she braced herself to step into the spotlight, heart racing in tandem with the vibrant beat of the music that resonated throughout the venue, ready to embrace the chaos and joy that the Queer celebration embodied.

As the backstage atmosphere crackled with a mix of excitement and tension, Freddie leaned against the cold, metal wall, eyes wide as he absorbed Mark's recounting of the awkward encounter between Sandy and Josephine, a glimmer of mischief dancing in his features. "What? Who is this chick?" he quipped, his brows lifting in exaggerated disbelief.

Mark, still shaking his head in disbelief, explained how Josephine had been making a scene, seemingly throwing herself at Zack like an uninvited guest at a party. "But I don't think Zack even notices," Mark sighed, rolling his eyes in exasperation, to which Freddie replied with a knowing chuckle, "Of course not. Zack didn't even notice their best friend was in love with them for ten years."

"Sandy handled it well; she kept it classy," Mark attempted to offer some praise, but Freddie was quick to underline the reality of the situation. "Oh, Sandy is a lady, but she will strike fast. Josephine won't even know what hit her. Sandy doesn't play about Zack and Zack don't play about Sandy," he warned, a playful glint emerging in his eyes as they both envisioned the impending showdown.

Meanwhile, in another corner of the dimly lit backstage area, Lisa was meticulously applying her makeup under the harsh glare of a fluorescent mirror, caught in a moment of self-reflection—quite literally, as Robin admired her from the side. "What's the point? Sandy wins every year. We're like her backup losers at this point, here to catch her roses before they hit the floor," Lisa lamented with a hint of sarcasm, her lips pursed in frustration.

Robin interjected, a warm smile breaking through, "Someone else's beauty doesn't take away from yours. You look beautiful." Lisa appreciated the compliment but felt a slight tremor of anxiety creeping in, "Thank you, baby," she replied.

"How do you feel about all of this?" Robin pressed, her concern sharpening as she shifted the topic toward the troubling whispers surrounding Val and her dubious dealings. "I mean, Val is the leader, so we have to follow her," Lisa asserted, though a trace of uncertainty tinged her voice. Robin's tone turned serious, "If Zack finds out, there's going to be hell to pay," her words carrying the weight of a warning.

Yet Lisa remained resolute, "Well, Zack won't find out," she assured, while a flicker of worry marinated in the air, lingering over the backstage drama like the scent of hairspray and ambition.

Back to the front, Charlotte took the stage, her authoritative voice slicing through the electric atmosphere, "Next up is best male threads. Let's see who has the style to get the judges buzzin."

Anticipation crackled in the air as male contestants entered confidently, strutting their meticulously crafted outfits under the harsh lights while the judges leaned in, ready to crown a winner amidst the brewing chaos of alliances and rivalries hiding just beneath the surface.

The judges selected a winner

"Can we have the best men's body come to the stage, please? Best man bod, who will it be? Could it be Scorpions, or Red Dragons, or perhaps another delicious treat?"

The anticipation hung thick in the air as Mark strutted out, impeccably fitted attire highlighting his sculpted physique. He's not alone in this quest for glory; four other muscular competitors from both the Scorpions and Red Dragons followed suit, each trying to catch the eye of both the judges and the jubilant crowd.

Centerstage, Freddie, waved his neon vote sign with wild enthusiasm, rallying the audience into a frenzy of cheers.

As the judges deliberated, the energy intensified. Moments later, Mark was announced the winner, a surge of excitement rippled through the crowd, culminating in thunderous applause.

Charlotte, sensing the heat of the moment, playfully quipped, "It's getting hot in here; someone turn up the heat! These boys aren't sweating enough." The audience laughed, fully engrossed in the festivities. With the first contest wrapped up, she seamlessly transitioned to the next competition, "Next, we have best pinup girl! Let's bring out all the dolls and queens. Ladies, strut your stuff! We want to see body on body. We want legs, hips, and all that sass!"

As the music pulsed louder, electric and vibrant, Maria, Lisa, and the other contestants glided onto the stage one by one—each moment building anticipation in the crowd. Their energy was palpable, but it wasn't until Sandy made her much-anticipated entrance that the atmosphere shifted dramatically.

All eyes gravitated toward her, captivated by the stunning silhouette she presented, and a wave of approval washed over the audience as they erupted into cheers. It was clear: the Goddess had arrived, and everyone else was merely basking in her radiant presence.

Adorn in a sexy, form-fitting dress that clung to her curves, the fabric was perfectly tailored to accentuate her waist while the daring high split showcased her long, toned legs. With each step she took, the dress shifted slightly, hinting at the mesmerizing femininity that radiated from her. Her breathtaking beauty was undeniable; it wasn't just the striking features of her face but the confidence that emanated from her every gesture.

Men stood gaping, awestruck and speechless, their admiration for her impossible to disguise. Even Zack, positioned front and center, was swept up in the excitement, waving their vote sign enthusiastically in support of her undeniable charm. With confidence radiating off her, Sandy owned the stage, engaging in flirty banter with the audience, her laughter ringing like music in perfect harmony with the pulsating beats. Effortlessly, she stole the spotlight from the other contestants.

The judges were glued to her performance, snapping their fingers, tens across the board.

"It's unanimous, daughter, Sandy still that bitch. Go get your award," Charlotte said enthusiastically.

Sandy basked in the triumph, and Zack was the first to congratulate her, a proud smile illuminated their face as they showered her with kisses.

The night continued, showcasing a vibrant collection of competitors vying for the titles of Best Hair and Best Dressed, each participant bringing their unique flair to the stage.

However, the energy peaked as Charlotte piped up, "You guys voted for this next one. Are you ready? It is Dreamboat of the Year!"

Trans boys and cis men confidently strutted their stuff, each showcasing their unique charms, but it was Zack who stole the spotlight with a show-stopping entrance. Shirtless, their chest glistened under the lights, sculpted to perfection with a six-pack that could practically rival a washboard. As they sauntered into the limelight, the sea of hair cascading down their face and those alluring green eyes piercing through the crowd created an unforgettable image that captivated everyone.

Zack exuded an otherworldly appeal, as if they had been chiseled by the gods themselves. Their looks were effortlessly handsome, but it was the undeniable charm that enveloped them that really sent the girls into a frenzy. They screamed, waved their vote signs, and fanned themselves in a desperate attempt to catch a glimpse of Zack's rippling physique.

Among the chaos, Josephine's amazed gasps echoed like sweet music to the surrounding audience; she couldn't help but wave her own vote sign fiercely for Zack.

Yet, even in the midst of their admiring fans, Zack's gaze was irresistibly drawn to Sandy. Their chemistry crackled like static, undeniable and magnetic, as Zack teased and flexed their muscles, drawing Sandy into their orbit.

The moment was electric. With a subtle yet bold gesture Sandy's fingers danced across Zack's chiseled chest, igniting envy in the hearts of the other girls, who watched with widening eyes, torn between admiration and jealousy. Their playful banter was charged with flirtation, creating an atmosphere that blurred the lines between performance and genuine attraction, leaving the crowd enthralled and yearning for the next act.

After an exhilarating showdown, the judges cast their votes, and named Zack as the winner, the pride radiating from Sandy was unmistakable. Charlotte beamed with pride, "Zack attack! Look at my son still giving you bitches wet dreams! Go on, Zack, get your award!"

The night drew to its climax as Charlotte introduced the final category, "Doll Face!" The air buzzed with excitement as she urged all the pretty contenders to hit the stage, each hoping to leave a lasting impression. One by one, they took their turns under the spotlight, Sandy, Maria, Lisa, and others showcased their gorgeous faces.

However, it was clear who was the star of the show. Sandy, with her striking features and undeniable charisma, exuded a level of confidence that seemed to radiate from within. Her flawless skin glowed under the harsh lights, and the carefully applied makeup only enhanced her natural beauty, casting a spell over everyone in the audience.

As Sandy stepped forward to present her face to the judges, the crowd erupted into an ecstatic frenzy, chanting her name in a chorus of adoration, their enthusiasm echoing off the walls like a tidal wave of support. Sandy moved with grace, and the judges, caught in her captivating smile, drew them in and held them rapt.

When the moment finally arrived, and the judges presented her with the coveted award, the applause was deafening. Sandy stood there, enveloped in a spotlight of triumph, basking in her dual victories. It was a moment of pure magic, cementing her status as the undisputed Queen of the Queer off. As she raised her trophy high, the room filled with cheers—an affirmation of her beauty and grace.

Backstage after a riveting performance, the atmosphere buzzed with lingering excitement and energy, as Zack hurriedly changed their clothes, sweat still glistening on their forehead from the exertion of their energetic show.

Just then, Josephine burst into the dressing area, her eyes sparkling with a mix of admiration and mischief.

"Hey, you, what a show," she exclaimed, her voice warm with genuine enthusiasm as she sought to connect with them amid the chaos of costumes and the distant sound of applause.

Zack, momentarily caught off guard by her presence, smiled, their heart still racing from the stage lights and the thrill of the audience's reaction.

"I'm glad you came. How did you like it?" they replied, eager for her feedback. With an infectious grin, Josephine leaned against the locker, eyes filled with lust.

"Well, I definitely enjoyed your show," she teased, clearly impressed, which made Zack's chest swell with pride.

"Thanks. Did you vote for me?"

She shot back confidently, "Of course, I did."

As Zack stood up and pulled their shirt over their head, her boldness escalated. She leaned in and whispered, "God, you are so hot."

Before Zack could process the shift, she stepped forward, grabbing them and kissing them passionately.

However, just as the world around them began to blur, Sandy entered through the back door, and everything screeched to a halt. The sight hit her like a lightning bolt, the sharp pang of betrayal slicing through her as words lodged themselves in her throat, rendering her momentarily speechless.

Just as she gathered her thoughts to confront the situation, Zack instinctively yanked Josephine away, anger flaring in their eyes.

"What are you doing? You know I have a girlfriend," Zack snapped, an edge of disbelief in their voice. Josephine shot back defiantly, "I don't care about her."

The hurt of her words stung, and Zack clenched their fists, shaking their head, their heart loyally tethered to Sandy despite the confusion.

"Well, I do," Zack remarked, wiping away the imprint of Josephine's kiss as if it were a stain.

"I love Sandy; I would never hurt her like this. Don't ever touch me again, Josephine."

With that, Zack stormed out, leaving behind a cascade of fractured emotions.

Sandy, witnessing Zack's fierce defense of their relationship, felt a wave of relief washing over her mixed with pride, delighted to witness Zack stand up for their love. But in the wake of this turmoil, Josephine felt a tap on her shoulder.

Turning around, she barely had time to register the threat before Sandy landed a fierce punch right to her face, eyes blazing with rage as she spat, "Stay away from Zack," and stormed out.

As the night wore on, it became clear that all good things must come to a close. Charlotte took the stage to address the crowd. "I want to thank everyone who participated in tonight's Queer Off! Congratulations to all of our winners!" her voice a melodic blend of joy and excitement, reverberating against the walls adorned with vibrant decorations celebrating queer culture.

"We're still raising money for the Queer House, so please drink up and keep partying," she urged, encouraging the lively crowd to revel in the moment as the scent of spiked punch wafted through the air, mingling with laughter and cheers.

With a playful wink, she added, "Let's cut a rug!" and the pulsating rhythm of the live doo-wop band filled the room, compelling bodies to move in celebration of love and community.

On the dance floor, Freddie and Mark twirled effortlessly, beaming with carefree energy, while Lisa and Robin gravitated toward each other, the space between them narrowing as they shared intimate whispers punctuated by shy giggles.

Nearby, Val attempted to coax Maria into joining the dance party, but Maria floated through the moment, her mind adrift thanks to the heroin Val slipped her earlier.

Amongst the throng, Dee, Halle, and an array of crew members showcased their joyous abandon, dancing with wild enthusiasm and uninhibited smiles.

Meanwhile, Zack relished a quiet moment on the sidelines, nursing a drink and watching the jubilant chaos unfold before them.

Sandy strode up to them with fierce determination and planted a passionate kiss on their lips, catching them completely off guard.

"What was that for?" they asked, their eyes widening in surprise and delight. "Just for being you," she replied with a playful grin that made their heart race. "Would you like to dance, beautiful?" Zack offered, their smile deepening as they extended their hand. "With you? Always," Sandy responded, her voice lilting with the carefree spirit of the evening, even as she teased, "I mean, it'll ruin my rep, but you're worth it."

As they made their way to the center of the dance floor, the world around them blurred, leaving only the undeniable connection between them. The soft music cradled them like a gentle embrace, the notes swirling in the air and wrapping around them as they began to move in harmony, swaying together in a slow dance that felt as natural as breathing. Their gazes locked, deep and unwavering, as if they were sharing a secret only, they understood. Zack, caught in the depth of her gaze, felt a rush of feelings surfacing; they were mesmerized. Sandy's eyes sparkled with curiosity and warmth, holding Zack captive in a moment that felt both timeless and fleeting.

"Why are you looking at me like that? Please do tell," Sandy murmured, breaking the silence.

"I'm just feeling lucky that's all, appreciating the moment," Zack confessed, their voice sincere, each syllable laced with the truth of their heart as they cherished the miracle of Sandy's presence in their life, a twist of fate that had brought them together.

"You could've had any man you wanted, but you chose me," Zack added, almost incredulously, as if the enormity of that realization struck them anew.

Sandy's expression shifted, a soft blush creeping onto her cheeks as the ambient lights flickered gently around them. "I didn't want just any man because I'm not just any woman. You are perfect for me, Zack, and I think I always knew that. It just took some time to see it, but I'm glad I did."

A smile spread across her lips, and her eyes sparkled with an intensity that took Zack's breath away. "You are everything I never thought I was worthy of. Happiness, a concept I long believed didn't exist for me, you show me every day that it's real." Her words wrapped around them like a warm embrace, filling them with a sense of belonging they had never quite felt before. They shared a passionate kiss that sealed their bond beneath the glimmering lights, the rest of the world fading to nothingness.

As they broke away slightly, breathless and smiling, Zack grinned widely and asked, "You want to get out of here?" Sandy felt excitement twinkling in her eyes, her heart racing and she nodded enthusiastically, responding, "Absolutely," hand in hand they slipped into the night.

Val stumbled alongside Maria, her heart racing as she frantically tried to keep her steady on her feet. Maria was disoriented and giggling uncontrollably, yet there was a dangerous edge to her laughter that sent chills up Val's spine.

"Come on, Maria, we need to get you up," Val urged, dragging her off the floor, where she had plopped down as if it were the most comfortable place in the world. Each movement felt like a challenge against an unseen force; the drugs coursing through Maria's veins dulled her senses and clouded her mind. Val's breaths quickened as she shouted for help, her voice trembling with urgency, but the pounding bass from the party drowned her out.

Meanwhile, in another part of the Queer House, Freddie stood next to Mark, his playful demeanor lightening the moment even as the weight of reality pressed down on them both. "Now that I'm seeing the best-dressed man in Queerville, I think I need a wardrobe upgrade," Freddie teased, eyeing Mark's impeccable style with envy. Amid laughter, Mark's aspirations bubbled to the surface,

"You know Freddie I really want to open my own shop."

"Well, that's going to be hard without a high school diploma or a loan from the bank. You need to finish school."

"I'm done with school. They don't teach us anything besides, living in fear and how to work for the man once you graduate. That diploma means nothing. I'll find a way, but it won't be your way."

Over in another corner, Lisa and Robin danced, caught up in their own world. Robin couldn't help but compliment Lisa, whose beauty seemed to shine even brighter in the moment; there was an electric energy between them, a tension that had finally found its breaking point as Lisa playfully encouraged Robin to close the gap between them. Their kiss ignited sparks that seemed to light up the dim room, but just as their intimate world began to expand, chaos erupted nearby, pulling them back to reality.

The commotion came from the bathroom, where Val hovered over Maria, panic etched across her face.

"She's overdosing," Val cried out.

As the reality of the situation settled in, Val's heart raced, each beat echoing her guilt and fear. The moment they had all been enjoying—the laughter, the music, the carefree essence of youth—had evaporated in an instant. Val felt the weight of despair heavy on her shoulders, her frantic cries piercing the air, yet her heart shattered with the knowledge that this was partially her doing.

Robin and Lisa busted in; their joyful moment extinguished by the grave nature of Val's news.

"What the hell, Val," Lisa said franticly.

"What did you give her?" Robin's angry words cut deep, a reflection of the panic swirling in the room. Lisa's voice was sharp as well, demanding answers, clarity she was too muddled to provide.

"Just help her please," Val implored desperately, her voice quaking with emotion, as if trying to wrap the words around the reality of Maria's situation.

In that frantic whirlwind, Lisa emerged a plan, "Get her into the shower."

They placed Maria in the shower and submerged her in cold water. Val's hands sought to revive Maria, her fingertips brushing against the pale cheeks that seemed so impossibly still. "Wake up, please," she whispered, guilt gnawing at her insides. Minutes stretched into an eternity, every second amplifying their fear as she slapped Maria's cheeks with gentle insistence.

Lisa's voice cut through the chaos, "We need to get her to the hospital now."

Together, they rushed Maria to the hospital, the gravity of their night bearing down as the vibrant colors of the party faded into a stark, sterile reality.

* * *

In the serene aftermath of a long night filled with laughter, conversation, and shared moments, Zack and Sandy found themselves in the cozy intimacy of their home, the air still carrying echoes of their joyous escape from reality. Sandy, weary from the day's demands, plopped on the couch and kicked off her heels. Zack, ever the attentive partner, kneeled to massage her sore feet, their fingers gently kneading away the tension.

"Awe, thank you baby. My feet are killing me," Sandy murmured, a soft smile graced her lips as she sank deeper into the comfort of the moment. Zack casts her a warm glance, "You know I'd do anything to make you happy," they replied, a hint of mischief dancing behind their words.

Sandy chuckled lightly, her curiosity piqued, "What's gotten into you today, huh?"

Zack feigns innocence, ensuring their eyes remain locked on her feet, 'Nothing." A playful air filled the room as Sandy, sensing the undercurrent of their secrecy, brushed off their evasiveness.

"Ah huh. You know I'm doing a double shift tomorrow. But if you want to go see a flick or go to a hop..." she trailed off, leaving the invitation hanging in the air.

However, her excitement met an unexpected wall as Zack interrupted, "No, you're not." The tension shifted. "What do you mean? Do you not want me to work?" "I told Charlotte that you won't be coming in for a few days." "Why would you do that?" Sandy asked, lost in confusion.

Zack grinned spread wider, "Because I'm taking you on vacation." The words tumbled out like a cascade of joy, and before she even processed them, Sandy erupted into a joyful scream, a blend of shock and exhilaration sweeping through her. "You are?" she gasped, practically leaping onto Zack's lap with excitement.

Zack nodded, "Yes, go pack a bag, we leave first thing in the morning." Sandy could hardly contain herself, her voice echoed disbelief and happiness, "Oh my god!'" Bursting with energy, she leaped from their lap and dashed off to pack.

* * *

The ~~dimly lit~~ police station was alive with the muffled sounds of rustling papers and the low hum of fluorescent lights. Officer Whitey, with a weary look etched into his face, sat at the desk, fingers lazily tapping away at the keyboard, filing reports from a shift that felt like it would never end.

Suddenly, the heavy door swung open with a gust, and Dawn busted in like a whirlwind, her breathless energy contrasting sharply with the stagnant air of the station. "We know where the drug warehouse is. But you'll have to come quick."

Her frantic announcement sent Whitey into a moment of confusion, the words tumbling out with such urgency that he struggled to piece them together.

"Dawn, I can't make out a word you're saying. Now calm down and try again."

Taking a moment to catch her breath, Dawn steadied herself, knowing that every second counts as the weight of the discovery hangs heavy in the air.

"I know where all the drugs are coming from. It's a warehouse in O Town; I can take you."

* * *

Meanwhile, at the local hospital, in the dreary waiting room, where Robin and Lisa sat in a tense silence, their expressions a mix of worry and regret. Maria was in the back, receiving treatment.

"The nurse said she's going to be fine," Val blurted out feeling relieved. "What the hell were you thinking giving Maria that stuff?" Tension crackled as Val's defensive tone rose to meet Robin's accusations. "She was nervous. I was trying to get her to calm down."

"That's what the Mary Jane is for."

As Lisa's remark hung in the air, a moment of realization passed between them, punctuated by Robin's sharp gaze, foreboding as she leaned in closer, "You better pray Zack doesn't find out." With that warning, Robin took Lisa's hand and stormed out, leaving Val to wrestle with the consequences of their reckless decision.

* * *

Outside the warehouse, police cars screeched to a halt, lights flashed in the darkness as officers sprang into action. Adrenaline surged through the air as they rushed toward the warehouse, determined to find the drugs that Dawn had so fervently pointed out.

Inside, however, the vast space was eerily empty; the shadows stretched long across the cold concrete floor. Dawn and Max stood at the entrance of the warehouse, their breath visible in the chill of the night air, confusion etched upon their faces.

"What?" Dawn muttered, scanning the area with disbelief, her heart racing with the fear of failure. Max, equally perplexed, shook his head and replied, "They were just here."

In that instant, the gravity of the situation settled heavily upon them, amplifying the impending dread; they were on the edge of something much larger than either of them had anticipated.

CHAPTER 10

Mississippi
1957,

The sun hung high over the Mississippi campus, casting long shadows on the ground as students moved about, bustling between classes, yet the atmosphere felt heavy with unspoken tension. Kelly moved briskly, hoping to avoid Martin, whose dinner with the Martins had left her reeling with discomfort, an emotional knot tightening in her stomach.

She could still recall the way his family had scrutinized her every word, their judgmental gazes making her feel like a fish out of water, gasping for air in a world where she didn't belong. Each polite smile handed her a fresh layer of anxiety, and she thought of the evening as a theatrical performance, where she struggled to find her lines amidst a collective script, she hadn't agreed to be part of. When Martin finally tracked her down amidst the crowd, his familiar voice shattered her momentary escape from the reality of that evening.

"Hey Kelly, I've been calling you," he said, a hint of urgency in his voice. She turned slowly; annoyance clear in her eyes. "I know, could you stop?" Her voice was strained, a mix of frustration and vulnerability. Martin's persistence only fueled her irritation.

"Now, why would I do that?" he replied, his tone light yet insistent. Their conversation quickly spiraled into a labyrinth of emotions, with Kelly expressing her discontent over trying to fit into his perfect family.

"I don't fit in with your highly judgmental family," she declared, her heart racing as Martin's response revealed his own struggles with familial expectations.

"Well, neither do I. I could never live up to my folks' expectations, so I don't expect you too."

"Okay, so what was the dog and pony show for?"

"It was the southern thing to do," he explained, attempting to justify the elaborate charade. Kelly scoffed, her frustration boiling over as she challenged him.

"I'm so sick of hearing what's the southern thing to do, what's the Christian thing to do. Do you people just do the right thing? Huh? Can you think for yourself?"

"I know my family can be a little Judgmental. But I thought a girl like you could handle them and you did."

"What do you mean a girl like me? You don't even know me." "Thick skin, you got thick skin Kelly."

"Oh, well, what's it to you?"

And just as the air thickened with unacknowledged feelings, Martin made an impulsive decision.

He grabbed Kelly and kissed her.

Queerville,
1957

The sun blazed high in the cerulean sky, its warm rays glistening off the waves as Zack and Sandy basked in the moment, reveling in the joy of a well-deserved getaway. Sandy lounged on her beach chair, looking effortlessly sexy in a vibrant two-piece bathing suit that hugged her curves perfectly, while Zack flaunted their athletic physique, shirtless in swim trunks, the breeze tousling their hair as they grinned at her.

Their laughter rang out, light and free, as a cheerful waitress approached with colorful drinks garnished with tiny umbrellas. "Baby, thank you for this trip. These last five days have been a dream," Sandy said, her eyes sparkling.

The tropical scenery served as the perfect backdrop for their impromptu getaway, where every moment felt like a page pulled straight from a postcard.

"It's beautiful, and I'm so glad we did this."

Zack smiled, their heart swelling with affection, admiration flooding their senses as they watched Sandy's face light up with joy amidst the vibrant colors of fruit and sunshine.

"You deserve it, Sandy. You're always working so hard. I want you to start having some fun, stop and smell the roses, okay?"

The sincerity in Zack's voice resonated deeply, echoing the sentiments that had brought them to this paradise in the first place—a shared understanding that life was fleeting, and sometimes, you needed to step out of the confines of routine to truly live. Sandy took a sip of her drink, the sweet flavors dancing on her tongue, making her momentarily forget the bustling diner and taking orders waiting for her back home. Here, away from it all, she could savor laughter, friendship, and the simple joys that often got buried beneath the weight of daily obligations.

A playful glint appeared in Sandy's eye as she teased, "Yes, daddy. You want to take a swim with me?"

Without missing a beat, Zack shot up from their spot and shouted, "I'll race you!"

They sprinted toward the inviting water, Sandy swiftly followed suit, and as she caught up to them, she expertly ducked Zack under the waves, laughter echoed in the salty air.

In the splashing chaos, Zack lifted her effortlessly, their lips crashing together, sealing their shared excitement and connection.

As evening descended, they found themselves in an elegant restaurant, enveloped in the intimate glow of candlelight. The atmosphere was alive with their joy, punctuated by smiles and laughter as they enjoyed a delectable meal, with Sandy sneaking bites from Zack's plate and feeding them in return, creating a rhythm of tenderness that wrapped around them like a warm embrace.

Outside, a charming chapel twinkled in the distance, illuminated against the night sky, setting the perfect backdrop for the spark of romance unfolding between the two. Moments later, they found themselves lost in a passionate kiss, Sandy's excitement spilling over as she exclaimed, "Are you serious?" Zack, a playful grin on their face, affirmed their intent with a soft, "Yes."

Sandy lit up, "Okay. Let's do it on the beach!"

The night embraced them as they sprawled on the soft sand, gazing up at the stars, sharing tender kisses, allowing the warmth of the moment to ignite their passion, rolling around as waves lapped at the shore nearby.

Eventually, they retreated to their hotel room, the moon casting its ethereal light over them as their bodies intertwined, Sandy bent over the balcony, her joyous screams filling the air with the essence of ecstasy as they surrendered to the night.

Afterward, they found solace and comfort in the quiet of their hotel bed, cocooned under the sheets as they wrapped themselves in each other's warmth, gazing into each other's eyes. "I love when you hold me," Sandy murmured, her voice softening as she felt the safety of Zack's arms around her, "I feel so safe with you."

Zack tenderly caressed her face, assuring her, "That's because you are. I would never let anything happen to you, Sandy." Their conversation took a deeper turn as Sandy reminisced, "Remember when we were younger, we ran off to the carnival and I went to see that fortune teller."

"Yeah, the crazy gypsy lady," Zack remarked.

"Did I ever tell you what she said?"

"Um, something about you getting married."

"She told me I would meet a man, and he would have hell in his eyes, but I would find heaven in his arms. And that would be the man I would marry." Zack, drawn into the depth of her gaze, smiled back as she confessed, "I think she was talking about you. I'm falling in love with you, Zack."

Witty banter ensued as they teased, "You're late to the party." "Oh, I forgot, Zack is too cool to express their feelings," she retorted, rolling her eyes dramatically.

Yet beneath the lightheartedness laid an undeniable truth that simmered just below the surface, waiting to erupt. To her surprise, Zack leaned in closer, their expression shifting to one of earnestness.

As they peered into her amber eyes and whispered, "Sandy Myers, I am absolutely, madly in love with you." The declaration washed over her like a wave, filling her heart until it felt almost too big for her chest.

Sandy had always known in her bones that Zack cared for her, but this declaration painted a vivid landscape of emotion that she had never dared to dream was possible.

Just as their lips met in a passionate kiss, reality struck with a sudden sneeze attack from Sandy, bringing a chuckle that momentarily lightened the intimacy.

Back home, Sandy found herself curled up on the couch, nursing a cold, with an array of cold medicine and crumpled tissues scattered across the coffee table. The sounds of chaos erupted from the kitchen as Zack fumbled around, the clattering of dishes mixing with the aroma of something burning.

"Baby, do you need my help?" Sandy called out, her voice laced with affection and amusement.

"No, I got it!" Zack's determined reply, followed by the unmistakable sound of something shattering. Sandy chuckled, amused by their antics and secretly grateful for their efforts. "I'll pay for that," Zack shouted, clearly recognizing their blunders. "Really, I feel a lot better. I can help," Sandy insisted, but Zack was adamant, claiming, "Help me and stay there. I got it, it's done already."

After a chaotic but endearing battle in the kitchen, Zack finally emerged with a tray full of care: steaming tea, comforting soup, a sandwich, and a handful of medication for Sandy. "Awe, thank you, baby," she said gratefully, a smile lighting up her face as they nestled down beside her and began massaging her feet.

"You're spoiling me," she teased, sinking deeper into relaxation. Zack, understanding the importance of caring for their lover, expressed their regret, "I'm sorry we had to cut our trip short. I had so much more planned for us. But I have to finish this custom order. The guy paid extra."

"It's okay, it's not like we could've stayed anyway, me getting sick in all." "That's right so no work. Take it easy and get better. Okay?"

Sandy chimed in, eyeing them imploringly, "If you keep massaging my feet like that, I promise I will." With a playful smirk, Zack insisted, "I'm serious no work today. I have to head to the shop, finish this cats ride, then I'm coming back."

"Can you bring back some chocolates?" she requested, her tone sweetening the deal. "Sure," they replied, leaning down to kiss her forehead tenderly, "I love you."

"I love you too. Have a good day at the shop."

* * *

As the sun cast a warm glow over Queerville, Dawn and Max navigated the vibrant streets, both of them acutely aware of the urgency that hung in the air like an electric charge. "We need to find where this new drug house is before they have a chance to set up again," Dawn said, her voice steady but laced with a sense of determination that Max admired yet questioned all at once.

They moved briskly, scanning the eclectic storefronts and familiar hangouts, but Max remained skeptical.

"Dawn, it could be anywhere," he replied, shaking his head as if the mere thought of the sprawling network laid out before them was overwhelming.

However, Dawn didn't waver; she knew that without leads, they were effectively hunting in the dark. "That's why we need to find Douglas," she asserted, her tone leaving no room for disagreement. Max frowned, unconvinced. "Douglas? He isn't going to tell us anything," he remarked, folding his arms defensively across his chest.

His doubt hung in the air, but Dawn's mind was already racing ahead. "I didn't say we would ask him," she countered sharply. "We need to find him and follow him again. He'll lead us to the new location; he always does." Max opened his mouth, about to launch into a tirade of objections, "I don't think so maybe that's why they moved it they knew we were on to them."
"No, that's not it."
"How you figure?"
"And I know for a fact there is someone bigger involved." The doubt in Max's eyes deepened. "Well, how do you know that?" he challenged, and she was

ready with her answer, her voice a mixture of frustration and clarity.

"How do you think they were able to move the drugs so fast? And what about the evidence against Val and Douglas magically disappearing? We need to find out who is helping them." Each point landed like a hammer, resonating with a truth that hung between them and pushing them further into the swirling fray of conspiracies and shadows that defined their world.

For Dawn, every passing moment felt like a ticking clock; the fate of Queerville, as fragile as glass, depended on their next move.

* * *

The atmosphere in Maria's home was heavy, tension filled the air as Val stood awkwardly in the living room, guilt etched across her face. "Are you okay?" she asked tentatively, her voice barely above a whisper, as if the very question could shatter the fragile peace that lingered on the brink of chaos. Maria's response was swift, laced with anger and hurt, "Am I okay? You drugged me."

The words hang between them, a stark reminder of the betrayal that had fissured their friendship. Val's defense was weak at best; she insisted, "I told you what was in it." but Maria's eyes blaze with incredulity as she retorted, "No, you did not. I almost died, Val."

Val's apology sounded hollow, almost pathetic, an empty gesture that fell flat against the walls of Maria's disillusionment.

"You're out of control," Maria declared, her voice rising with a fierce intensity, "I'm done being a part of this obsession you have with trying to be like Zack. How about you figure out who Val is?"

With those final words, Maria opened the door, firmly invited Val to leave, a symbolic act of closing a chapter that had become increasingly toxic and damaging.

* * *

Over at Zack's Auto Shop, the sun filtered through the windows, illuminating the various projects scattered about in a creative chaos. Zack was focused, finishing up a custom order when Josephine made her entrance, her sunglasses concealing more than just her eyes.

"Hey, Zack," she called out, but they were far from pleased to see her, an immediate tension palpable as they responded coldly, "Josephine, what are you doing here? I'm still not going to cheat on Sandy with you." The reminder of their complicated entanglement hung heavily in the air as Josephine's demeanor shifted; she seemed almost contrite.

"I'm sorry about that Zack. I really am," she replied, removing her shades to reveal a painful black eye.

"What happened to your eye? That's a bad shiner," Zack exclaimed, the vein of concern lacing their voice as they examined the damage.

"Your girlfriend has a mean right hook," Josephine quipped, her humor strained and defensive.

"Sandy, did that to you?" Zack's shocked response reflected their disbelief, the realization hitting them harder than anticipated. "When? Why?" they pressed, seeking clarity amid the chaos that had ensued.

"The night of the queer off."

"Oh, she must've seen you kiss me. She didn't say a word." Zack's acknowledgment of the situation added another layer of complexity to their tangled relationship.

Josephine, knowing the weight of her own actions, offered an apology that felt inadequate in the shadow of their shared history. "I don't blame her; I would've done the same thing too. I just wanted to come to you and officially apologize. I think it was the alcohol," she said, a weak excuse barely masked the reality of the situation.

Zack tried to brush it off, "No harm done."

Josephine, desperately seeking some semblance of normalcy, suggested friendship, but Zack's resolve hardened. "I don't think that's possible. Sandy would never trust you around me again." Her desperate plea, "She doesn't have to know," was met with silence, and in an act of finality, Zack turned their back to her, "Goodbye Josephine," signaling that their friendship was over.

* * *

Charlotte sat across from Mayor Lewis, a sense of anticipation hanging in the air as she considered the implications of their meeting. Mayor Lewis, exuding a blend of charisma and authority, broke the ice with a warm compliment, expressing his satisfaction at her recent election as chair. Charlotte beamed with pride, appreciating the mayor's recognition of her dedication to Old O Town, a community she holds dear.

However, the conversation took a sharp turn as Mayor Lewis revealed his desire for change, introducing a controversial topic that raised Charlotte's eyebrows.

"Well, after the events that took place up in the hills at that God awful conversion camp. A lot of the folks in this town have experienced a bit of anxiety. Now, I myself have witnessed such herbs bring these folks some relief and get through their anxiety. It's a little unorthodox but completely legal and safe."

Establishing a connection between his next point and the urgent need for relief among the townsfolk.

Charlotte listened intently as he discussed the positive effects of certain natural remedies—herbs, he called them—bringing solace to those grappling with their mental health challenges.

"Are you talking about some kind of medication to help the people deal with their trauma."

"Yes and no. You see this is not some pill or syrup you make in some lab. This is all Organic, it's natural, doesn't poison the body. It's marijuana."

When he boldly suggested marijuana as a potential solution, Charlotte's initial shock was palpable, a mixture of disbelief and intrigue crossing her face. "Mary Jane? You want to sell reefer to the folks in this community?"

"Why not? It's safe and its perfectly legal to grow."
The idea of legally selling *"Mary Jane"* to residents felt almost absurd, yet Mayor Lewis argued passionately for its benefits—highlighting that it's a safe, organic solution free from the synthetic concoctions of pharmaceutical labs.

As the discussion unfolded, Charlotte grappled with the implications of such a shift in policy; she recalled the strictures of the Narcotics Control Act, which her own values have aligned with for years, sparking a fierce inner conflict.

Yet, the mayor presented a compelling argument—why should the city lose out on the profits when the community is already turning to the black market? He painted a vivid picture of reinvesting the proceeds into initiatives close to her heart, like the Queer house project that could uplift vulnerable youth in the town.

For a moment, Charlotte found herself caught between tradition and the innovative, albeit audacious, proposal that could not only transform the landscape of Old O Town but also offer a lifeline to those suffering.

As she silently weighed her options, pondering the potential ramifications on both her personal ethics and collective community welfare, the atmosphere in the office thickened with the weight of possibility, leaving a lingering question: Is change worth the risk?

* * *

The Bronxville Devil's clubhouse reverberated with tension as members gathered in the dimly lit room, their unease palpable amidst the flickering fluorescent lights overhead. The air was thick with unspoken fears and whispered rumors, each member stealing glances at one another, trying to gauge the mood of the group. The wooden tables, scarred by years of heated debates and hasty decisions, stood as silent witnesses to the unfolding drama. As the clock ticked ominously in the background, the faint sound of muffled voices drifted in from the street.

At one end of the table stood Bobby, his authoritative presence commanding immediate attention as he leaned forward, his eyes narrowed in frustration.

"I want to know who this crew is that keeps hitting us," he demanded, exuding a mix of anger and desperation that echoed off the grimy walls.

Danny, leaning against the wall with a casual air that belied the gravity of the situation, scoffed, "Well, it's not the squares from O Town, and no one from the North is that stupid." Their conversation shifted quickly into speculation, "It has to be the Queerville gangs."

"No, never. Zack would never deal with drugs. Zack is the reason we don't sell in Queerville," Bobby remarked.

"Yeah, but Zack is no longer running the Red Dragons. The crews have been running wild for months now. No one has seen Zack."

"We need to be clear about this. Zack isn't someone you can just take out. If we move on Queerville and you're wrong. They'll be hell to pay."

"I'm saying there's someone new calling the shots and it ain't Zack," he insisted, emphasizing a crucial shift in power that had unfolded in Zack's absence, "I'll check with some people."

Bobby turned and faced his crew before saying, "Yeah, do that. The rest of you get ready for war."

* * *

Meanwhile, outside the gang's dark world, Dawn and Max scoured the streets in a desperate hunt for Douglas, their car weaving through the urban landscape. The night was alive with the neon glow of signs and the dull thud of music filtering from nearby teen hangouts, but these places offered no clues about Douglas's whereabouts. With each passing block, their anxiety mounted; the mundane backdrops of parks and fast-food joints provided nothing but sharp contrasts to the gravity of their mission.

They were entirely unaware of the machinations spinning in the city's underbelly. The vibrant nightlife, so full of laughter and carefree moments, held nothing but darkness for them, and as Dawn tightened her grip on the wheel, she couldn't shake the feeling that they were racing against time—and against forces far greater than they could imagine.

* * *

Back in the Mayor's office, the mood was tense as Mayor Lewis received an unexpected guest. As she shadowed the doorway, Mayor Lewis glanced up in horror to see Josephine, her countenance a blend of defiance and resolve.

The once opulent room, with its dark wood paneling and heavy drapes, now felt like a cage, a stark reminder of the entrapment she had found herself in by aligning with a man harboring ulterior motives.

Mayor Lewis, a steely glint in his eye, pivoted quickly from surprise to hostility, "What are you doing here? What if someone saw you come in?"

Josephine, refusing to be intimidated, threw back her shoulders and retorted, "It doesn't matter, it's over. Your plan didn't work. Zack isn't who you thought. They would never cheat on Sandy."

In the charged silence that followed, Mayor Lewis's dismissal was palpable as he insinuated, "Maybe you just didn't apply yourself adequately." "I applied myself adequately enough, alright. Zack is not dumb, and using

Zack's dead brother's name—what was that?" Josephine shot back.

"I knew Zack wouldn't be able to resist you with a little boy that shares the same name as dear Anthony."

"Yes, they bonded, but that was all. Zack is in love with Sandy." Yet the mayor's resolve hardened, his voice turning menacing as he stated unequivocally, "I need Zack to want Kelly back. Now you break them up, or I'll throw your ass back in that jail cell where I found you. I chose you because you have a pretty face, but there are other pretty girls around that can get the job done." The threat lingered in the air, and Josephine swallowed hard before asking, "Why do you want them back together so bad?" In a chilling moment that underscored the stakes, Mayor Lewis cupped her face in his hands, his eyes narrowing as he delivered his chilling answer, "It's the only way I can guarantee my survival."

* * *

As Zack quietly entered Sandy's home, keys jangling softly in their hand, they paused momentarily, taking in the familiar scent of Sandy's favorite vanilla candles that lingered in the air. The cozy glow of the living room created an intimate ambiance, setting the stage for what they hoped would be a restful evening.

"Sandy, I'm back," they called out, their voice warm, full of affection as they made their way further inside.

Sandy, seated on the couch with a smirk, glanced up from the book she had been reading.

"Hey baby," she replied with a teasing tone, an eyebrow arched. "I was thinking, you have keys to my place, but I don't have keys to yours."

A smile tugged at Zack's lips as they reassured her, "I'll get you a set tomorrow." Sandy's expression softened, and she responded, "I love it when my partner listens," her voice wrapping around them like a comforting blanket.

"How are you feeling?"

"I feel good enough to go back to work tomorrow," she answered confidently, but Zack knew her too well. They couldn't help but tease, "I figured you would say that."

With a playful gesture, they handed her a box of chocolate; her delighted expression was all the thanks they needed. But soon, the mood shifted as Zack took a seat beside her, a serious note edging into the intimacy of their previous banter.

"I saw Josephine today," they said, watching her face closely. The fleeting guilt that crossed her features didn't go unnoticed as they continued, "She was rocking a shiner."

Sandy's quick wit returned, her sarcasm lacing her words, "Really?" Zack narrowed their gaze, asking pointedly, "Do you know anything about that?"

Sandy's immediate head shake didn't quell the underlying tension in the room.

Finally, after a moment of hesitation, she confessed, "Okay, you got me." "Why did you hit that girl?" Zack probed. Sandy's defense was fierce and protective.

"Because she put her lips on you," she stated with an unwavering conviction. Zack sighed, rubbing their temples as they tried to articulate the situation.

"I had it handled."

"Yes, you did," she acknowledged, a proud smile breaking through her earlier guilt. "And I was so proud of how you handled it. But she needed to be punished for her actions." Zack chuckled, the tension dissipating into a lighter atmosphere. "You're badass," Zack remarked before taking a brief pause and continuing, "So, you're not mad that I didn't tell you?" they asked, searching for assurance.

Sandy leaned closer, her voice steady and assuring, "You defended our relationship and stayed loyal. As long as you keep doing that, there's nothing you need to tell me."

Their lips met in a tender kiss, sealing their unspoken understanding before she added fiercely, "If she touches you again, I'll stab her." Zack laughed softly, captivated by her fiery spirit. "I believe you."

In a playful tone, she ordered, "Now, get out of those clothes." Zack, caught slightly off guard, raised an eyebrow in confusion, "Huh?"

Sandy dragged a towel clad Zack into the bathroom, where had transformed it into a sanctuary, candles flickering around the tub, casting dancing shadows on the walls while soft music filled the air, creating a romantic atmosphere.

A bubble bath glistened, adorned with delicate rose petals, and a bucket held a bottle of wine and two glasses, completing the serene setting.

Zack stood taken aback at the enchanting display before them.

"Wow, what's all of this?" they asked, their surprise genuine. "Well, you work hard too, so I wanted to do something special for you," Sandy replied, her smile radiant as she beckoned them closer.

Zack settled into the warm water, a sigh of relief escaping their lips as Sandy washed their chest in a tender manner while Zack reveled in the affectionate moment.

"Is the water warm enough?" she asked, her fingers tracing lazy patterns.

With a flirtatious grin, Zack teased, "The water is perfect, but you're definitely raising my blood temperature."

"No... behave. I really want to do this for you," Sandy warned, trying to maintain her composure despite the undeniable attraction crackling between them.

"Thank you for all of this," Zack said earnestly, "I've always given love to other people, but you teach me every day how to accept it. You make it look easy." Sandy's gaze turned soft and sincere as she replied, "Loving you is easy, Zack."

They looked at her with an intensity that spoke volumes of unvoiced desires, and Sandy giggled, realizing the heat radiating off them. "Okay, you need some cooling down, I see," she remarked playfully, reaching for the wine, carefully pouring them each a generous glass. The deep crimson liquid sparkled in the soft light, they lifted their glasses for a toast, Sandy nodding for Zack to lead.

"To us, for finding our way to each other," Zack proclaimed, their eyes locked onto hers, the words resonating deeply between them.

Sandy couldn't help but smile, feeling a warmth spread through her as she added, "And to you, for finally accepting love," her tone playful yet sincere.

They shared a knowing look, smiles brimming with promise as they clinked glasses together, savoring the sweet sip. Zack playfully shifted gears, pretending to have a kink in their neck, "You know, I have this cramp in my back." "Where?" Sandy's caring instincts kicked in immediately, her approach tender as she leaned closer to assess the 'cramp.'

"Yeah, right there," Zack sighed in exaggerated relief, enjoying her touch more than they had anticipated. Her hands sought the tension in their back with gentle pressure, and Zack, in a moment of blissful surrender, let out a satisfied groan.

As her fingers worked their magic, their playful banter transformed into something far more intimate. The air thickened with chemistry as Zack's fingers intertwined with Sandy's, anchoring her closer to them.

In that moment, the world faded away, and all that mattered was the connection they shared. Leaning in, their lips met in an explosion of electricity, igniting a fiery spark that sent waves of passion between them. The playful teasing melted into fervent kisses, leaving them breathless, each moment unveiling the depth of their desire and affection.

Whether it was the warm water or the heady atmosphere, the kiss deepened as Zack pulled her into the tub, Sandy settling herself in their lap, their hands roaming freely, passion taking over.

"You still want to finish bathing me?" Zack teased, breathlessly, their words laced with playful mischief.

"Shut up and take me," Sandy responded, desire thickening the air around them.

In a swift, fluid motion, Zack positioned Sandy at the foot of the tub, their labored breaths mixing with the sound of splashing water as they entered her.

Sandy's moans filled the steamy room, resonating off the tiled walls transforming the bathroom into a sanctuary of raw passion. Each sound echoed with the raw intimacy that enveloped them. Water splashed out onto the floor with every movement, creating a cascade that mirrored the turbulent emotions coursing through them.

As Zack expertly stroked deeper, Sandy's cries of passion erupted in waves, punctuating the air with expressions of pleasure and ecstasy as they surrendered to the moment, lost in each other entirely.

* * *

Meanwhile, somewhere down a dark road outside of town, shadows danced under the pale glow of the moon. The chirping of crickets and the haunting hoots of owls filled the air, creating an eerie symphony that sent a shiver down Douglas's spine. He stood alone, the chill of the night creeping into his bones, his senses heightened as he waited. The sudden arrival of Danny shattered the stillness. With an aggressive glint in his eye, Danny approached, a sly grin forming on his lips.

"You on the wrong side of the tracks," he scoffed, his voice laced with disdain, as if sensing Douglas's discomfort in this gritty setting.

Undeterred, Douglas squared his shoulders and retorted, "I'm the one that called you," he shot back, his voice steady despite the racing pulse in his ears. Danny off guard momentarily, a flicker of surprise evident in his eyes.

"Oh, that was you. You're not what I expected," he admitted, momentarily disarmed by Douglas's unexpected assertiveness.

In the charged air between them, Douglas shifted gears, tackling the elephant in the room.

"Listen, I know you cats are looking for who robbed your shipment." Danny's interest piqued, he leaned in slightly, demanding to know, "Yeah, what about it?"

The tension crackled as Douglas posed a question that brought him perilously close to a line that, once crossed, would usher in consequences far beyond his control.

"What if I knew who it was?" he ventured, his voice low yet confident. Danny's posture stiffened, a mix of curiosity and menace as he replied, "Then it's best you tell me."

The stakes were clear, and Douglas couldn't help but wonder about the ramifications of his revelations.

"What happens to me? Are you going to kill me?" His apprehension was palpable as the weight of the moment pressed down on him.

However, Danny's response was chillingly calm, "You tell us who has our drugs, and I can guarantee that no one from Bronxville will lay a finger on you." With a heavy heart, Douglas decided to share the name, understanding that sometimes survival demanded risky wagers.

"It was Val, from the Red Dragons," he disclosed, watching carefully as Danny's expression shifted to one of contemplation, circling him.

Danny continued to probe, "I see. Tell me, did Zack have anything to do with this?" The tension escalated as Douglas felt the eyes of fate upon him.

"No, Zack doesn't run the Red Dragons anymore. It was all Val. What are you going to do?" he pressed, curiosity overcoming caution. A smirk appeared on Danny's face, but his reply felt ominous with malice.

"I guess you're going to have to wait and see." In that moment, Douglas realized that no matter the truth he had just spoken, he was now ensnared in a web of danger that extended far beyond his initial intentions.

CHAPTER 11

Zack laid cocooned in the warmth of Sandy's bed, but their mind was a tempest of turmoil, the darkness filled with haunting nightmares. In the thick of their restless slumber, they cried out for Kelly, her name escaping their lips like a desperate plea, echoing through the stillness of the night. Each utterance felt like a dagger in Sandy's heart, who was abruptly stirred from her peaceful dreams by the unmistakable sound of Zack's anguish.

As she came to, the pain of their cries resonated deep within her, a sharp reminder of the complexities of their relationship and the specter of Kelly that loomed between them. She instinctively reached out to them, wrapping her arms around them in a comforting embrace, hoping to soothe the turmoil that engulfed them and bring them back to a semblance of calm.

The morning sun broke through the windows, casting soft beams of light across Sandy's face as she sat alone on the couch, her thoughts still clouded with worry. She couldn't shake off the image of Zack calling out for another woman, and it troubled her more deeply than she cared to admit. Even as Zack awoke, blissfully unaware of the storm that had brewed in the night, they greeted her with a cheerful good morning that barely masked the heaviness settling in Sandy's chest. "Good morning beautiful, you're up early."

"Yeah, I couldn't sleep," Sandy replied softly with a yarn.

Immediately, Zack's expression shifted to one of concern, "Is everything okay?" Zack asked, their voice laced with genuine worry. "Yeah. Everything is fine, Zack," she replied, but the quiver in her tone didn't escape their notice. They leaned in closer, sensing the unspoken heaviness in the air.

"Okay, what's wrong? What did I do?" they probed gently, not wanting to let go but Sandy shook her head, a small smile trying to break through the tension.

"Nothing, Zack."

In a sudden burst of playfulness, Zack lifted her effortlessly, whisking her off her feet and placing her on the kitchen table, their hands wrapping around her in a firm yet tender grip that rendered her momentarily captive in their embrace.

"I'm not letting you down until you tell me," Zack declared with a mock seriousness that was almost contagious. Sandy took a deep breath, feeling a twinge of heartache at the sight of Zack's concerned stare, so familiar yet so urgent. "You were having nightmares last night. Do you remember?"

"No, did I hurt you? Did I do something?"
Sandy cupped Zack's face gently in her hands. The intimacy of the moment softened her heart.

"No, I was just worried about you."

Zack's cheerful demeanor remained unshaken, and they replied with a reassuring smile.

"I'm fine, baby. Really." Zack's smile was infectious, and for a fleeting moment, the doubt faded from Sandy's mind.

She shook it off.

Surely, it was just a dream; everything would be alright. She told herself.

"Now, I want my breakfast!" Zack said with a cheeky glint in their eye, leaning back into the chair, their erotic nature pulling Sandy back to the present moment.

Quick to catch on, Sandy responded with a flirtatious smirk that lit up her face. She teasingly unfastened her house gown, allowing it to slip down her shoulders, a gentle reveal that sent a spark of electricity through the air. She arched her back, leverage against the table accentuating her curves as she leaned back slightly, casually parting her legs and allowing them to drape invitingly in Zacks' direction, the very picture of allure and confidence.

Zack, unable to resist the magnetic pull of her sultriness, found themself leaning closer. As their head dipped between Sandy's legs, a gasp escaped her lips, the warmth of Zack's tongue cascading over her skin and igniting a thrilling sensation that coursed through her body. Sandy closed her eyes, and surrendered to the moment, her earlier worries momentarily forgotten as pleasure washed over her.

As Zack's strokes grew more fervent, Sandy's breathing quickened, her body responded instinctively. Each touch sent shivers through her, pulling her deeper into a blissful trance. The sound of her heart pounding filled her ears; she gripped a handful of Zack's hair, anchoring herself as waves of ecstasy started to swell within her.

The sensations overtook her completely, a blissful storm that erupted into a screaming orgasm, crashing over her like a tidal wave and leaving her breathless, her heart racing as she floated in a sea of pleasure.

Zack, thoroughly satisfied and with a relaxed smirk gracing their lips, leisurely licked their fingers, savoring the last remnants of Sandy's sweetness, the taste of intimacy lingering. "I'll see you later," Zack teased as they kissed her goodbye. As the door closed behind them, Sandy was left sprawled across the table, her body still humming with bliss, a mixture of breathlessness and satisfaction coursing through her veins.

* * *

Speeding down a bustling road, Val navigated her chariot with confidence, the afternoon air alive with the cacophony of revving engines and the sweet melody of birds chirping overhead; she was fully immersed in her own world, humming along to her favorite doo-wop tune, the kind that lingered in your head long after it had stopped playing.

Yet, in a moment that shattered her tranquility, she caught sight of a Bronxville Devil chariot pulling up alongside her, its occupants a group of rowdy young men whose laughter pierced through the ambient sounds of the road like an alarm bell. Revving their engine in a taunting display, they matched her speed, their faces radiating mischief and raw energy as they exchanged glances that hinted at some untamed mischief brewing amongst them.

Val gripped the steering wheel tightly, the leather hot against her palms, as she processed the chaos unfolding around her. In a sudden violent move, they rammed their car into hers, causing her vehicle to swerve violently before it slammed into a ditch at the side of the road. The impact rattled her, and Val's world spun for a heart-stopping moment.

Her car settled at a dangerous angle; the tires stuck in the earth. The Bronxville car came to a halt as the young men pour out, fueled by adrenaline and a reckless sense of power. They approached her vehicle, their intentions clear and intimidating. Val tried to gather her wits, struggling to open the door, but they were on her in an instant.

"So, you want to steal from us? This is what we do to cats that steal from us."

The men hauled Val from her car with a force that left her gasping, each jarring movement a painful reminder of her vulnerable position. She struggled against their iron grip, desperation clawing at her throat, but their laughter only grew louder, a cruel soundtrack to her helplessness. It was as if her pleas were a mere whisper in the face of their brutality, their dominance palpable as they began to rain down blows with a chilling indifference.

The strikes landed with brutal precision, each thud echoing in her mind, leaving behind a storm of pain that coursed through her veins, igniting a fiery agony that made it hard for her to breathe.

Danny leaned down, his voice cutting through the haze of her suffering like a knife. "Tell your crew we're coming for them. For all of them. Queerville dies tonight," his words dripped with menace, a foreboding declaration that sent a fresh wave of dread crashing over her.

As Val crumpled to the ground, the world around her darkened and blurred. The last thing she remembered was the sound of their mocking laughter echoing in her ears, a chilling reminder of the danger she found herself in.

Val was left to grapple with the reality of her choices.

* * *

As the sun began to rise over the dilapidated structure of the old O Town school, casting eerie shadows across the cracked pavement, Dawn and Max sat hunched over in her car. They had spent countless days combing through every corner of their little town, but the haunting specter of danger seemed to gather in one place: the very school that had once been the backdrop of their youthful memories. Max, his brow furrowed with concern, broke the tense silence, "Do you think they're in there?"

"We've checked every inch of O Town. This is the only place they could be."

"I really think we should tell Zack what's going."

"I promise we will. Once I know who else is involved."

"We should tell the sheriff about the school so they can lock it down."

"I can't believe this is how our senior year is going to end. Our hometown invested with drug addicts and crooked cops. This is like some kind of crime novel."

"Compared to last year's events I'd say this is a walk in the park."

Dawn looked at Max with a sympathetic stare.

"Yeah, that was a tough one."

Their moment of connection turned tender as Dawn leaned in for a kiss, but it was abruptly interrupted by the arrival of a mysterious car, sending adrenaline pulsing through their veins.

With instincts kicking in, they ducked down to observe as the vehicle rolled to a stop and the iconic figure of Mayor Lewis emerged, a sight that sent shockwaves of revelation through Dawn's mind. She quickly grabbed her camera, snapping photos with a trembling hand as panic coursed through her; the implications of the mayor's presence raised urgent questions. "Holy shit, it's Mayor Lewis."

Dawn pieced together the unsettling puzzle: the release of Val and Douglas from jail, the disappearance of crucial drug evidence—the mayor could very well be the orchestrator of this chaos. "This makes sense."

"There has to be some explanation for this."

"Oh, Max, open your eyes. It must be him. He's the guy."

Bewildered, Max couldn't process the implications.

"What? The one bringing drugs into O Town?"

"Yeah, think about it who else could've had Val and Douglas released from jail. And the drug evidence that went missing from police custody."

If the mayor, once a symbol of hope and integrity, now stood as the antagonist, who could they trust?

"The freakin mayor well who do we go to now if the mayor is the bad guy."

Dawn's expression hardens into steely resolve, an inkling of defiance igniting within her. "We go to a good guy that knows how to do a lot of really bad things," she declared, their eyes locking in mutual understanding.

* * *

Zack and Mark were bent over the hood of an old car, both covered in grease and deep in concentration as they tinkered with the engine, their camaraderie evident in the easy banter that flowed between them. "Sandy doesn't play," Mark remarked, breaking the silence with a playful grin, a comment directed at Zack.

"Yeah, that shiner was something serious." Mark's voice softened, expressing concern with a hint of sincerity, "You know I was a little worried. She was coming at you hard. I didn't know if you..." The unspoken question hung in the air, but Zack shook their head, firmly asserting, "No, I don't cheat. Especially not on a woman as amazing as Sandy. She's the total package; I'm not messing this up."

Mark nodded, visibly relieved. "I'm happy to hear you say that. I like you two together; you complement each other, and you both seem so genuinely happy."

Zack smiled, their heart swelling with pride and affection, "We are, and thank you."

Just as their conversation took a lighter turn, the peaceful ambiance was shattered when Dawn and Max burst through the door, their faces flushed, panting as they rushed into the shop.

Panic painted their expressions as they shouted in unison, but their words came out in a jumbled mess, leaving Zack on edge.

"Max? What's going on? Did something happen to Kelly? Zack's heart raced at the thought, a knot tightening in their stomach. "No, Kelly is fine," Max panted, clutching his chest as he tried to catch his breath. Dawn shot a glance at Zack, her eyes wide, "We have a big problem." The tone of her voice sent a chill through the room, the sunshine now eclipsed by an impending sense of dread.

* * *

Val laid on the ground, her body limp and riddled with injuries, each labored breath a painful reminder of the chaos that had unfolded. Douglas stood nearby, his mind racing with panic, completely overwhelmed by the gravity of the situation, knowing this was his doing.

"Okay, what do we do now?" he stammered, fear etching itself into every inch of his expression.

Maria, her face pale and quivering, shot back in a terrified whisper, "If the Bronxville Devil's know we're the ones that hit them, there's going to be a street war."

Lisa, trying to keep her voice steady, chimed in, "A street war no one knows is coming," her eyes darting anxiously toward Val.

Robin, perhaps too aware of the tension spiraling out of control, said, "Now might be the time to tell everyone."

Val, despite her injuries, mustered all her strength to grumble back, "No, we can't." The disbelief washed over Maria as she protested, "What do you mean we can't? You're lying there half dead! Bronxville cats are out for blood. We need to talk to Zack."

It was at that moment that Zack's voice broke through, ominous yet calm, "I'm listening," sending a chill down their spines. Everyone froze, panic gleaming in their eyes as Zack entered, their presence demanding attention and respect. "Zack?" Lisa gasped; shock written all over her face. Maria quickly added, "Zack, don't be mad," while Val's voice broke as she apologized, "Zack, I'm sorry."

Douglas, attempting to explain, faltered as the trio shouted in unison, "Shut up!"

Zack approached Val, their face a mixture of disappointment and concern. "What happened?" they inquired; their voice steady but laced with urgency. Val managed to respond weakly, "We robbed Bronxville Devil's for their stash. We sold it and flooded the streets with heroin. They know it was us, Zack."

The shock registered in Zack's eyes as they processed her words. "The mayor had you do this?"

"Yeah, it was Mayor Lewis," Val confessed, her voice weak. Lisa and Maria exchanged horror-stricken glances, mouthing, *"Mayor Lewis"* as Zack scanned the room, their gaze sharp and piercing.

"You all have no idea the can of worms you just opened. What could make you so fucking stupid?" they exploded, their tone dripping with disdain, "You flooded your own home with drugs and just undid the peace agreement we had with Bronxville. You wanted to hang with the big boys; congratulations, you all made it to the major leagues, and they're some heavy hitters coming."

Their heads drooped as guilt engulfed them like a thick fog, as if children caught misbehaving. Zack's next command was decisive, slicing through the tension like a knife. "Get her to the hospital now."

Douglas hesitated, "I don't think..." but Zack interrupted with an edge of anger in their voice, "You're right, you don't think. Get her to the doctor now."

Reluctantly, Douglas nodded, and scrambled to lift Val.

Maria turned to Zack, her eyes pleading, "What now, Zack. What else should we do?"

The answer came with finality as Zack's gaze sharpened, the gravity of their situation reflected in their alluring-green eyes. "Prepare for war." The words rolled off their tongue like a drumbeat, resonating with an ominous certainty that sent shivers down Maria's spine.

As the words hung in the air, heavy with gravity neither of them could ignore, a sinister soundtrack began to weave its way through the thickening atmosphere. The sound of tires speeding up filled the scene, each purring engine roaring like predators ready to pounce. An ominous fleet of chariots surged into view, tires screeching against asphalt as the gangs stormed in like a dark tide, signaling a battle that was unforeseen yet inevitable.

Sandy sat at the counter, her fingers nervously tracing the rim of her teacup, looking lost in thought as the afternoon sunlight filtered through the window, casting a soft glow around her.

Charlotte leaned in, her voice low and comforting, "What's got you lost in thought?"

"Last night I heard Zack crying out for Kelly," she confessed, her heart clenching at the memory. The weight of her words hung heavy in the air, and Charlotte's expression shifted from surprise to sympathy.

"Oh, baby, I'm sure it was probably just a nightmare. They went through hell together," Charlotte reminded her, her tone soothing, but Sandy could feel an unsettling knot tightening in her stomach.

"Yeah, that's what I keep telling myself, but it wasn't the first time," Sandy replied, a sense of despair creeping into her voice.

The thought of Zack's past didn't just linger in their memories; it echoed in their daily life. Charlotte probed gently, "Has Zack had nightmares before?" There was a quiver in Sandy's voice as she replied, "No, but I have heard Zack in the shower crying over her. I can't compete with a woman who's not even here."

A tremor coursed through her as she spoke, and her heart ached, fearing that she was just temporary in Zack's life—a diversion from the shadow that Kelly cast.

Charlotte's eyes were fierce, an unwavering support, as she leaned forward, insisting, "Sandy, Zack loves you." Sandy nodded, "Yeah, I know, but Zack is nowhere near over Kelly. I'm just a place holder, a distraction." The words slipped out, heavy and fraught with vulnerability.

Charlotte's resolve only hardened, "No, I won't hear of this. Zack is over the moon about you. Those nightmares are memories; they just don't go away, Sandy. Give it time. Don't give up on Zack."

Each word from Charlotte felt like a lifeline tossed into turbulent waters. Sandy took a breath, preparing to respond, but before she could find her voice, she was interrupted by a familiar voice calling out from behind her.

"Sandy, can we talk?" The shock of hearing Josephine startled her, and she turned around to face her unexpected visitor.

* * *

The atmosphere was thick with tension as Zack stood in front of a diverse gathering of gang members from THE SCORPIONS, TWO SOULS, LIPSTICKS, RED DRAGONS, HOUSE OF PROSPERITY, and the DRAG Queens. With a firm expression and unwavering resolve, they addressed the issue at hand, "I don't want to waste time with litigations. I'm taking back control of the Red Dragons and command of all the crews."

As they spoke, men began to haul in an impressive arsenal, their movements synchronized and purposeful as they prepared for what lies ahead. "First thing we need to do is provide safety for our people at places they're known to visit," Zack continued, glancing around to ensure they had their full attention. "I want Two Souls to cover the drive-in, and Lipsticks, you've got the high school. I'm going to reach out to Bobby, the leader of the Bronxville Devils to negotiate another peace agreement. Everyone else needs to hit the streets to make sure our territory is secure."

Their directive was met with a chorus of nods and murmurs of understanding as the gangs began to disband, each taking on their assigned roles with a renewed sense of purpose. Just as the last of them started to disperse, Dee from the House of Prosperity approached Zack, her demeanor a mix of hesitation and respect, "Hey, Zack, listen I know I've had my reservations about your leadership. But I'm glad you're back. I didn't see it before, but we need you."

"Thank you, Dee, but you were right. I was a loose cannon out for blood. I needed this time away to see things differently. But thank you for not giving up on me."

Their handshake signified a moment of reconciliation, a bridge built between past and present, as they stood together ready to face the challenges ahead with a unified front. The energy shifted slightly; it was no longer just about control but about protecting a community they all love.

* * *

Sandy couldn't hide her shock from seeing Josephine. As they stood facing each other, the tension was thick in the air, a palpable reminder of the betrayal that had occurred not long ago.

"What happened between Zack and I..." Josephine began, but Sandy's response came sharp and quick, a reflex born of hurt. "You mean when you forced yourself onto Zack?"

Her voice trembled with a mix of indignation and disbelief. Josephine's expression shifted, and Sandy could see the hesitation flashing across her face.

"It's not what you think. I'll admit it, yes, I have feelings for Zack..." Sandy shot Josephine a pointed look, the kind that clearly said: *Don't push your luck.*

Josephine, undeterred, pressed on, "...but any fool can see Zack is head over heels in love with you. Zack is a great catch; you're a lucky girl."

"I know that already. Where is this going?" she demanded, her frustration rising. But the next piece of news shook her to the core.

"What you don't know is the mayor hired me to get close to Zack and seduce them, to break you two up." Sandy's heart dropped, her pulse quickening as the weight of those words settled over her like a heavy blanket.

The words hung in the air, a dark cloud of betrayal overshadowing Sandy's heart as she uttered in disbelief, "What?!" The revelation shattered the fragile sense of security that had begun to form around her relationship with Zack, and Sandy felt a wave of emotions crash over her, forcing her to confront not only her feelings toward Josephine but also the precarious nature of her own happiness.

* * *

Zack drove through the sun-dappled streets of the picturesque Northside suburbs, the weight of the upcoming battle heavy on their shoulders. They had made this journey to seek out Duffus, the quirky, wiry, white boy with an unmistakable passion for chaos and a heart full of admiration for Zack. He had been vying for a spot in Zack's infamous Red Dragons, eager to

QUEERVILLE

prove his mettle in a tumultuous world that seemed always on the verge of conflict.

As Zack pulled up to Duffus's garage, they spotted him polishing his beloved car, the bright sunlight glinting off its glossy finish as Duffus enthusiastically chatted with his crew. The moment Zack emerged from their ride, Duffus's eyes widened in disbelief.

"Zack Calhoun am I dreaming?" he exclaimed, bounding across the garage with the kind of energy that only he could muster. "How's it hanging, Duffus?" Zack replied, a half-smile on their face.

"What brings Zack Calhoun across the tracks? Not that I'm complaining!" His excitement palpable, Duffus leaned in, eager for the answer.

"I'm in a bit of a dilemma," Zack stated, the gravity in their voice drawing Duffus in. Instantly, the thrill of anticipation surged through Duffus; this was his moment, his chance to prove his worth.

"Just tell me what you need," he practically shouted, ready to leap into action. The thrill of anticipation flooded Duffus's heart, and a grin spread across his face like wildfire.

Zack took a deep breath, feeling the weight of their request as they prepared to lay it all on the line. "I have to do some really bad things to some real bad people."

Duffus's face broke into a devilish grin, a gleam in his eye that promised mischief. "Are we talking morgue or the hospital?"

Bronxville, USA

In the sweltering afternoon heat of Bronxville, tensions hung like a thick fog, as Zack strode toward the Bronxville Devil's clubhouse, their demeanor unyielding and menacing, a dangerous glint flickering

288

in their eyes that dared the fifty odd men surrounding them to challenge them. Each of them cast death stares sharp enough to cut glass, a silent testament to the animosity that simmered just below the surface—each one wishing they could bring an end to their life. yet Zack walked unabated. They made their way, undeterred by the hostility that crackled in the air. Reaching the makeshift table where Bobby waited, Zack casually tossed a bag of drugs at his feet, "There are your drugs. What's left of them."

"You gotta be shittng me that's not even half of what was stolen."

The tension was thick enough to cut with a knife, and Zack's calm demeanor juxtaposed sharply against the backdrop of anger radiating from Bobby and his men. Despite the grave implications of their presence here, Zack attempted to broker peace, attributing the chaos to their gang's misguided choices.

"There's cash in there as well. That should make us even." "Even?" Bobby scoffed, baffled by Zack's audacity.

"Look, my crew got out of hand. They were led down the wrong path, trusted the wrong person," Zack admitted, an undercurrent of desperation lacing their words as they seek some semblance of truce. "I'm hoping we can come to some sort of agreement, so there's no more bloodshed."

The men around them snickered, the tension diffusing momentarily into derision, one of them mocking their plea— "No more bloodshed? That's funny coming from someone who flooded the streets with Bronxville's blood searching for their brother's killer."

With steely resolve, Zack fired back, "And I'd do it again," their words a stark reminder of the violence that had marred their world.

* * *

Meanwhile, the narrative shifted inside the police station, where Dawn burst in, urgency fueling her every movement as she implored the officers to intervene.

"I need to speak with the sheriff. There's a bunch of Bronxville cats headed to the diner, and they're not going for the milkshakes!" Her frantic declaration echoed, underscoring the brewing storm just outside.

Back in Bronxville, Zack asserted, "Don't mistake me being here trying to come to an easy resolution as a sign of weakness." "What else am I supposed to take it as?"

"Stalling," Zack murmured with a grin.

In a twisted moment of fate, the shout of engines filled the air as the Queerville gangs rolled in, guns blazing, and chaos descended.

Zack's reflexes sharpen, as they pulled their weapon, shooting Bobby squarely in the chest before unleashing a torrent of gunfire on the surrounding Bronxville men.

Duffus and his Northside crew rolled into the chaotic scene with a level of intensity that seemed almost otherworldly, their vehicle's tires screeching against the asphalt as they barreled through men. It was a calculated chaos as Duffus wasted no time in unleashing a storm of bullets from his sidearm, the deafening crack of gunfire echoing through the streets as he focused his aim on the men positioned on rooftops.

One by one, they collapsed, bodies plummeting to the ground like raindrops caught in a tempest, each fall punctuating the moment with chilling finality. A wicked grin blossomed on Duffus's face, a semblance of pleasure swirling in the madness as he felt the power surge through him with every fall of a foe.

As he emptied his clip, the adrenaline surged through his veins, driving him to leap from the car with the ferocity of a predator unleashed. He charged into the fray, throwing punches with an almost primal energy, his fists connecting with bone and flesh, sending more of his adversaries sprawling to the ground. Each strike was fueled by a mix of rage and exhilaration, a fierce determination to dominate this brutal encounter as he fought to take down as many men as possible.

In that moment, amidst the cacophony of gunfire and shouts, with his crew rallying around him, Duffus became a whirlwind of violence and chaos—an unstoppable force determined to carve his mark into the annals of street legend. The battle unfolded in a chaotic frenzy, the sounds of flesh meeting flesh and the distant sirens wailing a chilling symphony in the background.

Dee, ascended into the fray, returning fire with unrestrained ferocity from the rooftops, the air reverberating with the cacophony of gunshots.

As the Queerville gangs stormed the clubhouse, the stakes escalated into a full-blown shootout. Amidst the chaos, a Bronxville thug suddenly had Robin in his sights, but Lisa acted with blinding swiftness, her shot ringing true as it found its mark in the thug's head.

Robin, stunned by the sudden turn of events, turned to Lisa, who blew her a cheeky kiss, igniting a spark

within Robin, who then unleashed her fury, taking aim
and fired with vengeance at every Bronxville Devil in
sight, Lisa hot on her heels, back-to-back, the two of
them a whirlwind of vengeance and solidarity in a
deadly ballet of gunfire.

The afternoon exploded with violence, the lines of
loyalty and enmity blurring in a whirlwind of
gunpowder, blood, and unrestrained rage as the streets
of Bronxville bear witness once more to the cycle of
violence that defined their existence.

* * *

The diner hung heavy with tension as Sandy leaned
across the table, her brow furrowed in confusion and
fear. "Why? Why would the mayor care about breaking
us up?" she exclaimed, her voice trembling slightly.

Josephine, glanced around nervously as if searching
for answers in the fading decor of the diner, replied
with a tight-lipped expression, "All I know is that it has
something to do with some girl named Kelly." At the
mere mention of Kelly's name, a familiar pang shot
through Sandy's heart, a blend of jealousy and
bitterness that made her stomach churn. The ghost of
this girl loomed large in Zack's life,
an uninvited specter casting a shadow over Sandy's
hopes and dreams.

Just then, the front door of the diner burst open, and
in stormed Freddie, his face flushed and eyes wild with
panic. "Everybody get out! Now, get out!" he shouted,
his voice slicing through the air like a siren. The sudden
chaos erupted as he hurriedly ushered the startled
customers out, their confusion morphing into a clamor
of questions that went unvoiced. Sandy fumbled her

coffee cup as she shot a questioning look at him, bewildered. "Freddie, what's going on?" Charlotte hurriedly wiped her hands on her apron, her eyes darting to the door.

"Freddie are you out of your mind chasing away my customers?" she protested, incredulous at the chaos. But Freddie, his expression stern and filled with urgency, shook his head vehemently, "Look, Zack sent me to get you guys out of here." Frustrated by the lack of detail, Sandy pressed on, "What? Is Zack okay?"

Her heart raced as Freddie's voice turned grave, "We're at war with Bronxville right now and it's bad." The gravity of his statement hung in the air like an impending storm, and Sandy felt a chill run down her spine, "Where is Zack? What is going on?" she urged, her voice trembling with urgency. The word "war" struck Sandy like a lightning bolt, and she glanced anxiously at Josephine, knowing they needed to find Zack immediately.

"We need to get to Zack," she insisted, her protective instincts flaring. Yet, Freddie was resolute, "No, Zack told me to keep you safe. We have to go now." The urgency cut through the diner's din, and the girls hastily gathered their belongings, the weight of the moment pressing down on them.

Suddenly, Freddie rushed to the window, a look of horror spreading across his face. "Oh, shit. Get down!" he yelled just as gunfire erupted outside, the deafening sound of bullets smashing through glass and tearing through the diner walls filled the room, sending shards flying; shattering the tranquility of an ordinary afternoon and plunging them all into a fight for survival.

CHAPTER 12

The deafening sound of gunfire erupted outside the diner, echoing through the streets of Queerville like a scene torn from a Al Capone movie. The Bronxville Devil's unleashed a torrent of bullets toward the diner, sending shards of glass flying and splintering the once-vibrant windows into a mosaic of chaos.

Inside the diner, the atmosphere became one of sheer hysteria as Sandy, Charlotte, Freddie, and Josephine dove under tables, their hearts racing with fear. Each bullet that found its mark pierced through the diner as if it were made of mere tin foil, transforming the comforting hub of camaraderie into a perilous war zone.

Sandy's pulse quickened in her throat, knowing they were trapped in a maelstrom of violence.

A sickening smell began to saturate the air as gas leaked ominously from the punctured lines, mixing with the crackling sparks dancing from the exposed electric sockets lining the walls—an impending explosion lurking just beneath the surface.

Meanwhile, outside, the screech of tires reverberated as Zack, Lisa, and Robin came barreling down the street, their arrival marking a frantic shift in the dangerous balance. As they returned fire, the onslaught from the Bronxville men momentarily dwindled, pushing back the chaos and granting an unexpected pause to those cowering within the diner. The Bronxville men retreated.

Zack burst through the doors of the diner; their eyes wide with urgency as they called out for Sandy amidst the rubble of the frantic scene.

The sound of her name sliced through the panic, and Sandy, her heart soaring with relief, leapt up, rushing into Zack's arms, the warmth of their embrace a stark contrast to the violent atmosphere surrounding them. Their hearts beat in sync, filled with relief.

"Are you okay?" Zack asked, their voice low and filled with genuine concern as they looked deeply into Sandy's eyes. "Yes, are you?" she replied, the heaviness of their reality momentarily lifting as they sought solace in each other. "Yeah, baby. I'm fine."

In that fragile moment, they shared a passionate kiss, a brief distraction from the nightmare unfolding around them.

"Is everybody okay?" Zack's voice broke through the lingering silence, filled with anxiety as they scanned the surroundings for familiar faces amidst the carnage.

Charlotte spoke up, her irritation cutting through the thick tension like a knife, "Yes, but I'm very angry. My dress is ruined. Lord, look at my diner."

Her concern was comically misplaced among the horror, yet it brought a sliver of levity to the grim situation.

The sobering reality hit again as Josephine emerged with a tremor in her voice, "Just a day in the life of Zack Calhoun." "Josephine? What are you doing here?" Zack asked, the surprise evident in their voice, momentarily pushing aside their rising dread. "Long story, I'll tell you later," Sandy replied, glancing anxiously around, "Freddie is here too." Panic surged through Zack, their heart pounding with urgency as they began to search frantically, calling out, "Freddie!" Their voice echoed through the debris-laden room, desperation clawing at their throat, until they finally located him curled beneath a booth, wounded and unnaturally still.

"Shit, Freddie!"

Their heart raced as they pulled Freddie from beneath the debris. Sandy's scream pierced through the chaos, "Oh my god. Freddie!"

Zack checked his pulse. "He's alive, we need to get him out of here now." "Oh, my baby," Charlotte gasped before the aroma of gas caught her attention, "Do you guys' smell that?"

The reality of their dire situation hit harder as Zack inhaled the unmistakable scent of gas. "Get out of here; the place is going to blow," Zack exasperated.

"I'm not leaving you, Zack." Sandy demanded, refusing to leave Zack behind, her heart torn between loyalty and survival.

The urgency in Zack's voice escalated, "Charlotte!"

Charlotte's maternal instincts kicked in as she grabbed Sandy, "Come on, child," hustling her towards the entrance. "No! Put me down Charlotte." Sandy cried out, desperate to turn back, her heart racing as she thought of Zack's safety.

As Zack hoisted Freddie onto their shoulder, the path to the door became blocked by falling debris. If they didn't escape soon, they might be trapped in the wreckage. Zack looked around for an alternative way out. They spotted the exit sign for the back entrance.

Just as Zack ushered Freddie through the back door, the diner suddenly exploded, sending a shockwave of terror through the hearts of those in front.

The diner erupted in a catastrophic implosion, a violent farewell to what once was a beloved diner. Sandy's frantic cries pierced the air as she watched the building collapse, her body straining against Charlotte's grip, begging to go back inside, the panic swelling inside her.

"Zack! NO!" She tried to dart back inside, but Charlotte's grip held her firm.

"Charlotte, let me go. Please! Zack…"

Just as hope seemed to evaporate, Zack emerged from the back, cradling Freddie in their arms and laying him down gently on the ground as relief flooded Sandy's face, a tide of emotions washing away the tension that had gripped her heart.

In an instant, she dashed into Zack's arms, wrapping herself around them with an urgency born of fear and gratitude. "I'm okay," Zack murmured, their voice a soft reassurance against the chaos that surrounded them. Sandy pulled back slightly to scrutinize their face, the worry etched in her brow spilling over as she retorted, "You scared the shit out of me," her voice trembling with the remnants of panic.

"I'm sorry I couldn't make it to the front door; I had to go out the back," they replied, a familiar hint of guilt coloring their tone as they glanced back at the scene they had narrowly escaped.

Just then, Charlotte interjected, relief flooding her features as she quipped, "Zack, you must have nine lives," a nervous laugh punctuating the weight of the moment.

"We need to get Freddie to the hospital," Zack ordered, the urgency in their voice propelling them into action.

Lisa's car roared to a stop, the engine's growl matching the frantic beating of their hearts as Robin and Zack carefully placed Freddie inside.

"Get him to the hospital, quick. I'm right behind you," Zack urged, their eyes darting back and forth, scanning the surroundings for any signs of lurking danger.

Sandy, still tethered to Zack by an invisible thread of concern, blurted out, "Where are you going?"

"I need to take you somewhere safe."

Sandy's eyes burned with defiance, her voice firm and unwavering as she retorted, "Zack, I'm not going to stay in some hideout while you're running around fighting for your life." "Sandy don't fight with me on this," Zack countered, desperation creeping into their voice.

"Zack, no. I'm not leaving you," she pleaded, the sirens in the distance growing louder, a bitter reminder of the urgency that cloaked their predicament. As the wailing of the approaching sirens grew closer, Charlotte's voice cut through the tension like a knife: "Zack, get out of here; the fuzz is coming." Zack grabbed Sandy's hand and left the scene.

* * *

Over at Sandy's home, Zack hastily shut all the blinds as if locking out the world outside that had just proven to be so dangerous. Sandy's heart raced in her chest, a mixture of fear and confusion swirling in her mind as she turned to Zack, her voice trembling slightly, "Zack, tell me what is going on."

Frantically checking her surroundings, she felt the rush of adrenaline still coursing through her veins. Zack, clearly worried, took her hands in theirs, their grip firm yet gentle, trying to ground her as they looked deep into her eyes, "Are you okay?" Sandy felt a flicker of comfort in Zack's presence,

her hands, tremors beneath their touch. Sandy pulled away slightly, frustrated as she reiterated, "Yes, stop asking me if I'm okay and tell me what's going on!" she demanded, her voice steady but laced with an underlying panic. Zack couldn't help but notice the way her eyes burned with fright.

"Breathe. You're safe; I won't let anything happen to you," Zack reassured her, enveloping her in a comforting hug, cradling her against them as if to shield her from the unfolding chaos outside their sanctuary.

"I was so scared," she admitted, her voice muffled against their shoulder, and it broke their heart to know that she had faced such turmoil.

"I know, baby. I'm sorry you had to go through that," Zack murmured as they sank into the couch.

After an agonizing recap of events, Sandy finally processed the revelation regarding Val's betrayal, her bewilderment evident. "I can't believe Val was behind all of this. What was she thinking?" she questioned, disbelief coloring her voice. Zack shook their head, "I don't know. A better question is, why does Mayor Lewis want to break us up?"

The realization of the mayor's involvement only deepened the mystery, as Sandy recalled, "I thought you had a relationship with the mayor. Him helping with the carnival and all." "Yeah, but I couldn't do what he wanted me to do," Zack replied, their eyes shadowed with the weight of unshared burdens.

Just as Sandy prepared to probe further, her phone rang, an unwelcome interruption that pulled her from the depths of their conversation. "Hello... Okay, I'll tell Zack," her gaze flickering back to Zack, anxiety tightening her throat. She hung up, the news heavy on her heart, "Freddie just went into surgery." Panic surged in Zack's chest; their instincts kicked in.

"I have to be there. Please stay here; I need to know you're safe." The sincerity in their tone was unmistakable but it was mixed with a tender plea that made Sandy's heart ache. "Fine, just please be careful," she conceded, anxiety bubbling at the thought of them rushing off into the unknown.

Their eyes locked for a lingering moment, and they shared a passionate kiss that spoke volumes of their love each promising the other silently that they would return unscathed. "I love you," Zack whispered, a vow laced with desperation. Sandy responded fervently, "I love you, too. Come back to me in one piece," the gravity of the moment settled between them as she watched Zack leave.

* * *

On the other side of town away from all the chaos. The afternoon sun spilled through the glass storefront of the jewelry shop, casting a warm glow over the myriads of glimmering displays showcasing exquisite pieces.

Daron stood at the counter; his youthful face painted with determination as he perused a selection of engagement rings. The soft chime of a bell signaled his presence to the salesperson, who greeted him with knowing curiosity.

"What's the occasion, young man?" the salesperson inquired, flashing a friendly smile that betrayed a hint of skepticism regarding Daron's age. With a broad smile on his face, Daron replied, "Engagement rings?" The salesperson's eyebrows lifted in surprise, "Engagement rings? Aren't you a little too young."

"I'm a young black man in America. I don't have much time left. And I want to marry the woman I love as soon as I can." His words hung in the air, heavy with the implications of his reality—time is fleeting, and love waits for no one. The salesperson softened, recognizing the fire beneath Daron's bravado; he admired the young man's desire to embrace life fully, despite the uncertainties that loom. "A man that lives in the moment," he nodded appreciatively, before leading Daron to a display, retrieving what he claimed was the perfect engagement rings.

Daron's eyes widen as he explored the curated collection, each ring an emblem of devotion and promise.

Finally, he settled on a simple yet elegant gold band, adorned with a sparkling diamond that seemed to capture the essence of his emotions.

"This is the one," he declared, conviction radiating from his every syllable. "Can I get it engraved?" The salesperson eagerly encouraged his request, genuinely invested in Daron's dream. "Sure, what would you like it to say?" Daron's face softened as he pondered for a moment. With a wistful glance, he stated, "To my one true Rose."

* * *

As Zack anxiously walked the sterile corridor of the hospital, they couldn't shake the gnawing sensation of dread that curled tightly in their stomach. Freddie's surgery felt like an eternity, and every minute ticking by was a reminder of the precarious tightrope they walked every day in their tumultuous life. When they finally spotted Charlotte, her face was a mask of worry and confrontation.

"How is he?" Zack asked, the urgency in their voice barely masking their distress. Charlotte's brow furrowed, her voice laden with concern as she updated them on Freddie, "We don't know he's still in surgery. What is going on Zack? And why is my diner burnt to a crisp?"

Zack exhaled dreaded to tell Charlotte the truth.

"Val got tied up with the mayor to deal drugs."

"Drugs?" she exclaimed in disbelief.

"Yeah, she had the crew steal the Bronxville Devil's shipment, so they retaliated. Look, I'm sorry about the diner we can rebuild." "No, don't you worry about rebuilding. The diner could use a break. I'll take the insurance money and put it into something new."

Zack nodded in agreement as they stood in the waiting room while Freddie fought for his life.

* * *

303

Sandy busily rummaged through a hodgepodge of books on the shelf, searching for a long-lost novel that had always brought her comfort. Amidst the dusty tomes and well-worn pages, her fingers grazed something unexpected—an envelope tucked away within the crevices of Zack's belongings, her heart racing slightly as she wondered what secrets it might hold.

Opening it she discovered documents. Sandy flipped through the papers; her eyes widened in disbelief. The documents detailed an experimental drug aimed at enhancing memory retention, a glimmer of hurt in her heart as she realized that Zack had been working tirelessly to find a solution to help Kelly regain her lost memories. Just as she contemplated the implications of Zack's research, a firm knock on the door pulled her back to the present. Instantly on edge, she wiped her hands on her jeans and strode to the door, opening it to reveal the stern yet familiar figure of Mayor Lewis.

"Mayor Lewis? What are you doing here?" she asked, confusion mingled with a hint of apprehension in her voice. He looked at her intently, his expression serious.

"Ms. Sandy Myers, I presume?" his tone formal yet laden with an urgency that made her stomach twist. A million thoughts raced through her mind as she nodded, instinctively moving aside to let him in, her heart raced not just from the unexpected visit but also the heavy weight of the documents in her hand.

"What brings you here, Mayor Lewis?" she asked, trying to maintain a semblance of composure despite the growing dread within her. The mayor's expression remained serious as he leaned closer, lowering his voice to a near whisper, "I think you'd be interested to know what's coming."

"Why is that?" she inquired curious.

"Because Zack's fate lies in your hands." he stated, leaving a chill of uncertainty rippling through the air.

Sandy's heartbeat quickened; *what did he mean by that? Had he uncovered something about Zack's research, or worse yet, was there a deeper implication about the lengths Zack was willing to go to for Kelly?* The weight of the mayor's words settled heavily on her shoulders.

"What are you talking about. What do you want with Zack?" she asked afraid of the truth.

Mayor Lewis flashed her a devilish grin, stating, "We are long overdue for a much-needed conversation."

* * *

Dawn busted into the bustling police station, once again. She clutched a manila envelope tight against her side—a silent weight carrying the truth of a conspiracy that stretched to the highest office in Queerville.

The sheriff, his brow furrowed in frustration, stood behind his desk, sorting through seemingly endless paperwork amidst the din of ringing phones and murmurs of officers discussing the latest tragic events plaguing the town.

"Ms. Parker, I told you without the evidence we don't have a case," he stated, his voice laced with exhaustion.

"All we have now are a bunch of dead Bronxville teens and a burned-down diner that no one seems to know what happened to." His words sank in like a lead weight, amplifying the urgency in Dawn's veins.

With a steely resolve, she took a breath, meeting his gaze. "What if I give you these?" she replied, pulling the envelope from under her arm and sliding it across the desk. The sheriff raised an eyebrow as he retrieved a collection of photographs. Dawn's heart racing with the adrenaline of revelation. As he flipped through the images, a deep frown etched across his face, capturing the unmistakable likenesses of Mayor Lewis, alongside Val and Douglas, all standing with bags filled with illicit substances.

"The mayor was at that school when these drugs were present?" he asked incredulously, trying to piece together the shocking implications. Dawn nodded; her voice unwavering, "Yes, and you can also see who's with him. Sheriff, the mayor is bringing a drug war to Queerville." Each word felt like a detonator, poised to blow open a scandal that could upend the very foundations of their town, sending ripples of fear and urgency through the thick walls of the station.

"Well, Ms. Parker I must say you do have a knack for taking down powerful people."

Dawn gave a knowing mischievous grin.

* * *

Meanwhile, in a completely different realm of tension and expectation, Rose prepared for the evening ahead. She stood in front of the mirror, her delicate figure adorned in a beautiful slim dress that hugged her curves perfectly, enhancing the soft glow of her skin. The anticipation of a date with Daron left butterflies fluttering in her stomach, as she recalled the laughter they've shared and the promises of what was to come.

Daron, on the other hand, looked effortlessly handsome in his dress slacks and a neatly patterned button-up shirt, his attire reflecting a youthful charm that complemented Rose's elegance.

A smirk played on his lips, admiration flashing in his eyes as he took in the breathtaking sight of Rose as she ascended the stairs.

"Oh my… you look beautiful, Rose."

"Thank you, you don't look too bad yourself."

Daron drew her closer, swooping her in his arms and kissing her.

They exchange playful banter, the air around them charged with romance, oblivious to the chaos brewing beyond their world. With each glance, each lingering touch, they were swept away in the magic of possibility, creating a stark contrast to the dark realities that Dawn was about to unveil at the police station, where lives were hanging in the balance amidst a brewing storm of corruption and crime. The city outside may be shrouded in secrecy and shadows, but within this intimate bubble, hope and yearning flourish as they stepped into the night together.

* * *

The sheriff and his deputy stormed into Mayor Lewis's office, their presence commanding and authoritative. The mayor, caught off guard, looked up from the pile of paperwork cluttering his desk, confusion evident on his face. "Hey, what's this all about?" he stammered, his voice tinged with an unsettling mix of defiance and disbelief.

The sheriff stepped forward, his demeanor serious, yet unfalteringly calm. "Mayor Lewis, you are under arrest for drug trafficking, endangering the lives of juveniles, blackmail," he stated, methodically listing the grave charges that had finally caught up with the man many considered untouchable.

"And I'm sure there's a whole list of other crimes we'll get to later." It was as if the walls themselves had ears, soaking up the momentousness of this event; the mayor was no longer the untouchable figure behind the polished facade of his office, but just another criminal being handcuffed and led away, his legacy crumbling as the cuffs clicked shut around his wrists, sealing his fate. The office, once a hub of power, felt hollow as the officers hustled him out.

* * *

Dawn and Max sat on the floor, surrounded by graduation paraphernalia, discussing what the future held for them. Max turned to Dawn, his expression one of awe mixed with pride. "Dawn, you just took down the mayor," he exclaimed, unable to contain his excitement.

Dawn, though still processing the whirlwind of events, caught his gaze and responded, "We, just took down the mayor," her voice echoing the weight of their collective achievement.

Max then shifted the conversation to their imminent futures, "What's next for Dawn Parker?" he inquired curiously.

"Well, Max," she began thoughtfully, "I think I want to study journalism," the sincerity in her words revealing her desire to uncover the truth in a world shrouded in deceit. Max chuckled, playfully dubbing her, "O Town's very own Nancy Drew," yet the humor was tinged with nostalgia.

"There is no more O Town," Dawn replied, her tone turning sentimental as the reality of their small town's transformation settled in.

Max nodded, reflecting on how bizarre it felt to write out mail now, replacing the familiar *O Town* with *Queerville.* The conversation shifted back to Max as Dawn asked, "So, what's next for Max Hamilton?" Max spoke of rekindling his passion for basketball, sharing a glimmer of hope for future pursuits, though when she inquired about his family coming for graduation, a shadow crossed his face as he revealed, "No, they never want to step foot back in this town."

A shared understanding lingered in the air as they contemplated their extraordinary lives beyond the confines of their small community, bound by their experiences yet eager to carve out new identities in the world.

––––––––––––––––––

As they walked hand in hand, Daron took the lead, guiding Rose along a path decorated with delicate rose petals that led to an intimate dinner set for two. The atmosphere was enchanting; soft, twinkling lights surrounded them, and a live band played romantic melodies in the background, creating a dreamy ambiance.

As they arrived at their secluded table, tucked away from the hustle and bustle of the world around them,

Rose couldn't believe her eyes. This was so much more than anything a boy had ever done for her.

Her heart swelled with a mix of surprise and delight; the thoughtfulness and effort Daron put into the evening spoke volumes about his feelings for her.

The two settled into their seats, and the waiter presented them with a menu filled with mouth-watering options. They indulged in a delicious dinner that sparkled with flavors, sharing bites, laughter, and meaningful conversation as they enjoyed each other's company.

Once the plates were cleared and the candles flickered gently in the soft light, Daron took a deep breath and prepared for the moment he had been anticipating. He rose from his chair and walked around to Rose's side, his heart racing with excitement and nerves. With loving determination, he got down on one knee before her. In that moment, the world around them faded away, leaving just the two of them in a bubble of love.

With eyes shining and voice steady, Daron began to speak from the heart. He delivered a beautiful testament to his love for her, recounting the moments they had shared, the laughter and joy they had experienced together, and how she had transformed his life in ways he never thought possible. As he finished, he unveiled a stunning ring, glinting in the soft light, and asked her the question she had secretly dreamed of.

"Rose, will you marry me?"

Overwhelmed with emotion, tears of joy filled her eyes as she eagerly nodded, her voice barely above a whisper.

"Yes, yes, a thousand times yes!" she exclaimed, throwing her arms around him. The moment was pure magic, sealing their love with promises of a beautiful future together. The cheers and applause from the nearby diners filled the air as they celebrated this joyous occasion, marking the beginning of a wonderful new chapter in their lives.

* * *

Sandy's home was thick with an unsettling silence, shattered only by the sound of the front door creaking open as Zack stepped inside, a hopeful smile graced their face as they called out, "Sandy, baby!" but their heart dropped into the pit of their stomach as they were met with an eerie stillness.

The once vibrant space now felt cold and empty—her clothes, once draped casually around, were missing, her toiletries all gone, as if she had never existed in this space at all.

On the table, a single letter, a poignant contrast against the backdrop of her absence.

With trembling hands, Zack picked up the letter and began to read, each word striking like a nail to their heart and echoing with the unmistakable finality of Sandy's farewell—*"Zack, first let me say, I love you in ways you've never been loved."* Those words tangled with the bittersweet memories of their time together, memories that flickered like the last embers of a dying fire, warming their heart even as they threaten to extinguish them.

Zack continued to read, *and more than you could ever imagine...You have made this last year the happiest my life has ever been. I've never felt love like yours before and it's something I will always treasure. But your heart belongs to another, and I can no longer fill her place. I know you love me, but you need her, so go get your girl. I hope you don't hate me after this. Just know this was not easy for me to do. But I love you too much to watch you in pain. Forever yours, Sandy.*

With each sentence, the weight of her decision settled heavier upon them, until the ink on the paper seemingly blurred with the welling tears in their eyes. They dropped the letter, a profound sense of disbelief enveloping them like a shroud. Zack screamed into the emptiness, a raw, agonizing sound that bounced off the walls, echoing their heart's devastation.

Their knees buckled from under them, they wailed in agony but then something strange happened. The fire returned to their belly. Zack stood up, wiped their tears, and their alluring green eyes, now blood red.

Zack picked up the phone and made a call.

* * *

Meanwhile, Maria entered a starkly lit hospital room, her heart heavy with relief as she found Val awake, though still weakened. "I'm glad to see you're okay," she said, allowing a fragile smile to break through the tension that hung in the air. Val's response, laced with guilt and concern, revealed a whirlwind of emotions as she asked about everyone else, remorseful for the chaos that they have endured.

"Everyone is safe thanks to Zack," Maria reassured Val.

"The Bronxville cats will probably retaliate but the worst is over. The mayor has been arrested. Do you think he'll talk?"

"I don't know." Val sighed, before batting sympathetic eyes at Maria. "Maria, can you forgive me?"

"Depends on who am I forgiving?"

"Some dumb kid. Who thought they had to be someone they're not."

Maria pondered before answering, "Yeah, I can forgive some dumb kid," with a warm smile.

As they shared a tender kiss, the chaos of the world outside momentarily faded, yet one unresolved question remained unaddressed: "Will you be my girl now Maria?"

———————————

Under the moon glare, the cool silver light bathed the secluded dirt road in a surreal luminescence, transforming the unpaved path into a hauntingly ethereal backdrop to Zack's standoff with Douglas.

The air was thick with an almost suffocating sense of anguish that wrapped around them as they stood face to face, the shadows of tall trees casting elongated shapes that seemed to emulate their strained expressions.

Zack's eyes bore into Douglas, searching for signs of guilt or remorse, desperate for some acknowledgment of the consequences that had unfolded. It wasn't just about Val's safety; their reputation was at stake, tangled in the aftermath of reckless decisions made in the heat of the moment.

Douglas leaned against the rough bark of a nearby tree, attempting to project an air of indifference, yet his voice quivered slightly as he spoke, betraying the nerves he tried so hard to mask. "Zack, I did what you told me. I took Val to the hospital. She's going to be fine."

"How did the Bronxville cats find out it was Val?"

"I don't know maybe they just thought, who else could it be," he stammered.

The dance of accusation unfurled as Zack circled him, demanding the truth, each question laced with danger.

"I find it funny that they knew exactly what road Val would be on." Zack's tone transforming from curiosity to accusatory, causing Douglas to squirm under the intensity of their stare.

In a moment fueled by fear, Douglas attempted to flee, but Zack's wrath found its mark as they brandished their weapon—a dark metallic symbol of death—and without a moment's hesitation, pulled the trigger, each shot resonating with a clarion call of irreversible consequences that shattered the stillness of the night. Zack moved closer and sent a single bullet through Douglas's head.

* * *

The stark, sterile environment of Val's hospital room was charged with tension as the officer Whitey entered, his heavy boots resounding on the linoleum floor, the bright fluorescent lights casting harsh shadows across Val.

"Valarie Johnson, you are under arrest for drug trafficking, distribution, and armed robbery, along with three counts of murder." The weight of his words hung in the air like a storm cloud, ready to burst. Val's eyes narrowed with a mix of defiance and disbelief as she quickly repeated, "Murder? Now you know you don't have any bodies to put on me." Her voice was laced with an incredulous laugh, a clear challenge to the charges laid against her. Officer Whitey's eyebrows shot up, a smirk appearing at the corners of his mouth.

"Oh, was that a confession?" he teased, probing for a reaction. Val straightened, the fire in her suddenly sparking bright as she shot back, "No, it was a fact."

Val was cuffed to her bed.

* * *

Mark sat vigil by Freddie's bedside, his eyes glued to the rising and falling of the machines that surrounded him, hope flickering like the heart monitor's fluorescent green light. Charlotte, immersed in her magazine, hadn't noticed the palpable anxiety that surrounded them until Zack staggered in, their face ashen.

"Hey, where is Sandy?" Charlotte queried, her casual tone betraying the seriousness of Zack's demeanor.

"She's... gone," they replied, their voice trembling with raw emotion, "She left me."

The words fell like heavy stones, the reality of the moment anchoring her disbelief. "What do you mean she's gone? Gone where?" she pressed, refusing to accept the depths of their despair. "Well, you can go check her home if you don't believe me," Zack shot back, raw and vulnerable, tears glistening in their eyes.

"Everyone I love leaves me," Zack continued, their voice cracking with vulnerability that was at odds with the anger bubbling within them. "I'm done... from now on I only want one thing."

Charlotte felt her breath hitch in her throat, the revelation looming ominously before her. "And what's that?" she asked, though a part of her already dreaded the answer.

Zack glared, a fierce intensity radiating from their gaze, giving Charlotte goosebumps as their expression hardened and they murmured, "Blood."

In that moment, Charlotte could see that there was more to this pain than simple heartbreak; it was a swirling tempest of grief and fury, a yearning that threatened to consume them whole, and she found herself not only witnessing their unraveling but entangled within it, anxious about what this darkness might mean for her friend.

An unsettling silence enveloped them, fueling Charlotte's next desperate question. "Zack, you can't give up on..." But just as that question hung in the air, a heart-stopping beeping broke the moment—Freddie's monitor flatlined. Mark sprang to action, instinct kicking in as he yelled, "Freddie, don't you do this!" Zack echoed the plea in horror, "WE NEED A DOCTOR NOW!"

In an instant, the sterile calm of the hospital room morphed into chaos as doctors rushed in like a whirlwind, their hurried movements eclipsing any lingering fear. But for Zack, amidst the confusion and chaos, all they could see was the shadow of loss, a suffocating blackness that consumed any flicker of hope.

As monitors blinked and alarm bells rang, they stood on the edge of a precipice, caught between the despair of losing another loved one and the spiraling fury that threatened to engulf them like a storm. In that moment, surrounded by frantic movements and desperate pleas for life, it became painfully clear: the weight of grief was an unrelenting force, dragging them under, leaving them gasping for air in a world that felt increasingly void of light.

Callisto Robinson

Present Day,
1960

The diner was a husk of its former self, remnants of past warmth overshadowed by the weight of tragedy as Zack worked alone, attempting to mend what existed within both the structure and their soul. Their hands moved mechanically—until a familiar voice pierced through the haze of their despair.

"Oh wow, what happened here?"

The tone jolted them; it was a melody from a distant past they never thought they'd hear again. Zack's heart thundered as they turned around, the shock evident on their face.

There stood—Kelly, the love of their life, seemingly untouched by time, lighting up the dim diner like the sun breaking through clouds. Memories flooded back—the laughter, the quiet moments, the dreams they once shared. The room melted away, leaving just the two of them enveloped in their own world, suspended in nostalgia.

"Kelly?" Zack whispered, ensuring they wasn't dreaming, their voice trembling under the weight of emotions long buried. She flashed, a warm, radiant smile that cradled their heart. "Hi, Zack."

In that very moment, the diner transformed; the past and future collided, and despite the shadows lurking in their lives, the flickering flame of hope glowed anew.

* * *

Back at the hospice, the atmosphere was heavy with a mix of sorrow and quiet acceptance as nurses tended to dying patients, their gentle hands trying to ease the pain and suffering of those nearing the end of their journeys. The air was thick with the scent of antiseptic and the muffled sounds of heart monitors beeping in harmony with labored breaths.

Yet, amidst the somber backdrop, the unthinkable occurred. Frank Calhoun, a man who had long been presumed lost to the grip of death, suddenly opened his eyes, jolted back to life as if resurrected from the depths of despair.

His gaze was not one of confusion or fear; instead, it burned with an intensity that sent shivers down the spines of the nurses who rushed to his side. It was a fierce and uncontrollable lust for revenge that coursed through his veins, igniting a fire within him that had been dormant for far too long.

For years, in a coma trapped in a hell of his own making, reliving the torment of Zack's betrayal over and over again, each recollection a dagger twisting deeper into his heart. The thought consumed him: he wanted to obliterate everything that Zack had built, to watch it all come crumbling down as a fitting punishment for the deceit that had stolen his life.

With every heartbeat, the desire solidified into an undeniable resolve.

Frank had emerged not just from a coma but from the clutches of despair, and he now harbored a singular, all-consuming mission—KILL ZACK!

DEATH TO ZACK CALHOUN
WANTED DEAD OR ALIVE
BOOK 4

Coming soon!

Made in the USA
Las Vegas, NV
26 October 2024